Witness Trap

Does she really want the truth?

Rosie Elliot

This is a work of fiction. Names, places, events and
incidents are either the products of the author's
imagination or have been used fictitiously. Any
resemblance to any person living or deceased is purely
coincidental.

A CIP catalogue record for this book is available from the
British Library.

ISBN: 979-8-5923-4010-9

Also available as an eBook
rosieelliotbooks@gmail.com

DEDICATION

For dad, Carol, Jane and Dawn
I still miss you

ACKNOWLEDGMENTS

Simon Drysdale, my partner in life, thank you for all your support along the way - I couldn't have done it without you by my side; Lucy Clare for your encouragement right at the start of this project.

Geoff Robinson for his wonderful cover photos; Robert Crompton for such helpful advice and feedback; Jonny Halfhead for the initial inspiration to put pen to paper; Helen Baggott for proofreading and editing (helenbaggott.co.uk).

Many thanks to George Wicker for help with the technical side (GWCS Business Writing & Web Design).

CHAPTER ONE

The crooked gate was already open. The eyes of the two seven-year-old girls met in mutual questioning before inspecting the overgrown path that led to the front door. Through the drizzle evidence of past paintings could be seen from a distance, the flaking edges of the layers displaying multiple shades of grey and beige. Narrow patches of bright yellow around the knocker hinted at former happy times. Either side of the door small-paned grimy windows stared back at the girls. Filthy, torn net curtains sneered at them as they took in the scene, the excess length pooling around the windowsill inside. The house was daring them to take a step closer.

Without fail there was a churning in the pit of Jess's stomach every time she approached another door. It never diminished, and when faced with having to knock at such a scary house it was that much more intense. There could be anyone in there; a madman that drags them inside only for them never to be seen again, a spiritualist that starts talking in a strange language, a murderer.

With eyes down as they cautiously crept along the path Jess could see piles of household rubbish trapped under the thorn bushes. Dented tins, cigarette packets, torn up letters. A soggy newspaper dated almost a year before lay beneath, its announcement that some Earl is sought in a death mystery just readable through a layer of dirt.

Skipping over a pile of furry cat mess to her left almost made her lose her footing but Nerys's firm handhold steadied her. It would never do to get her new shoes dirty so quickly.

"Shall we do it? Or just leave?" Halfway down the path Jess voiced in a hushed tone what they were both thinking, "I really don't like the look of this one."

But they both heard the correct response in their heads: everyone needs to be contacted, not just the people who live in nice shiny houses with cars on the drive. Everyone is deserving of this important information. Today it was up to them to deliver it. It was a matter of life and death.

Nerys, the braver of the two friends, reached out to lift the weathered knocker but with lightning reaction Jess slapped her hand down and whispered desperately, "Don't knock on the door, silly. Ring the bell. It might not have any batteries in it. At least we could truthfully say that we called."

With one hand in Jess's tight grip, Nerys raised her other hand to the bell. Jess turned her feet in anticipation of a quick flight. A loud 'Ding Dong!' rang out somewhere in the depths of the house, an oddly cheerful sound in the gloom of such a place. Too scared it would actually bring someone to the door the girls bolted back down the path, over the mess, careful not to slip, and through the open gate.

Nervous laughter escaped their lips as they recounted their experience to the group leader, pronouncing that particular house an 'NH' – Not at Home. Jehovah's Witnesses had abbreviations for everything. They almost had their own language.

*

The Truth. Being in the Truth. That's what Jess was. Two words that suggested any other belief system was completely false.

*

I love the ministry. I get to see my friends and when we're finished, after about two hours, we go back to a brother or sister's house and have lemonade and biscuits. The other kids in my school don't do this on a Saturday but Mummy says this is the 'real life'. She says they are materialistic (*that means they love things more than they love God*). No, at the weekends they go out playing sports and shopping. Katy is doing her cycling proficiency and lots of the girls in my class have ballet lessons.

But if they are so busy with all these things they won't have time to worship God. And then if they don't please him he won't choose to keep them alive when Armageddon comes. He'll kill them along with all the other wicked people.

At the meetings there are lots of talks from the Elders about how bad the world is getting. All those that are not Jehovah's Witnesses are liars, cheats and deceitful adulterers, whatever that means. It must have something to do with kissing because that's what's in the pictures in the magazines. They steal things too and are totally selfish. They even murder other people who have annoyed them. What a horrible world we live in!

I don't want to mix with people like that. They are

'bad association' as First Corinthians 15 verse 33 says. The Elders say that if we mix with people like that then we will become just like them and that means Jehovah won't like us anymore. No, it's all right to talk to people at school and down the shops but not a good idea to go and play with them at the park or go swimming with them. It's just not worth the risk.

I can't wait for the paradise to come. Once all the bad people are out the way and the devil is put into a cage we will tidy up the whole planet and make it beautiful again. The pictures of the paradise in the *Watchtower* and *Awake* magazines are brilliant! So colourful! I'm going to have a tiger, a polar bear and probably some snakes in my house. Oh, and an elephant so I can ride on his back everywhere. And it will be so peaceful and I won't be afraid of anything. I can sleep in the middle of the woods if I want to all on my own and I won't be scared.

Other pictures in the magazines aren't so nice though. When Armageddon comes people will be struck by lightning and great big balls of fire will shoot down from Heaven like fiery rain. It will be scary but Jehovah will protect all the Witnesses. We are the only ones that he'll save because we have stayed faithful and we've gone to all the meetings and gone out on the ministry.

I know how important it is to warn people about Armageddon. If I don't tell them then that would make me blood guilty. (Mummy explained what that means – that if I keep the Good News all to myself and don't give people the chance to change their bad ways then God will kill me too.) But I don't want to die.

Sometimes I have bad dreams. I see men and

women and children running down the street on fire. They are screaming and screaming and screaming. Their clothes are on fire and they try to tear them off as they run. No one helps them because everyone else is on fire too. It's horrible. Babies are left in their prams while their mummies are lying on the floor dead. It makes me wake up crying sometimes but I go into mummy's bed and cuddle up to her. It's only a dream but it does scare me sometimes.

And what about the resurrection? Well! Granny's getting old now and when she dies she'll just be in a deep sleep and when she wakes up she'll be in the paradise! I've prayed to Jehovah and asked if he can make sure I'm at her graveside when she climbs out. I want to be the one to tell her all that's happened and that now we're all in the New World.

I wonder about Shakespeare and Tutankhamun. Will they be resurrected too? I've asked the Elders cos they know all the right answers and they say that people like Hitler and Henry the eighth probably won't because they were bad people, murderers and adulterers.

I know everyone thinks I'm weird. I feel like the odd one out at school sometimes. We don't celebrate Christmas 'cos Jesus wasn't born on twenty-fifth of December so I go into a different classroom when they're doing something Christmassy. I don't actually know what they are doing but I just get on with my project or read my Kings and Queens book, the same things as when I sit out of assembly every morning.

Going on the ministry on Christmas day is great though! It's the best time because people are at home and are naturally thinking about Jesus and will be happy to talk or to buy a set of magazines for thirty pence. I usually place loads of mags and sometimes a householder will give me a packet of sweets. Some people are nasty and shout and swear at us for disturbing them on Christmas day but most people are nice.

Last week when the whole school was in a special Easter assembly I was in my classroom tidying up the reading books and I looked out the window. I could see lots of teachers walking around hiding cardboard bunnies. I didn't know what they were doing that for. Assembly must have finished cos I saw all the children running around looking for the bunnies. Mrs Wynn-Jones called to me through the window and said I should come and help find them too. So I did. I wasn't sure if I should join in or not 'cos it was an Easter activity but I did it anyway. I knew exactly where all of them were; under the bird table, in the branches of the tree, under the flowers in the flower bed and under the wooden bench. When we all got back into the classroom and all our eggs were counted up it turned out that I was the winner 'cos I'd found the most. The prize was one enormous chocolate egg with Smarties inside! I was a bit scared to tell Mummy how I got the egg but she just laughed and said I'll know for next time that I shouldn't join in 'cos it's a pagan tradition.

I love my teacher Mrs Wynne-Jones. She's pretty and kind. During lunchbreak on a Wednesday she teaches me how to play some chords on my guitar. I'm the only one that has a guitar lesson, perhaps nobody else wants to learn. Daddy got me my guitar. It's just the right size for me. The other one I had was Diane's and it was too big to get my arm round. I have to be careful carrying it into school and I put it in the stationery cupboard to keep it safe.

I get called names at school like Jovo and Hovis and it usually doesn't upset me but sometimes it does. The boys are the worst. They shout those names from right across the other side of the playground and everybody looks at me. I don't like it. But this is all part of being a Jehovah's Witness. People will hate us and will turn against us and make fun of us. But we've got to turn the other cheek like Jesus said, pray for help and carry on.

Philip Star is my favourite Elder. Not just because he's got a great name but he's funny and always has little stories to tell. But I should love all of the Elders 'cos they are chosen by God to look after his congregation. The Holy Spirit tells them what to do so everything they teach must be right. Mummy thinks so and she says we must always do what the Elders say, even if we think it's wrong. They know best and they care about us so much just like Jesus does.

*

It was all true. It must be true. Jess heard the Bible being used to support every aspect of the religion repeatedly at the meetings and Circuit Assemblies and District Assemblies. Her young mind absorbed all it was exposed to and she willingly soaked it up.

The same couldn't be said for the rest of the family.

*

Two years earlier Jess found herself wedged into the family Cortina Estate and along with her six siblings, Mum, Dad and the dog Silkie, they made their way to the south coast for their summer holiday. The boys were Marianne's and the girls, Ben's, and then there was Jess – the product of them both. For a stepfamily, the kids got on very well and Jess, being the youngest of the seven, was thoroughly spoilt with attention.

Overstuffed suitcases bungeed to the roof threatened to burst open even though Ben had secured them as best he could. The excited chattering of the children at the start of the two-hour journey from Uxbridge soon turned to pushes and moans as each tried to get comfortable. Some were on the back seat, and the ones that sat on cushions on the ridged metal floor of the boot moaned the loudest and begged Dad to stop so they could swap around. But they were all happy to be going away to have some familiar fun by the sea.

The summer of '73 was particularly hot and dry and the heat in the car was unbearable. On arrival at the campsite everyone was anxious to get out and get moving. The erection of three canvas tents and the connection of the gas bottle ready for the week ahead was all the kids were willing to help with before heading off in different directions.

Jess and her teenage sisters Karen, Jackie and Diane announced they were heading for the beach. There was one main road to cross outside Cannons Camping Site in Pevensey Bay, and once through the familiar streets of bungalows and around the Martello Tower they hopped over the hot sand straight down to the sea. They all had their swimming costumes on under their clothes and Jess with her rubber ring around her waist didn't hang about for her sisters but ran straight down into the chilly salty water. The girls jumped and stumbled through the water splashing each other endlessly. Jess squealed with delight and had no fear.

Jackie was the one that always tidied Jess's long hair, scraped it back off her face and wrapped a bobble around it or a colourful ribbon. She was gentle and loving and Jess was happy to let her play with her hair no matter what she was doing.

In the sea Diane tried to get Jess to float on her back unsupported: "Put your head back and look up at the sky," she instructed, "and push your bottom up."

It worked and once back home she took Jess to the pool regularly and taught her to swim.

The four girls looked for tiny creatures in rock pools all afternoon and gathered an assortment of shells. Jackie said that dad could put a hole in each one so they could make a necklace and Jess thought that was amazing. She couldn't wait to wear it. He was handy like that, always making or fixing something.

The boys were probably getting up to no good, lighting fires, pushing each other off the groynes into the choppy deeper waters while the sun beat down. Their favoured, more sinister activities of trying car doors and pickpocketing they thankfully left at home for the week.

The two older boys had really become out of Marianne's control. She'd done her best to get them back on track but they bounced off each other and the dangerous group they'd got into back home were only going to take them down one path. Marianne's mother had them living with her for some time back in Ireland to try to get them out of the situation. It was felt the change of environment and a separation from the gang they were involved with would set them straight but once they were back home it was as if nothing had changed. At home Jess had opened the door to the police on a couple of occasions and overheard the neighbours' shouts at mum and dad for not keeping their kids under control. Any trouble in the neighbourhood was always blamed on the boys and more often than not they were the perpetrators.

With tummies grumbling all the kids congregated later in the afternoon at the ice cream van and the girls found a café and bought two cups of tea to take back for mum and dad.

*

The summer was always a difficult time for Ben to get through: with Marianne's fair complexion, ginger hair and freckles the heat irritated the hell out of her, made her sweat and feel unclean, in need of a bath every hour or so and a change of clothes. Ben knew she would rather stay in the shade, but for the sake of the family holiday she put up with the discomfort. In contrast Ben loved the heat. While all the kids were occupied the parents had a chance to sit back and relax – Marianne under the sunshade – to watch the world go by, and to talk.

Ben was from London, born and bred in Paddington. His work was in a factory making asbestos panels and his preferred shift was 10pm till 6am as it meant he could top up his tan whilst sleeping in the garden when he got home. A wiry man, short at five feet four inches, he was as strong as an ox. Afraid of nothing and no one. But strangely he felt he had to tread carefully where Marianne was concerned. Scrambling around for the right description in his head, the only way

Ben could describe Marianne's ways was that 'she suffered with her nerves'. His tough, no nonsense city background did not allow for such things to get in the way. Growing up in post war London there was no time for melancholy, not when putting bread on the table was the main priority. Ben had watched his younger brother die of malnutrition despite his mother's best efforts to feed the family after his dad had walked out.

Before they'd married Ben had listened patiently as Marianne had explained that her strict Irish Catholic background had left its mark on her. He understood that she'd had it hard with the fear of sin and punishment being drummed into her at church, at school and at home. Educated in a convent school she heard the screams of the young girls as they gave birth and witnessed the tears and ongoing trauma as their babies were taken away from them.

Pregnant at nineteen and unmarried her father rained down shame and eternal damnation on her. She was a whore and would burn in hell for sure and he wouldn't have her under his roof anymore. She'd made her bed, now she had to lie in it. She was out.

"Get out! Get out of my house!" were his final words to her, unless, of course, she did what he said and had an abortion.

With the little money she had she bought herself a ticket to England. Hiding her pregnancy she found a job in a typing pool at an office in Great Portland Street in the heart of London. Efforts to disguise her condition were not good enough though as most mornings without fail she'd rush from her seat at the back of the room all the way to the front to escape to the toilets to vomit. The other girls guessed her plight and one of them, Irene, took her under her wing.

Years later Marianne was looking through some old paperwork and discovered her parents had married in September 1935. Her birth was in January 1936. He might not have ever forgiven her for disgracing the family but she never forgave him for his hypocrisy.

Her bouts of depression – which Marianne herself referred to as 'funny turns' or 'down times' – had plagued her all her life. It was a weakness that had run in her family on her father's side, everyone called him 'mad' and the way he dealt with it was to hit the bottle and go to bed. Forget going to work and forget spending the little money they had on essentials, he needed to escape from his torment. Marianne wasn't a drinker like her father but her go-to was her bed. Sleep. Oblivion. From what he could see Ben could add to the affliction migraines and a generally foul mood. And when it was her time of the month he would volunteer for extra shifts.

Ben knew she had spent time searching for something to believe in. She said she still had some kind of belief in a higher being but wasn't sure how to frame it. Buddhism, Hinduism and Greek Orthodox faiths had stirred an interest in her but not enough to get her hooked. She stopped searching on the day two seventeen-year-old girls knocked on her door with some magazines. It was as quick as that. She'd found it! The true religion! The Truth.

The group was called Jehovah's Witnesses and everything made so much sense to her. The questions she'd had no satisfactory answers to were now being answered and backed up by the Bible. Those two girls had so much knowledge, they really knew their scriptures well. A week after their initial call she asked Ben to drop her off and pick her up from the meetings three times a week and it wasn't long before she was going house to house preaching about God and the end of the world. It was happening too fast for Ben to come to terms with, this sudden persistent visitor that wouldn't leave. It dominated every conversation and the religious literature was always visible when friends came round – it was embarrassing.

*

"Marianne, when are you going to stop this fucking nonsense? It's too much. My girls don't want it rammed down their fucking throat as soon as they get home from school. I don't want it brought up in every bloody conversation we have, and I don't want to see those magazines lying around. Next time I see any round here they're going on the fire. I'm not putting up with it anymore. If you're going to continue with this religious shit, I'm off."

That's what Ben wanted to say. But he had learned that it wasn't advisable to put Marianne in a bad mood and risk her spoiling the rest of the holiday for everyone else because she couldn't pull herself out of it. And boy could she spoil it! He needed to be tactful in his approach.

"It's not for me, Marianne. To be fair I have been to a few of your meetings and seen what goes on and, I just think, you know, it's… it's just not for me."

"But you haven't really given it a chance, Ben. Perhaps if you had a proper regular Bible study with one of the brothers in the congregation you'd get a better idea. I mean, yes, you came to the meeting but you sat there and brazenly lit up a cigarette! You would quite happily have smoked it if I hadn't told you to put it out. Smoking is not acceptable to the Witnesses and you know it. Do you really think that's good way to start?"

"A Bible study? Me? I don't think so. I wouldn't have time for that what with my shifts. By the way, the girls have told me they feel a bit awkward about having their studies. It's hard for them, you know, they've been at school all day, they've got their exams soon, and the last thing they want to do when they get home is more study. It's too much, Marianne. Can't you just leave them be?"

"But it's my responsibility as a Christian... actually it's your responsibility as head of the house, to teach them about the Bible. If you're not going to do it then I must. I'm committed to this, Ben. I've found something that's worthwhile and I want to share it."

A westerly wind had picked up. Clouds were starting to gather on the horizon. The colour of the sea and the sky had melded and Ben wondered where all the kids were and what they, especially the boys, were getting up to.

"Anyway," Ben ended the conversation, "let's get some tea going, the kids will be back soon." The two of them headed back to the tents and set about preparing a meal.

Something was left hanging in the air between them as it often was, yet another version of the same conversation that was 'to be continued...' They carried on with the practical chores despite knowing that this wasn't going to go away.

After tea the darkness fell quickly and tired bodies lay down in their sleeping bags after a long day. Sleep arrived for the youngsters but Ben lay awake contemplating the future with this woman and her obsession. It was as if he didn't know her anymore. She wasn't the woman he'd married almost ten years ago.

*

The following day saw the hot sun alone in the deepest blue sky. Seagulls made their yodeling cry and swooped down to fight over a discarded sandwich near the bin. Families took their places on the beach and dogs chased the waves in and out, snapping at the froth. Armed with a pile of towels, a flask of tea and a couple of books the parents unfolded their sunbeds and settled themselves down. The kids were already off enjoying themselves. Ben wondered if he should wait for Marianne to resume the only item on the agenda, but then decided to make the first move. It had to be done.

"It's not just the studies, Marianne, why don't you let the girls have their friends round anymore? They told me you've also stopped them from mixing with their school mates. What's that all about, then?"

"Ben, it's a dangerous world out there, you know. Our kids are precious and need protecting. We don't want them to get into the wrong company and end up doing things they'd regret. Look how the boys are turning out, can't you see I regret letting them get into a bad crowd? Let's not allow that to happen to the girls. There are plenty of good, respectful kids their age at the Kingdom Hall who'd make great friends, genuine friends. Perhaps I should invite some of them round so the girls can get to know them."

Ben could see the wisdom in what she was saying but why did it have to involve God and Bible study? Where was this going to end? It felt like Marianne had another man in her life and Ben had been put to one side. But his priority must be his girls, Karen, Jackie, Diane and Jessica. Desperate for their married life to return to what it was, but not really believing that could be possible, he considered what life would be like if they split. The older ones were almost finished school and could go out to work, but what would he do with Jessica?

He persevered for another two years and during that time even moved the family to Eastbourne for a fresh start in a place they loved, by the sea. With better surroundings than the city and a new set of friends, maybe Marianne would come to her senses and find another hobby just as fulfilling. Something like... yoga? And art class or cookery class? But it didn't happen that way.

Chapter Two

Suddenly at the age of seven Jess's family split in two, half the people she had been with all her life were gone. The two older boys continued their journey of self-destruction and found themselves tucked up in Borstal. That left Marianne, Peter and Jess. And Silkie the dog.

Whenever Jess asked where daddy was Marianne told her he was staying at gran's for a while, and every Saturday when she got her swimming bag ready for Diane to take her to the pool Marianne had to explain that her sisters were staying at gran's too. It took a long time to sink into Jess's mind that they weren't coming back.

One afternoon she came running in the back door shouting breathlessly: "Mummy! I've just seen daddy down the big shops. I shouted to him but he didn't hear me. I shouted and shouted but he walked away." Tears welled up her eyes and a blink released them down her freckled face.

Holding Jess in front of her Marianne explained: "That wasn't daddy, dear, it must have been someone who looked like him. Jess, sit down a minute, I need to talk to you." It was time to spell it out for her.

*

Ben visited twice for half a day in the following months but Marianne's letter informing him of Jess's distressed reaction to his visit, made him think seriously. He was torn between leaving his daughter in peace and feeling scared that, being brought up in this weird religion, her life would be at risk if she ever needed a blood transfusion. He considered going for custody but knew he'd never win as he had to go out and earn a living and there would be no one to care for Jess properly. He made the difficult decision to stop all contact.

The quiet sadness that overtook Jess was noticed by her teacher Mrs Wynne-Jones, young and newly qualified. While the class was in assembly each morning, excluded from attending Jess usually got on with some of her project about the Tudors but now she divided her time between scribbling in the back of her book and staring out the window. And she looked tired, so tired.

Concerned about her wellbeing Marianne talked to Jess about how she was finding school at the moment and that's when she told her about the bad dreams she had most nights. The demons hid from her in dark corners grabbing at her as she passed. While fireballs rained down from the sky, she tried to gather up small wounded animals and protect them from ferocious wolves. She looked around in hope but there was no one to protect her, she was completely alone, crying and calling out for help. Some nights she woke up sweating and checked under the bed for monsters, convinced she was going to be attacked. Marianne would occasionally wake to find Jess curled up in bed next to her, the covers pulled right up to her chin.

Marianne was at a loss as to how to help her daughter and thought the best thing would be to just carry on. Being absorbed in spiritual activities was the only answer. There was no choice for Jess. There was no option to stay at home while her mum and Peter went to the meetings and out on the ministry. She was only a child, she had to go.

*

The Kingdom Hall in Eastbourne was a large room above a fish and chip shop in the town centre right next to the public toilets. Fortunately, they were far enough away for the smell of disinfectant not to reach inside the Hall. The oily aroma of frying food however was another story. Every Sunday morning during the middle song the first whiffs from downstairs made their way into the building and if the window happened to be open it was simply torture. As the speaker droned on with big words Jess didn't understand she sat there picturing a plate of white fluffy fish in a crispy batter, a pile of greasy chips sprinkled with vinegar, a squirt of tomato sauce on the side and a glass of lemonade. She often saw herself racing down the stairs the second the final prayer was finished and grabbing a table for Sunday dinner. It never happened though as Marianne didn't have the money for such a feast.

Through the side door into the Kingdom Hall a flight of stairs rose to a green carpeted space that seated about seventy people. A centre aisle separated two blocks of very uncomfortable orange plastic seats and the slightly raised platform was fronted by a row of raised planters holding fresh leafy plants. It was said that they were placed there in the 60s to hide the Sisters' legs when they wore their miniskirts. Marianne scoffed at the contradiction: Sisters were not allowed to wear trousers but it was fine to show their legs and knickers off!

Many had their regular seats and refused to sit anywhere else. Just to prove a point, on occasion, mostly when she was in a confrontational mood, Marianne sat in one of the 'reserved' seats only to be greeted with scowls and huffs on the arrival of the seat's usual bottom. But she wouldn't move. She liked to stir things up sometimes, prove a point.

These were the same pedantic individuals who believed that the end of the world was coming in 1975. According to Bible chronology, that year was the six thousandth anniversary of the creation of man, therefore highly appropriate from God to begin Christ's thousand-year millennial reign at the start of man's seventh millennium.

The Governing Body strongly implied in the magazines that Armageddon was going to take place and the urgent warning was preached from door to door. Not only did this lead to a significant growth in numbers of Pioneers and new Bible studies, but active Witnesses took to selling their houses, cars and other valuable items so they could spend the profits. Many took out loans knowing they wouldn't need to pay them back. When 1975 came and went with no Armageddon the numbers rapidly dropped off as people, feeling they had been deceived, left in their droves.

Marianne wasn't one to listen to gossip. She just carried on with her spiritual routines with the view that God will bring Armageddon when he feels like it. And anyway, there would be signs to look out for leading up to it, so where were they?

At the Hall, the literature desk was tucked away in an alcove at the back and was where Jess queued to pick up their regular pile of bi-monthly magazines. Most of them were for Marianne's 'return visits', people who wanted them delivered each fortnight. According to which experimental printing method was being used at the time glossy slippery paper or dull rough leaves all had their different smells to Jess. The pictures on the front covers were delightfully detailed no matter what the main subject was and were designed to stir or shock the public into having a conversation.

Presenting the magazines on the door-to-door ministry a fluffy paradise scene with lions and sheep playing together would produce such comments as: "No, I don't believe that'll ever happen." Vivid scenes of a gunman in full swing or pictures of starving children holding out empty bowls would elicit a shaking of heads and, "I don't know what the world's coming to." From those prompts she had learned how to take the conversation forward and steer it to spiritual things and the wonderful future God promises the righteous.

Jess devoured each article and she learned to read very well, both silently and out loud. Mrs Wynne-Jones, observant as she was, noticed Jess's reading was very expressive. She could see Jess was settling down, coming out of her shell and smiling a bit more and thought being cast as the narrator in the school play would be perfect for her. It's not a Christmas play so she should be all right with it. She decided to look out for Marianne when she came to pick Jess up to make the suggestion, eager to get rehearsals underway.

"Yes, she is a very good reader. So, what's the play about?" Marianne asked.

"It's a shortened version of *Charlie and the*

Chocolate Factory."

"Ah, that's her favourite book, that and *The Railway Children*," said Marianne, smiling. "When are the performances and what would the rehearsal schedule be like?"

"We've still got some arrangements to make but rehearsals would be Tuesdays, Wednesdays and Thursdays for about an hour straight after school. The plays are in December for two weeks on Thursday and Friday evenings. It's going to be great. We've got our "Charlie" on board and he can't wait to get started!"

Marianne could feel Mrs Wynne-Jones' excitement but already knew Jess would not be able to join in. She'd been very kind to Jess, keeping a close eye on her but this was not going to happen. She let Mrs Wynne-Jones down apologetically but firmly.

"Oh, what a pity. Our meeting nights are on Thursdays so I'm afraid Jess won't be able to do it."

There was no contest. The meetings came first. God came first.

Jess was extremely disappointed and as she sat in the audience watching the final performance her heart was heavy thinking how much she wanted to be up there, on the stage doing as good a job herself. She had to keep telling herself the meetings were much more important than any school play. She came to accept it.

*

There were many things Jess would have chosen to do in her life but her naturally developing skills were quashed by purposely not being encouraged. In fact, they were actively discouraged. She was good at gymnastics, poetry, story-writing, crafts, playing guitar, swimming, but the time that would be spent on any of these would be better spent on spiritual pursuits, she had learned that at the meetings. The Organisation's efforts to produce Christians totally devoted to doing God's will, allowing no distractions to creep in was working very well on Jess.

As she grew Jess's views and outlook were firmly shaped and reinforced at every Jehovah's Witness event she attended. As she observed others in her class getting their BAGA certificates for gymnastics and going on school trips she grew to feel like an outsider, so different to others. But she was encouraged to feel proud to be so different. Jesus himself was seen as odd and he suffered because of it, and so it was to be expected that his followers would suffer the same. An alien in a foreign land, living a restricted life in a world that will soon be destroyed.

*

While Marianne was trying to do right by her children by getting them absorbed in the Truth she could see there was a growing problem with gossip and back-biting and outright lies in the congregation. Her strong sense of right and wrong told her this sort of thing has no place in a Christian setting. After having taken her concerns repeatedly to the Elders they were still doing nothing to sort it out and Marianne was not going to put up with it.

So, five years after Ben and the girls left, Marianne made the decision to move her depleted family to a more spiritual congregation and to have a fresh start, make some new friends. After much prayer she knew it was definitely the right thing to do for her family when the chance of a council exchange came up.

They left their beautiful home by the sea and headed for a dying steel town in the Midlands. Marianne constantly reminded Peter and Jess that their move was for the right reasons, not about the type of town they were going to. Unemployment was very high and many of the Scottish families that had migrated for the work at the steelworks now found themselves on the poverty line. It was a dire situation, but Peter started working within two days of the move. He went from door to door (such a handy skill to have developed, approaching strangers) and built up his own window cleaning round, perfectly flexible so it would fit around the ministry. She was so proud of him. He would make a good catch one day.

Jess started in the nearest secondary school and one or two of the young Witness children also went there. Marianne was pleased she wasn't alone.

The new congregation was bigger and had a wider age range than their previous one. It was spiritually strong and united, very loving and had a solid base from which to grow and Jess did indeed grow. She made plenty of new friends of all ages and was never short of someone to work with on the ministry. The social side of the Truth was better here too. Picnics were arranged now and then, country walks and visits to the JW headquarters in London. There was even a yearly trip to the British Museum where one of the tour guides was actually a Witness. This meant that the information from him about the Assyrians would be accurately tied into the Bible. How blessed they were!

*

It wasn't too long before Peter's day came round. He had met Janey at a weekend visit to a friend's in Hornchurch. When he saw her walking down the stairs he'd described it as 'love at first sight' which made Jess retch. After dating mostly by phone and letter for about four months they married and Jess was one of the bridesmaids along with Nerys. It was a happy day but her brother's move down to Essex left a big gap in Jess's daily life.

Peter was no longer there in the evenings for dinner, poking fun when Jess left sloppy green vegetables on the plate. The house had always been quite lively especially when his friends came round and now a stillness, an emptiness, had settled on the place. He'd passed his driving test at seventeen, just before they left Eastbourne, and now Jess and Marianne would need to get buses to the Hall. That was fine, a bit chilly in the winter, but it also meant that they couldn't give anyone a lift home and be invited in for a cuppa and biscuits after the meeting. But Jess was glad he was happy and she adored her new sister-in-law, Janey.

*

Life was beginning to get fuller and richer for Jess as time went along. She bonded particularly well with Cassie, a couple of years her senior and they shared many interests: they both liked music and carefully chose new records from the 'reduced' stand at the local newsagents. No songs about sex, violence or the occult was the general rule and that meant they needed to buy *Smash Hits* and inspect the lyrics before buying a record. Consequently, their collection of singles was quite small.

Cassie's mum, Cally, was a great knitter and was always willing to show Jess the complicated pattern she was working on. The huge balls of wool she used looked so thick and warm, as if they had come straight off the back of a sheep. Cooking became a regular activity when Jess stayed over at Cassie's and they came up with some bizarre creations to delight her parents. Their attempt at making a cheese sauce, however, was never very successful. No matter how many times they tried, it just wouldn't thicken up.

With almost every aspect of her life having changed Jess found herself feeling truly happy, the happiest she'd felt for a long time. It had taken a while to settle into her new surroundings but the past three years had been full and exciting, hard at times, but she got through it. Although she missed her old friends, especially Nerys, their exchange of letters and the occasional phone call kept their friendship alive. She also missed being near the sea but made regular use of the local swimming pool.

*

"It won't be long now till you're applying for jobs and making a start on your career," said the careers teacher when the fourth years had just finished with their mock exams. Interviewing each pupil individually he enquired:

"So which route have you decided to go down, Jessica?"

There was plenty of support and advice to be had for any career Jess wanted. This could have been a turning point for her and she decided she had to play along. But she knew wholeheartedly what she wanted to spend her time on but how could she possibly explain it? It would sound so alien to any teacher, even laughable.

A long time ago Jess had decided that when she

left school she wanted to become a Pioneer and that meant devoting at least sixty hours a month to the preaching work.

There was never any question of staying on at school for sixth form. It was pointless working towards going to university. The end of the world is coming so what use would a career be? 'Why polish the brass on a sinking ship?' was a common phrase which needed no elaboration. Pioneering was the most worthwhile activity to be engaged in for sure.

"Well, I want to stay on for sixth form, of course, doing French and Business Studies and then go into translation or interpretation."

It sounded good. Would have been nice, travelling, meeting new people, having a career with decent money. She might even meet some nice French guy and have some little French children one day.

"Well, you've obviously thought long and hard about it. Most pupils I've spoken to haven't got a clue what they want to do," he mumbled. "As far as I'm aware there are lots of opportunities in that field so you shouldn't be stuck. I wish you all the best, Jessica."

How deceiptful she was! But it's all right to lie if it's to support Kingdom interests.

For a Pioneer's hours to be officially recorded and included in the worldwide figures they needed to be a baptised Witness. And Jess's baptism was set for the following weekend.

*

Round about her fifteenth birthday, in April of 1983, Jess had reached a point in her life where she felt ready to make a dedication to Jehovah. This she did in prayer,

27

promising to spend the rest of her life in his service, doing what he required and enjoying the protection and blessings he would bestow upon her. She then approached the Elders and informed them that what she desired more than anything was to be baptised. That's the procedure and she followed it to the letter.

Shortly after, three separate visits by three different Elders were carried out at Jess's home and she was asked the set of eighty questions taken from their baptism book. She'd had the religion instilled in her almost from birth and their tricky back to front and reworded questions didn't catch her out. She guessed they needed to check that all candidates understood what they were doing – that they had repented of their sins and that their baptism would identify them as one of Jehovah's Witnesses in association with God's spirit-directed Organisation.

She knew the Truth inside and out. Had known nothing else her whole life and felt she had a good grasp of Christian principles as well as the rules of the Organisation.

She knew the subservient role of women and accepted that she would never be able to preach or read the Bible from the platform. As a Sister she would never be called upon to carry out any supporting tasks such as organising the literature, passing round the microphone, apportioning the territory for the ministry. There would never be an opportunity to progress to a caring organisational role or a decision-making role of Elder or Ministerial Servant. Those positions were fulfilled by males only, as they were in the Bible. However, Jess did recall reading about a Prophet and Judge of Israel called

Deborah, and what about Miriam, the sister of Moses and Aaron who led the Jews out of exile in Egypt? *Curious…*

She understood the difficult subject of blood transfusions and how that, if she was ever in need of blood to save her life or her child's, it would be right to refuse. Blood is sacred and God has instructed that it must not be eaten (or taken into the body). Always a touchy subject on the doors it was one that she would try to avoid. The best she could do was *hope* that she would do the right thing at the time. *No one could ever be sure though, could they?*

No trousers for Sisters including culottes. And no beards for the men. *But that was strange because Jesus had one. Hmmm. OK.* No eating chocolate eggs at Easter time or hot cross buns. No black pudding as it contained blood. *(That's an easy one, it looked disgusting anyway.)* No more than one piercing in each ear. No tattoos or other body piercings. No ankle bracelets – they are the mark of a prostitute. Minimum make-up to be worn.

She knew it all…

Discos are where the devil resides and while people are in a drunken state he influences them to engage in all sorts of heinous activities. Obviously, Christmas and birthdays are out of the question – she is quite used to this.

No watching *M*A*S*H*. It's all about patching up soldiers so they can go back out and kill more people.

No watching or joining in with any Morris dancers – they try to scare away the devil with all their bells.

And definitely no further education. Mixing with worldly students and their drinking and late-night sexual activities culture is certain to drag the most spiritual person away from the Truth. So, forget it.

*

Approved for baptism, the day arrived and was held as part of the Circuit Assembly programme the following December. The assembly, which catered for about a thousand local Witnesses, was currently held in her home town at the Civic Centre which, conveniently, was right next to the swimming pool. There were two others from Jess's congregation doing the same thing that day. It was something to be celebrated indeed – one of the few things that was acceptable to recognise and take delight in. Presents and cards came Jess's way and tight hugs from her mum and friends. Cassie bought her a silver chain holding a tiny silver hedgehog which she treasured and wore to every meeting after that for years.

Marianne was relieved. This meant that Jess was truly under the safe protection of the congregation and she would be able to bat away any problems that came along. She was a baptised Witness now! Sister Jessica!

Jess was pleased too as it meant that all her ministry hours would now count; she could submit a monthly report and all her ministry activity would be sent to the worldwide headquarters in New York. She felt elated and was in such high spirits for the following few weeks. She held her head a little higher and wore a smile on her face at school for a change and no one knew why. She threw herself into the Truth as much as she could, making an increasing number of return visits. Some progressed to a weekly Bible study and Jess was happy to be passing on the life-giving message she'd been learning about all her life. It was truly satisfying.

She was proud of what she was doing and wanted to continue to improve.

Jess knew her mum was relieved that she was now under the safe protection of God and the congregation, but one day Marianne's duty-bound words of caution puzzled her, "You know, Jess, for about the next six months you'll need to be extra careful."

"Extra careful?" Jess asked, frowning as she put her *Watchtower* aside.

"Yes, don't you see your baptism has really angered Satan the devil? He's so cross with you for having made a stand against him and taken Jehovah's side. He's got his eye on you now and will be looking for ways to trip you up, to cause you to be unfaithful."

"Oh, right." Jess wondered how that would translate.

She had never seen this in any literature or read a supporting scripture, but it seemed understandable that the devil would be angry. There had reportedly been so many newly baptised ones that had fallen at the first hurdle and left the Truth after some temptation had come their way. Jess would need all her wits about her to watch out for any attempts to destroy her faithfulness.

It was quite a sobering thought, that the devil himself was on her back. She lay awake at night trying to pre-empt what the next day would bring and prepare for how she would deal with it. Perhaps she would be offered a cigarette at school or one of the boys next door would ask her out on a date. Or maybe she would be invited to investigate how a Ouija board worked. It was with these disturbing thoughts she would go to sleep – and wake with the same ones whirring through her mind.

After nights like that the mornings would begin with an extra expressive supplication to God and she would steel herself ready for the day ahead at school. She had worked hard at her spiritual goals, had chosen suitable people to mix with. She wanted to reach out for Missionary work one day and so wanted to stay on the right track. She didn't want anything to get in the way.

At times the pressure and the fear were too much to bear and she would spend her lunchtimes alone at the back of an unlocked classroom away from everyone. And no one knew or would understand the pressure she was under. How could she possibly concentrate on her lessons throughout the day when at the back of her mind was the fear that someone was going to try and trip her up, get her to sin against God and make the devil laugh?

Marianne was quite accurate when she'd said, "Six months."

Chapter Three

1984. This summer is a hot one. Jess's final exam had been in May and there is nothing to do except sunbathe in the back garden. And go out on the ministry.

As she lays there with her skin zinging as the baby oil is heated by the sun (some bright spark had assured her that baby oil would produce a great tan), she ponders her new status: no school to worry about now, all she needs to do is find a little part-time job cleaning or some office work then she will have time to pioneer. Such freedom! No need to mix with those worldly kids at school anymore, hear their plans to go to college to get a hairdressing qualification or to fry their brains with a computer programming course. It will all be a waste of time for them. Such a shame. Armageddon's just around the corner, if they'd only listen.

Poring over adverts in the jobs section of the local newspapers keeps her occupied for only a few minutes a day, there's so little about. So far the distribution of her CV and covering letter has not produced anything positive, no replies, no upcoming interviews. It's a bit disheartening but something should come up soon. And while she's waiting she's going to enjoy relaxing in this glorious sunshine and listen to the birds.

Some of her time she spends preparing for meetings or sorting out her ministry bag, making sure she has enough magazines and leaflets that cover the most common subjects: blood transfusions, where are the dead, why do we grow old, that sort of thing. It's best to be prepared as she could meet anyone out there. Maybe the first house she calls on will be someone who's just lost a beloved pet and wants to know if they have a soul. At this time of year many householders are out tending to their gardens and so Jess would steer the conversation towards creation and ask the person if they believe there is an intelligent designer out there. All good techniques she learns from the Thursday night meetings.

Sometimes she rearranges the furniture in her room or sorts through boxes of old school stuff. Her English books she's been keeping since junior school but maths and science books can go in the bin. What about her pencil case full of wood shavings? As she pulls at the zip and sniffs the contents, she decides to keep it, not really knowing why.

Food shopping when Marianne's not up to it and some hand-washing keep her occupied too as does an occasional trip on the bus to the record shop in town. She doesn't really see anyone outside of meetings and ministry except Cassie now as the others her age have managed to find jobs. Due to her health conditions Cassie is struggling to find a suitable working environment and a boss who understands her limitations. Diabetes has affected Cassie for much of her life. She manages it well and doesn't make a big thing of it, but Jess feels sorry for her having to inject twice a day and constantly watch what she eats. Epilepsy too has her in its grip and despite medication, Cassie still suffers occasional fits resulting in bruises and cuts from where she's fallen.

One or two of the young ones are pioneering and Jess has a regular arrangement for a Tuesday with Faye who has been a Pioneer for a year now.

"If we meet on the territory at nine we can start our time early," she'd instructed.

Jess had grown to understand that pioneering is all about hours and minutes. 'Time' starts with the knock on the first door and extends to the last conversation in the day, deducting chunks of time for lunch. Jess always thought it was cheating, of the five and a half hours she recorded on a Tuesday only a fraction of that could truthfully be said to be spent preaching, actually conversing with a non-Witness.

"But we're being *seen* out and about," Faye had said. "That's what makes it all right. When anyone spots us and says, 'they must be Jehovah's Witnesses,' that counts as preaching too. It's not all about standing on doorsteps."

Still, it didn't feel quite right to Jess.

*

The patio is far too hot to walk on barefoot. Jess wonders how the cats manage. Sophie, the most beautiful white-haired cat in the world in Jess's eyes, had recently produced a litter of four kittens. Sophie is so observant of her young ones and trusts Jess enough to let her touch her babies to wipe away their dribbles or to place them nearer to her.

Little squeaks emerge from their cardboard box in the wardrobe and Jess can hear their tiny scratching sounds as they try out their new claws. She sits and watches them often, sees the way that, gently but firmly, Sophie holds each kitten and licks its fur, biting an ear or laying down a heavier paw when necessary to keep it still. Then she rolls over to find another, each one getting the same loving care and attention. They are protected and cared for until it's safe to start exploring out of the confines of their cardboard box.

As the kittens' confidence grows they make their way into the garden and play together inside a lid-less yellow swing bin tipped on its side. Hide and seek! Rough and tumble! Crouch and pounce! Their playfulness is simply adorable. Jess lays on her side on the blanketed grass with her arm bent under her head and watches them for hours. It seems that mother and babies are so close and in tune they have their own private language and their little squeaks become louder as they get bolder. Sophie is less and less able to control them as they take to wandering about the garden. They will grow and they will make their way in this world alone. One day.

*

Sitting up Jess folds her legs to the side and grabs her *Watchtower*. She turns to the article to be studied at the meeting the following Sunday.

'Where Can We find Unity in This Strife-Torn world?' She answers it automatically in her head:

In the Truth.

Flicking through to the article for the following week she finds: 'How Important is Prayer to You?'

"Very," she says out loud to no one.

This is all very familiar stuff and it's a struggle to get anything new and fresh out of the magazines these days.

A big sigh escapes as she leans back against the

warm fence and shields her eyes from the sun. Her ears prick up. Coming from next door she can hear George Michael asking not to be kept hanging on like a yo-yo. Three teenage boys live there and their parents are away running a pub in Peterborough. The boys look after themselves from what Jess can see and she wonders if they miss their mum and dad or are having the time of their lives with so much freedom.

David's nice. If she happens to be in the garden when he's going out he waves through the fence. Sometimes he'll put the milk bottles at the end of the path along with theirs as the milkman doesn't always see them. Jess wonders if she should ask him what he's doing now the exams are finished. Maybe he'll stay on at sixth form. Or go to work at his parents' pub.

The boys play music at all hours, and at all levels. Jess doesn't actually mind as it's the only way she gets to hear what music is around at the moment. Marianne hates the disturbance and has told them many times to turn it down. Where music is concerned Jess has got a huge bone to pick with the BBC; they really couldn't have chosen a worse time to put *Top of the Pops* on – seven o'clock on a Thursday evening! That's meeting night! How could they?!

Another big sigh escapes.

A giggle is starting to bubble up from somewhere deep inside and Jess suddenly lets out a spurt of laughter, making the kittens jump and scurry away. That talk at the meeting last week that was all about self-abuse! How did anyone manage to keep a straight face? Lanzo had volunteered (he actually offered, can you believe it?) to prepare a few words to say about his personal habit! He explained that with lots of prayer and keeping busy in the ministry he manages to keep it under control. Bah ha ha!!! She so wants to go up to him at the next meeting and whisper in his ear: "Hi Lanzo, how's your personal habit these days?"

She wonders if Alan has a personal habit.

Alan is two years her senior. Tall, dark and handsome. Yes, it's a cliché, but it's true! She had fancied him forever. The meetings have a different element to them more recently and it's becoming increasingly difficult to concentrate. She is conscious of him from the moment she arrives till the moment she leaves – where he's sitting, who he's talking to, what he's wearing. And when he passes by, she takes the smell of him deep into her lungs. Her nerve endings are constantly fizzing with the thought of him and the possibilities ahead. Is she old enough to date? Sixteen, yeh, she thought so.

She'd grown up on advice from the platform about how to be a good friend and all the dangers surrounding dating. That dating was for one singular purpose; with a view to getting married. She understood the necessity of a chaperone, had absorbed all the wise information from the scriptures about how to be a good wife, one that a husband could be proud of, one that wouldn't nag and who would always perform her marital duty. What were her good points and what would Alan look for in a girlfriend? A good strong, faithful sister in the Truth. Friendly. She has time for the older ones in the congregation, gives the Brothers and Sisters practical help when needed and takes her turn cleaning the Kingdom Hall. What's not to like?

But the reality is Alan doesn't give her a second glance. There's not even the slightest eye contact. Why doesn't he notice her? And how can anything grow from nothing?

Lying there in the heat an image of dancing gathers in her thoughts. Not a youth disco or an after-school social night, something she'd never experienced, but one of the few barn dances she'd been to. They were held in a sports centre in Northampton and although organised by a worldly group it was considered that as long as everyone stuck together it would be all right to attend.

It was usual for the dozen or so Brothers and Sisters to meet at Jess's house prior to travelling out of town. Everyone just turned up and then they sorted out seats in cars. Wondering if she was actually abusing the wonderful gift of prayer, which is supposed to be for help with real problems, Jess asked God that Alan be put in the same car as her, preferably right next to her, please, so she can breathe in his scent and hear his deep voice. She would be so close to him he couldn't possibly avoid eye contact. It never happened.

At these dances it was the only chance she had to be really close to him, hold his hand if only for a fleeting moment while 'passing him by' or 'stripping the willow'. Each dance was over all too soon and she wished she could keep hold of his hand forever.

With Alan's continual blanking of her Jess eventually has to accept that God thinks she's not ready for a relationship yet. But, no doubt, he'll have someone ready for her at the right time, so she just needs to be patient. Keep doing what she's doing to the best of her ability and it will all work out.

But as the sun beats down and she's lying there in her bikini, body glistening with all that oil, she can't actually stop thinking about him: he's there, in her thoughts, in her heart and all she wants is to be enveloped in his arms and held tight. She imagines Alan with one hand around her back and the other holding her head against his chest and he gently rocks her as if to a soothing tune that no one else can hear. She could stay like that forever, wrapped up warm and secure. She knew that if he just held her for a moment he would realise she was the one. There was no need to keep searching anymore, they'd found each other. Within other imaginings she strays to a stirring deep inside that moves Alan's hands around her body. He wants her and he lets her know. She can feel him against her as his arms tighten around her waist. She looks up into his dreamy brown eyes. It's time…

Ice cream! Jess is sure there's some ice creams in the freezer compartment and quickly goes to have a look. Back out in the garden the sun has moved round and she sits down on the fold-up chair with just her feet in the sun and her Mini Milk in her hand and with each lick she can't help but think about Alan.

*

The kittens are still playing and she still needs to get her pen out and underline the answers in Sunday's *Watchtower*. But it's far too hot to concentrate on anything heavy, especially not the mind-bending prophecies of Ezekiel. She just wants to lie in the sun and relax, listen to the birds, follow the vapour trail of an aeroplane high up in the sky and imagine where it's going, or where it's been. Her exams are over, her time is all her own to choose what to do with. The last few months had been hard what with the mocks, her baptism and her final exams. Now she deserves some time to let her mind rest.

*

Sophie looks down on Jess and miaows.

"OK, Sophie, you hungry?"

On her way out to the kitchen to get the tins of cat food she notices a brochure laying on the mat. It must have just been posted through the door. It's colourful. Thick. A quick flick through shows it's a company that sells all manner of household products from radiator brushes to heated foot pillows and collapsible buckets. *Looks like there are some really useful things in here*, thinks Jess, as she works from back to front. Others appear totally unnecessary and just gimmicks that people would buy as presents. Like the bobbly floor polishing slippers and the snazzy washing machine cover available in pink or blue. Good prices though, she has to admit.

A sticker on the back cover says they are looking for agents in the area. Jess is used to going from house to house and street to street, she can do that with her eyes closed. A little job like this would do for a while. Anyway, it's not like she needs to earn a lot.

Running it past her mum the following day, Jess walks down the road to the phone box with a handful of ten- and fifty-pence pieces and dials the number. Following a short interview with the area supervisor she's offered an initial package of fifty brochures to see how she gets on.

*

Marianne is relieved that Jess will now be working. In

these few weeks since school had finished she could have got herself up and out on the ministry a bit more. She can see she's trying to build up her hours and has a sensible regular arrangement with Faye but still, she could be doing more. At least now she'll be occupied with something sensible and won't be lolling about in the garden all day playing with the kittens.

It's good for the young ones to have goals, thinks Marianne. So, Auxiliary pioneering this year at sixty hours a month then Regular pioneering next year, that's ninety hours. The next step would be a Missionary somewhere abroad or going to work at the Organisation's headquarters in London. *What wonderful opportunities are open to her! Oh, to be a youngster in the Truth! Think of all those lovely Brothers and Sisters she will meet all around the world, the chance to travel and help people to study the Bible,* muses Marianne. *Then she'll be asked up onto the platform at District Assemblies in front of thousands to relate her experiences. She might even make it into one of the magazines and be hailed as a young Witness who puts the Truth first in her life!*

Marianne loves her daughter and wants the best life possible for her.

*

"Mum, I'm off out to deliver these orders," Jess announces the following week. She'd diligently delivered the brochures in her designated area the week before and the customers' orders had been dropped off at her house a few days later. Matching up the goods with the duplicate order forms doesn't take a lot of brain power and loading up her large company bag she's ready to head off.

"Have you got many?" shouts Marianne from upstairs just catching Jess before she closes the front door.

"A few," comes her reply, not knowing how long it would take her as this is her first delivery. The sky is pigeon-grey and a gusty wind has developed. A welcome respite from the heat but now it's muggy and hard to breathe with a dusty orange hew all around. She takes a bottle of water with her and an umbrella just in case. Her ministry tactics come in useful as she takes a steadily paced walk towards the address the furthest away so she can work back towards home.

It's not taking that long really and her bag, now slung over her shoulder, is getting lighter and lighter with each delivery. She feels a temptation to write down how long it had taken her but shakes her head and tells herself not to be silly. This isn't the ministry, it's work! The rain has held off but the dark clouds are still there, threatening to burst before she gets home.

She left off delivering the brochures last week at the end of the even numbers in Gainsborough Street. She looks at the threatening sky and thinks if she's quick she can just post a few more brochures starting on the odd numbers before the heavens open.

Approaching number eighty-three down the long front path Jess is startled as the door suddenly opens ahead. The knocker clatters loudly with the force and a large man stands wildly gesturing and shaking his head. With a final scowl he firmly bangs the door closed. *No, OK,* thinks Jess, *you don't want one, that's fine*, and she moves on to the next house. In the following week the same thing happens at more properties, sometimes through an open upstairs window or from the front garden with the householders shouting:

"Don't want that rubbish here." "Not interested." "You can piss off with that nonsense."

Thinking it all a little odd she makes a note of the houses and reports it to her supervisor who is completely bewildered.

"We've never had our brochure turned down before. I don't understand why. I'll have to contact the house owners and find out."

But after a little thought Jess had worked it out. Her face was just too familiar on the estate.

*

The month of June passes by, uneventfully. Lazy days. She knows she's been slacking where the ministry is concerned but it's so hard to stay motivated. Faye is away on holiday and others try to make plans with her. It's easier not to make firm arrangements in case she changes her mind. She doesn't want to let anyone down. No, it's better if she just turns up at the ministry group meeting at half nine then she can be put with someone random. That does carry a certain risk though; she could be paired with a person she really doesn't like and be stuck with them for the whole morning. Ones that take over her conversation or, at the other extreme, expect her to do every door.

A few weeks in and Jess is getting into a good routine with her job. It's easy work and going from door-to-door feels so familiar, it's really no hardship. And the money's nice to have even though it doesn't stretch very far. After paying her board and bus fares to the meetings there's not a lot left but she's hoping it's enough to get something new to wear for Norwich District Assembly coming up mid-August. The theme this year is: 'Kingdom Increase'.

*

Carrow Road Football Ground. Capacity 25,000. Not a place to get lost. The annual assembly means four days of talks, demonstrations, singing, praying and note-taking. Jess is an excellent note-taker; she's had years of practice and has invented her own kind of shorthand, one that only she understands. These assemblies are hard work. It's the early mornings, trying to get through the crowds, queuing for food and the toilet, let alone trying to concentrate on the programme. If it's hot weather too, it's especially exhausting, and in the afternoons very difficult to keep from nodding off.

*

Jess suspects that Marianne won't be going this year. From the frequency of her mood swings and the amount of time she's been in bed Jess can tell her mental health hasn't been good lately and she probably wouldn't be able to cope with an assembly. Socialising is expected, it's an unwritten rule – what a wonderful opportunity to meet Brothers and Sisters from other congregations and make new friends! But when she's having a bad time, Marianne unwittingly wears a particular look which screams, 'Leave. Me. Alone.' It's hard for someone in good health to get through the punishing four days.

Jess will take plenty of notes though, so her mum won't miss out on any important information. She will bring back all the new books and brochures released and recount the many experiences the Brothers and Sisters

45

have had in the ministry over the past year.

Jess is sixteen now and old enough to be responsible for herself. She doesn't need her mum around like she used to.

A large group from Jess's congregation have chosen to stay this year on a campsite out on the Norfolk coast and will drive into the city each day. Cassie's parents have said the two girls can share a tent next to their campervan so she'll be safe enough. They know she's a good girl and would be no trouble.

*

As the assembly approaches Jess feels for the first time ever, that she actually doesn't want to go. It takes her by surprise. It's not just because her mum isn't going but, well, she doesn't really know why exactly. She'd been feeling quite empty over the last couple of weeks, a flag hanging lifeless on a windy day, with no energy or enthusiasm.

Was it down to boredom? Her job was going well, a little monotonous but it was all right. Her spiritual life was just the same as ever, she didn't have anything to complain about there. So what was it? She couldn't put her finger on why she felt so flat. But, after having a stern word with herself in the mirror, she knew that the coming four days of spiritual food will make everything all right. Hearing others' uplifting experiences will give her the boost she needs and she can go back home with a clear plan in her head about her future. *Yes,* she thinks, *this assembly is all I need.*

Chapter Four

At eighteen Ray is tall, lanky some may say, and is the image of Nick Heyward of *Haircut 100*, especially when he wears his hat.

Oldham born and bred his dad had been working at Agecroft colliery in Salford when cutbacks were announced. Ray's parents were unavoidably caught up in the miners' strikes that began in Yorkshire earlier on in the year. It was a serious situation and half the country's mineworkers had walked out. Money was short and it was a case of relying on the Union not just for help with paying the rent but also for their daily essentials. Some days Ray came home from his shift at Toy and Hobby absolutely ravenous only to find there was something on toast again for tea. While Ray's wages brought in a little extra on top of his dad's, the family was really struggling. Thinking about the bigger picture he had an idea that might just make things a little easier.

*

To ease the burden on their parents Ray and his brother Dane decided to travel for a while till things settled down. They were good boys, thoughtful and observant. They were confident they could earn money doing bar work, fruit picking, cleaning. Discussing the idea together with their parents they agreed that they would be prepared to try their hand at anything that came along. It would be challenging, not having a solid plan, but exciting, and who knew where it would take them? The decision was made.

Their journey started as they said goodbye to their parents at the front door. The lads looked back as they walked down the path, rucksacks thrown over their shoulders. Ray fought to swallow the lump in his throat. He saw his parents waving from the threshold, arms round each other, their faces heavy with emotion. He would miss them, of course, but tears wouldn't have been helpful to his mum at that moment.

They headed south on the local bus towards Macclesfield, an old market town only about twenty miles away. They didn't want to make their first stop too far away in case there were any problems which meant they needed to go back. Ray had been told by a mate there was work going at the Shell garage so that was their first stop. Straight in, first shift was the following morning. *This is going well*, Ray thought.

It was simple work – stocking shelves, filling up customers' tanks and serving at the till. Dane managed to talk himself into a job at Sainsbury's on Exchange Street. He had the gift of the gab, and a cheeky face, and people found him instantly likeable.

Their digs were at the home of a relative of a friend of Ray's, Mickey, who knew of their adventure and offered to put them his spare room for a while. It was really kind of him considering he had never met them. He had a telephone on the wall in the hallway and allowed Ray to use it to phone home as long as he threw a few coins in the pot by the kettle. Ray's dad, kind but strict, let the lads know the score:

"Yeh, best you be behavin' yourselves there, I've told that fella he can clout you round the head if you make a mess."

"We'll be fine, Dad," Ray assured him, and told him the good news that they'd both found work already.

"You and Mum gonna be all right?" Ray asked in a soft voice.

"We'll manage," he says, "no matter what happens with the pit, we'll get by, so don't you stay away if you get stuck, you hearin' me? You come straight back if you need to, lad."

*

Two weeks in and Ray and Dane are looking at the map making plans for their next stop. A hot summer spurs them on to try and see a bit of the country, perhaps get to stay by the sea somewhere. A swim would be good after a day of hard graft.

They moved on to Hartington in the Derbyshire Dales and were taken on in the Charles Cotton Pub. Lucky enough to be able to stay on site they stored their, as yet unused, tents in the cupboard on the landing. The landlady and landlord were such easy-going people and very interested to hear of their adventure. Long shifts behind the bar and a bit of waiting tables meant they are both shattered by the end of each evening, but not too tired for a walk down by the river and along to Thor's Cave.

One evening, Dane, a young starter with cigarettes, sat puffing on the shelf of the cave overlooking the beautiful landscape. The sun was just starting to dip below the trees and shadows of the branches danced around in the breeze. Ray sat on the grassy bank down below with his feet in the cool water, trousers rolled up, watching it bubble up through his toes.

"Nice 'ere i'nt it?" Dane shouted down to Ray. "I could stay here for a while meself."

"Thought we were heading for the sea? Summer'll be over soon, want to get there before the picking stops." Ray kicked a few pebbles under the clear water.

"Another few days, yeah, then we'll look at moving along."

Ray being the older brother had the final word.

Fruit picking. There'd be loads of work available in Norfolk. Apple orchards, strawberry and raspberry fields, cabbages, gooseberries and rhubarb. Easy work. That's where they were heading next.

*

On the day of the boys' arrival at Lea Malling the weather breaks. Thunderous clouds boom ferociously overhead as they hurry along the gritty road towards the Golden Sands campsite entrance. The bus couldn't get them any nearer. Backpacks sodden in the short time it takes to get to the site reception they hope the waterproof tent bags live up to their name. They'd been very lucky with the weather so far with not a drop of rain since leaving Oldham.

A quick visual sweep across the site through the hammering rain shows the boys there's a space in the far corner, just big enough for their two-man tent. They keep running though, and crash through the double doors into the seated area of the clubhouse and dump their packs on the floor.

Through the rain-streaked windows Ray can see the site is busy with pricey-looking caravans all down one side. Further away sits a row of static caravans looking as if they've been there for many years, set in their ways. Some of them wear a cheerful skirt of white picket fencing and display an assortment of plastic plant pots in the private patch at the side. A long nylon washing line stretches between two short lamp posts and holds a multicoloured mixture of items, now completely soaked. In the opposite corner there's a brick building with tiny windows housing toilets and showers.

It feels comfortable. As long as it's true about there being plenty of work Ray feels it could be a place to stay for a while.

Their long, disjointed journey down from Derbyshire had taken most of the day and their stomachs are now rumbling. In between making their coach connections there wasn't time to grab anything substantial to eat, just crisps and a chocolate bar from the kiosk. The café offers basic food, sausages, burgers, chips, eggs on toast so Dane goes to the counter and orders two meals and two big mugs of tea.

"Any picking work down here?" asks Ray of the man as he sets their plates on the table.

"You want to look at the advert in the shop window. Always looking for hands this time of year. Be quick, mind, season finishes in a couple of weeks," he informs them as Ray reaches for the tomato sauce.

Just in time then, he thinks. *Great stuff. Should make a bit of money.*

*

Standing in front of the shop Ray reads the sign: 'The truck to Bardon Fields leaves at 8am. Bring your own bottle, water will be provided. Payment at 5pm and not before.'

The old rattling farm vehicle they clamber into the

following morning has a tin roof over the trailer and is stifling in the heat. The bodies packed in along the benches either side adds to the heat and his brother's water bottle is almost empty before they are halfway there. Ray hopes the journey isn't too long.

Ray peers out from the back of the truck as they pull up and he can see the field of strawberries stretching far away. Laid out in rows alternating with dried earth and straw the rich red of the fruit flashes as the strengthening breeze blows the leaves. One or two weeds have made their way in and look alert and happy to have had a good drenching yesterday.

They jump out of the dusty truck and are quickly assigned a task. There is a strong, sweet, inviting smell, and as Ray breathes it in is reminded of home; toast with strawberry jam for breakfast, and his mum. He can't help wondering how things are back home. *Will Dad be on the picket line today?* he wonders.

The work is back-breaking, even for strong lads. Crouching with their legs folded underneath is too uncomfortable so they shift frequently to find a position to stay in for longer than ten minutes. Whoever said this was easy was lying, it's damn hard work. By midday their hands are aching especially their thumbs as they take each punnet back to the supervisor to be weighed. As they get familiar with how much each one should weigh the times they get sent back to top up underweight punnets grows fewer. A ticket is issued for each punnet of the correct weight and by the end of the afternoon each lad has a fistful.

Ray is a fast worker and puts his tickets safely in a zipped pocket in his shorts. Dane has to stop to have a fag at the edge of the field far too often, which means he's earning less, but, that's his choice. Their arrangement is they go halves on the site fees, food and drink. Travel costs they fund individually and if Dane needs fags, he buys them himself or goes without – Ray is very strict with that. He made it clear from the start he would not be supporting his habit, no way.

The week continues and the pot is filling up. The boys are quite chuffed with themselves for having come this far under their own steam. It was the right decision: to move along and let Mum and Dad concentrate on things back home unburdened by them. Ray feels a responsibility towards Dane and now they've reached almost the end of the summer he has to start thinking about their next move. North, south, east or west? He needs to decide.

*

Jess's journey to Lea Malling on the Norfolk coast seems endless. The view is flat and uninteresting.

Cassie's dad, Andrew, a true Scot with a beard, set of bagpipes and a kilt, is using their converted-by-hand Ford Transit named Bodger's Lodge. The envy of others in the group of having it all on wheels, it plods along the A47 at a steady fifty miles an hour towards Norwich. Cally, a cuddly lady who always smelled of freshly baked bread, is in the front and Cassie and Jess in the back, buckled up into the hand-crafted stowaway seats. The design, all Andrew's own, really was something to behold. He'd built cubby holes in the backs of the seats, pockets behind doors, means of securing lose items whilst on the road. He'd thought of everything.

Jess looks out of the side window at a landscape so

uninspiring her mind wanders onto one much more appealing. She rests her head against the glass and thinks of Alan. He is eighteen now. She doesn't know which assembly he will be going to this year. His family's not one for camping; they'd rather travel there and back each day and sleep in their own beds at night.

The previous week she'd made a special purchase with her wages, and as she had packed it away in her case attached to it the hope that Alan would be knocked off his feet when he saw how gorgeous she looked in it. The calf-length dress was a luscious red with moderate shoulder pads, a narrow white band around the short sleeves, hemline and neckline. It gave her skinny form, a womanly shape helped along by the wide white shiny belt, elasticated at the back. Ecru tights and white stilettos complete the outfit. How would he be able to resist?

*

For the Thursday, the first day of the assembly, Cassie's mum has prepared a huge pack-up, enough to last the four of them all day; a variety of sandwiches, snacks and drinks. They take their own battery-operated fans but usually receive tuts from those around as they emit an annoying whirr, a distraction to those trying to listen to the speaker. The narrow wooden seats in the stands are just so uncomfortable that after the first twenty minutes a numb bum was to be expected, so Jess and Cassie's job is to find the end of the long queue for the cushions that are lent out for the day.

Andrew and Cally take all the bags and go off to choose some seats high up in the North stand telling the girls where they'll be. It should have been a quick procedure but the girls get delayed bumping into numerous people they know from neighbouring congregations and everyone wants to stop and talk. Of course, Jess keep an eye out for Alan too. There's no time to chat and so they arrange to meet their friends at lunchtime at the entrance to seating blocks R-S-T. They hurry along with the cushions and arrive in their seats just as the first song is about to start.

Jess made sure she'd pinned her name badge to her cardigan that morning. Not for security purposes; the gates are always open around the ground and anyone is free to walk in. It's for each other to know who they are and which congregation they come from, an opportunity to make new friends. It's all one big brotherhood after all and totally safe.

Jess thinks it's awesome to be amongst such a huge crowd. There are thousands upon thousands there and they are all Jehovah's Witnesses! Every one of them her spiritual Brother or Sister! She feels at home here surrounded by such honest, loving people.

During the first prayer following the opening song Jess opens her eyes and peers through the rows in front to see the tiny people doing the same on the opposite stand. Her eyes struggle to take in the enormity of such a place, even though she's been coming to football stadiums for as long as she can remember. The rich green of the manicured pitch contrasts with the multitude of colours everywhere and the whole spectacle is a feast for the eyes. The sound system has a persistent echo and it is hard to tune her hearing in to catch the words but once the first talk is over it gets easier.

*

Before Ray takes his shot he leans down. Arms outstretched with a striped ball and the white lined up he takes aim with the cue and nods at the top left pocket. Being tall has its advantages when playing pool – his long legs, long arms and long fingers all mean he doesn't have to stretch as much as others and, once he's got his eye in, well, it's usually game over for most of his opponents. His skills could keep him on the table at the youth club back home all evening if he wanted; rarely did anyone beat him. But he takes it all in his stride, it's just what he does.

One irritated opponent had once suggested he join a league – he could make some money – but he didn't want the pressure and the commitment. Then the competitiveness and the expectations would take over and spoil it all. No, he is happier to keep things as they are: an enjoyable game now and then with anyone who wants to take him on.

The last game he plays at the campsite clubhouse that Thursday evening in August takes him completely by surprise. He'd not seen her before. She's standing with a group of people she knows and is knocking back a, what was it? A shandy? Hanging around on the outskirts of the group she takes her back off the wall and moves in a little as her interest in his game increases. He's conscious of her following him round the table, bending down when he does, looking at the line-up from different angles. Sometimes she gets in the way and he coughs, looks pointedly at her then she moves. He wins the game as he'd expected and looks around left and right for his next opponent.

*

Jess pulls her back off the wall and holds her hand out to take the cue from the loser. She takes her time with each ball and for each of the striped balls Ray pots, Jess pots a spotted one. As she takes her final, triumphant shot and pots the black in the named middle pocket she hears a voice from behind her:

"Whoa, cracking shot!" It's Dane.

She wears a sheepish smile. Embarrassed, Ray shakes her hand and congratulates her.

"Well done, you've obviously played before." Jess looks him in the eye and stands tall.

"A few times, not many. Want to play again tomorrow night?" she asks him hopefully.

"Um, can do." Should he risk defeat again? In front of his brother? "Yeh, I'm out working all day tomorrow but should be here after tea."

"Working? You not on holiday?"

"Not really a holiday, we're down for the picking, then we'll be moving on. Got another couple of weeks' work."

From her left Jess hears a slow, deep voice laden with warning speak her name. Maureen, the mother of one of the other young Witnesses on the campsite can see what is happening; Jess is getting far too friendly with this worldly boy. This is how it all starts: one innocent conversation leads to the next and before you know it someone's pregnant.

Jess turns her head and looks at Maureen, who clearly thinks her function is to stand in her mother's place and holds her gaze pointedly and expressionless. Giving a slow blink she turns her head back to Ray.

Their conversation continues, and they take it out

into the cool night air as he slowly walks her back to her tent.

*

Ray is a gentleman, polite and caring. She could tell from that very first moment she saw him. He didn't boast about his pool skills and he has the manners to walk her home even though the tent is only at the far edge of the site.

They say goodnight and exchange smiles and Jess enters the tent.

"Where've you been, Jess?" asks Cassie.

"Down the clubhouse, there's a few playing pool down there. I had a couple of games. Didn't you want to come down?"

"Nah, I'm tired and I needed to eat, my levels are not too good. There's some beef stew left over if you want it. And bread too in the bag over there. Jess? What you smiling at?" enquires Cassie.

A grin has spread across her face which she hoped Cassie hadn't noticed. She wipes it off immediately and sets about getting her food. Sleep won't come tonight, she knows. She lays awake in the silence of the tent and listens to the wind whipping round the site, a tin can has escaped from someone's bin and is being blown from one end to the other. She blames the persistent buzz in her head on the half pint of shandy she'd had earlier, but it's not only in her head, it's in her chest too.

Replaying the evening in the clubhouse when she should have been remembering the wonderful spiritual food she'd had at the assembly makes her feel guilty but she doesn't stop. She can't. The games of pool. The conversation. The looks. The walk home. She'd never had this much attention from a boy before. *What's going on?*

*

As the second day of the assembly gets underway and Jess settles in her seat the thought of being stuck here till teatime makes her feel quite trapped. *Why do they have to make the days so excruciatingly long?* But she sets her mind to absorb all the next eight hours has to offer and dutifully gets her Bible and notebook out of her bag.

Talks follow demonstrations, the public address follows a song then a prayer then someone relates their fascinating experience in the ministry: they came across a distressed man who had just been praying for help and then guess what?

"I knocked on their door with the good news of God's Kingdom! I studied the Bible with him, he got baptised and look! Here he is right now, walking on the stage!"

By their noisy extended applause the crowds show they are thoroughly impressed by the news of how fast the Organisation is expanding and how widespread the Kingdom message is becoming. There are now Witnesses in over 350 countries, so many new congregations have been formed and incredible numbers of newly baptised ones. The boasting continues for a whole hour. Jess struggles to get all the information and figures down in her notebook to show Marianne. She glances over to Cassie's notes and hurriedly copies the last few. Her writing is just about legible.

The programme is varied but Jess's concentration drifts many times and the smell towards lunchtime of burgers and frying onions doesn't help. There are burger vans around the stadium and she makes her mind up to get something really greasy for tomorrow's lunch. But right now she's starving and can't wait for the morning session to finish so she can dig into the pack-up.

Excited chatter and the smell of coffee surround her as she eats and as soon as Cassie has finished they make their way to the meeting place and wait for their friends. The afternoon passes slowly and Jess watches the sun make its way round the stadium as the hours go by. A lone seagull circles the pitch then, finding nothing to stop for, scoots off over the top of the north stand.

*

Another day at the stadium has passed and back at the campsite dinner is on. The heat hasn't eased, but rather intensified and there's a heaviness in the air, an oppressive weight. The small children in the group have stripped off their tops in an effort to cool down. Driving back into the site earlier in the campervan Jess had spotted Ray by the entrance gate. He was walking purposefully towards the clubhouse with his brother Dane.

Jess gets changed out of her smart clothes, has a quick shower, feeling lucky there was one free in the toilet block, and towel dries her hair. It's naturally wavy and in this heat, would dry very quickly. A brush through and a bit of dinner and she'll be ready to go down for another game of pool. She feels excited but is careful not to show it in any of her body language. There would be questions.

She'd learned a bit about the game when Peter visited. After his move to Essex his new job as sales rep for designer eyewear took him all around the south and

Midlands. Often turning up at the house unannounced, which was such a lovely surprise, he would take Marianne and Jess out for dinner. He explained the rules of pool to her and a few games in and Jess had got the bug.

*

She knows it's wrong, hurrying to see Ray. Very wrong. On so many levels. She's here with Cassie and her parents and they're the ones looking out for her. But actually, they're not. They haven't been down the clubhouse once since arriving. Cassie is Jess's best friend and really they should stick together, but Cassie wants to stay back at the tent and Jess finds that boring. But above all that, Ray is a worldly boy and the constant warnings of getting involved or 'unevenly yoked' with a non-Witness are ringing in Jess's ears. Everyone knows that a short conversation with a non-Witness of the opposite sex will only lead to disaster. *But it's only a game of pool for goodness sake, there's no harm in that*, she tells herself.

Worldly people are not all bad, she reasons in her head. She remembers a girl back in her junior school: the girl's father was very poorly and was confined to a wheelchair. It was just the two of them as her mum had died from complications after childbirth. There was no one else to help. Every day when the girl got home from school she would do the jobs that her dad wasn't able to do: the vacuuming and polishing, taking the rubbish out, walking to the shops for bits they needed, sorting out the washing and doing all this before sitting down to do her homework. She spoke about it at school but never complained. She loved her dad.

Jess thought that if the Elders knew about that girl's life they would say it's all right to mix with her as she's a good person, surely? How can someone as giving as that possibly be regarded as 'bad association'? She guesses it must be just easier that way. Everyone that isn't a Witness is on the side of the devil so it's clear cut really, but such a pity as many of her classmates seem quite nice.

Ray is a worldly boy. It's a fact. He's a no no. Yet despite conducting a fierce conversation with herself and imagining what her mum would be saying she finds her feet pointing towards the clubhouse.

Chapter Five

Their conversation this time as he walks her home is just as friendly, just as polite but with a touch of urgency. What is it about him that makes her want to get her words out quick? She'd had another couple of shandies and he'd been drinking beer, only two pints she'd noticed, and he seemed… nice. Just really nice. Uncomplicated. Not like the Witness boys whose conversations are only about Witness things. *Are you out on the min tomorrow, Jess? I've run out of Awake magazines, have you got any spare?* Not like Alan who doesn't even look at her let alone talk to her.

Ray is kind and attentive. He smiles at her. He'd noticed her and she can tell by his manner he likes being with her. Halfway across the campsite Ray takes a sudden right turn and follows the dirt path away from the tents. Jess looks about her to check that no one is around and decides to follow him. The path leads to a low wide metal gate into the next field. They stand there resting their forearms on the cool bar and together watch the darkened orange sun sink lower in the sky. It had been another hot day but a gentle breeze has now picked up and wisps of hair blow across Jess's face. She tucks them behind her ear as she looks shyly at Ray. There is whispered chatter. There is gentle laughter. And there are smiles.

*

"Where have you been, Jess?" Cassie asks as Jess

stumbles into the tent. It's almost dark and Cassie sounds cross as she looks up from her book, torch in hand.

"I've been down the clubhouse." Although she hasn't noticed how late it is she's not going to avoid the conversation. She knows Cassie is only looking out for her.

"The others were all back ages ago. Where were you?"

"I went for a walk with a boy I met down there."

No need for details. In fact there isn't that much to tell.

Cassie looks back down at her book. Nothing else is said but Jess can tell she's annoyed. Night has fallen and another long day lies ahead after, she hopes, a good night's sleep.

*

It's Saturday. Baptism day! It's so exciting, seeing these new Witnesses dedicating their lives! On some occasions the candidates are whisked off by bus to the nearest swimming pool but Jess likes it best when they set up a big round pool at the edge of the pitch. To get a clear view of the action she needs to stretch and move around in her seat and peer through rows and rows of bodies all doing the same thing.

Each candidate climbs the steps at the side and is then helped down into the water to the two brothers assigned to do the baptising. As she watches she feels the coolness of the water swirl around their legs as they descend. On a swelteringly hot day like today she's quite jealous. She can almost hear the brothers' instructions as one places his arm around the candidate's shoulders:

"Pinch your nose with your left hand and hold your forearm with your right hand." As the body is lowered the other brother checks the feet in case they rise above the surface, necessitating a second dunk. It is supposed to be total immersion after all.

Watching the candidates being submerged, she wonders about the practical things. Have they put chlorine in the water? Has anyone actually pee'd in there? And why does everyone wear a swimming costume or trunks and then also cover up with a white T-shirt? It's too hot! If they are just being modest, well, no one could possibly see any pubic hair sticking out from way up here in the stands so they shouldn't really worry about it.

Prolonged loud applause rings out in the stadium after each one emerges to a Sister holding out a large towel. That job is always given to a mature, responsible Sister. *Not a difficult job,* Jess thinks. *Anyone could do that.* She watches to see if she can see the Sister's lips mouthing 'congratulations' as she wraps the towel around their dripping shoulders. The volume of the applause increases as an elderly man steps out. He deserves a special clap because he must have made some major changes. All his life he has been living under the devil's influence and now he's turned it all around. Now he has a chance of living forever – but only if Armageddon comes before he dies.

The applause is louder still when it's a child.

The Organisation has always criticised the Catholics' practice of baptising infants pointing out that a child is too young to understand what baptism really means. Now it looks like they don't mind so much. How old was that boy that had just dedicated his life to the God of the whole universe? About eight years old Jess reckons, but she doesn't question it out loud for some time. The Witnesses claim to follow Christ's example in everything so Jess reasons that a good age to get baptised would be thirty, just like Jesus. If he chose not to do it at eight there must have been a good reason.

She thinks back to her own baptism the previous year at fifteen. Was that too young? She didn't think so at the time. It was all very confusing.

*

Once the baptism is over the day passes as slow as the others. Jess is tired and her note-taking requires extra effort. Today she doodles on the edge of the page as she lets her concentration lapse and her mind wander back to the events of last night.

What is she doing? Playing with fire, that's what she's doing. There is a feeling in her chest that remains unnamed regardless how hard she tries to frame it. It has never been there before, she knows that. A mixture of intermittent fluttering of excitement, an unfamiliar pain, a deep ache and at times a sensation of utter peace and calm.

She should not see Ray tonight. She's gone too far already. It's pointless making a friend of him – after tomorrow they'll never see each other again. No, she must pray for help to deal with this and to put him firmly out of her thoughts. A determination rises in her to do the right thing and she finds the words and speaks them in her head, forming them into a fervent prayer. Recalling the stern look and admonition from Maureen on the first night at the clubhouse Jess now feels like a little girl again. For the rest of the session she obediently listens to a mishmash of super-spiritual words reverberating around the stadium and tries to take more notes for her mum.

But her thoughts stray again.

Just stay near the tent. Don't go to the clubhouse and he won't see you.

Jess shakes her head and tries again to get her attention back to the present in this vast metal stadium. She looks at Cassie to her left whose eyes are glazing over. The heat is getting to her, Jess can tell, and hands her a bottle of water from the picnic bag. The roof of the stand casts a shadow across the seats in a straight diagonal line. It will reach them soon, maybe ten minutes or so, then it should feel a little cooler.

*

Back at the campsite Jess knows she needs to keep herself busy and visible.

Swingball and hide and seek occupy the younger ones after tea and some of the adults join in, lolloping about, not putting much effort in. Jess sees some packing up taking place. There's only tomorrow left and some are heading back home straight from the stadium. Others, including Cassie and family, are leaving Monday morning so there's no point packing now.

The sun is sinking and the children are beginning to wind down, playing sit-down games on the grass. A pack of cards is shuffled and dealt, a pencil case of felt tips emptied out and Jess can hear the frantic scribbling of a four-year-old. Outside the mess tent the adults gather their fold-up chairs into a circle and chatter in hushed tones, slurp tea and flick through notes taken during the day. Jess and Cassie are in between the two scenes. At their age they're unsure which group to join. Three other teens saunter over and they talk about other teenagers in the congregation before turning the attention to Cassie.

She had got baptised earlier in the year and her parents were just so proud. They understand Cassie's health restrictions but are helping her to increase her hours in the field ministry as much as she can. She's now studying with two people each week and her magazine placements have gone through the roof! Jehovah is certainly blessing her efforts as last week she'd been offered an interview for the office job she wants. Things are starting to go well for Cassie.

As the chatter continues Jess takes a moment to wonder just how well she's doing herself. Right now she feels quite proud that she's managed to get through the evening without giving in to her thoughts and feelings about Ray. She's doing well. There's only tomorrow left then she'll be going home on Monday morning with no harm done.

*

At last, it's Sunday! The final day of the assembly and everyone is shattered. Jess can see it in their sullen faces and the kids are walking around with much less bounce.

Halfway through the morning session the need to sleep is almost too hard to resist. Jess needs an excuse to get up and walk around and conveniently there's a song at that point. Without sitting back down as the last words ring out Jess nudges Cassie:

"I need the toilet, Cass, you coming?" she mouthed, trying not to draw attention.

There is no handrail to guide their walk down the deep stone steps and Cassie is swaying slightly. Jess puts her arm through hers to support her. They descend more steps into the darkness of the inner concourse. The change in brightness makes them both pause as their eyes adjust. *What are all these people doing wandering around and standing in groups chatting?* Jess wonders. *They should be in their seats listening to the programme.* It's as busy as a shopping centre on a Saturday afternoon down there! It's the same every year. They take a left turn and shafts of light from each of the tunnels up ahead shine through as they make their way along to the toilets.

"Wanted to go before the Drama starts," explained Jess. "Are you OK?"

"Yeh, can't stand the heat. I'll ask Mum if we can sit on the other side tomorrow."

Back in their seats, the music volume is increased indicating the Drama is about to start. Jess puts all her books and pens away except her songbook so she's ready to leave for lunch as soon as the final song is over. The spectacle is played out on one corner of the pitch, not in the middle where everyone would have a better chance of seeing it. It comes in the form of a popular Bible story but with a modern-day twist, with a lesson to learn or an example to follow. The bright colours of the costumes set against the rich green of the pitch makes a pleasant change to staring at the tiny speaker on the platform so far away. A recording of the voices is played (the accents are American) and the actors mime along to it, throwing their arms around for extra emphasis when needed. And the music, specially recorded for the event, is stirring when played extra loud. And of course, all the men are wearing false beards. There is always something to learn from the characters about how to put God first or be more forgiving. It's the most lively part of the whole assembly.

*

After a long hard final day at the stadium the evening is spent in the mess tent with Cassie and family and several others. Jess helps with the dinner – spaghetti bolognese, a convenient camping meal – but there's no cheese to put on the top. *Have to have cheese.*

"I'll run to the shop, just give me a minute," Jess offers, and she rushes out of the mess tent and down the dirt path to the campsite shop. They've got everything there, it's very well stocked. Even a variety of cheeses, not just one type. She chooses the mature cheddar, pays for it, calls thank you to the shopkeeper and heads for the door and straight into the path of Ray.

"Hey Jess. Didn't see you last night. You OK?" he enquires.

"R-Ray!" she stumbles. "Er yeah, thought I'd better spend some time with Cassie last night. Played with the kids. What you up to?" Damn, she shouldn't have asked that! She can't bring herself to look him directly in the face.

"Just had some chips in the clubhouse and me and Dane are going to the beach in a bit. Wanna come?"

She pulls her eyes up from his chest to look into his and in that very moment she feels all her determination, all her resolve, all her supplicated steadfastness unravel through her body and pool on the floor around her feet. There it is. Down there. She should bend down and gather it up, wrap it around her body and tuck all the edges in. But something makes her step to one side.

"Meet you by the gate in twenty minutes," she mumbles as she walks away.

*

The three of them can see the horizon just over the concrete bridge up ahead. The sand dunes run from left to right as far as the eye can see and the sheer vastness of the landscape stands in sharp contrast to the confines of the small tent Jess has been staying in. Families are packing up their belongings after a day of fun and splashing, hungry and sore where the sun has bitten them. A young married Witness couple approach with their towels draped over their arms having just been for a chilly swim. They clock Jess with these two unfamiliar male faces. She smiles at them as they pass by and continues to walk towards the inviting shore, shedding her flip-flops along the way.

Jess looks over to the two lads. *They must be sharing a private joke*, she thinks, and watches as they shove each other into the lapping foam, laughing.

The splashing reaches her legs so she joins in, running away from Ray as he chases her along the shore. Dodging lumps of wet sand thrown in her direction, she grabs handful after handful and lobs them back, laughing all the while.

"Jess!" She hears her name. It's Cassie. With her dad. "Jess, you coming back, we're going to have a sing-song at the camp?" Her dad's stern look takes her by surprise as she'd never seen him like that before. That couple of do-gooders must have reported her whereabouts. *Thanks a lot*, she thinks, *just when I was actually beginning to have some real fun.*

She slips on her flip-flops and like the obedient girl she has always been walks back to camp, though not one single part of her wants to leave.

It isn't Ray calling her back that made her stop suddenly. Nor is it the thought that she might have left something on the beach. It is an idea that filled her mind in the time it took for lightning to strike, sudden and immensely strong. There is no doubt, no hesitation, when her feet turn in the sand. Breathless, she runs up to Ray as he stands ankle deep in the water.

"I'm coming back! Next week! I'll ring the clubhouse." And off she runs with a burning in her ears and a padlock on her lips. Jess has got a secret.

Chapter Six

On Jess's return Sophie bounds up to her, more like a dog than a cat, and rubs her whole body around her legs emitting a deep loud purr. She'll get loads of fuss now Jess is back. Marianne doesn't give the cats much attention, maybe a distracted stroke if one should climb into her lap while she's watching the TV but that's about it. Although it's only been a few days it looks like the kittens have grown while she's been away. The smallest one can now climb up and get in the box. Their little legs are getting stronger every day, their cries a little louder and Sophie allows them a longer range before she calls them back.

*

Marianne receives a call from Cassie's dad who feels it's best she knows about Jess being on the beach with two worldly boys. She thinks about it but decides not to bring up the subject. Her daughter knows that kind of behaviour is wrong so what's the point in discussing it? She's been listening to the same advice all her life at the meetings, it's up to her to put it into practice. Anyway, she's back now and no harm has been done.

*

Ray is on Jess's mind from the moment she wakes up each morning. It appears to Jess that Marianne doesn't notice anything, she never does. She comes across as totally self-absorbed and oblivious to her surroundings, aloof and distant so much of the time. There is absolutely no question of her confiding in her mother, expressing these strange new feelings she has. No way! Jess knows she's treading a fine line and to go ahead with her plan is sheer madness, she doesn't actually need anyone to tell her this.

As a dutiful daughter Jess goes through most of the assembly programme with her mum, reading her notes out loud and telling her the scriptures that were used. She pauses when Marianne holds her hand up and reaches for her Bible as she wants to see for herself what each one says. Impressed by the large attendance and even more so by the number baptised Marianne commends Jess for her attention and comprehensive note-taking. And then life goes back to normal.

Witness normal.

Meetings. Ministry. Meeting preparation. Study.

This is the real life after all.

Jehovah's Witnesses are by far the happiest people on earth. They must be; they know the truth about what God has in store for the planet. So why is Jess feeling so down? She thought the assembly would have given her the boost she needed, a good spiritual banquet to feast upon, to absorb and to move her to action. But her sadness is still there and now it has an added dimension. The flutters she felt in her heart back at the campsite have not lessened since arriving home, they have grown stronger. She can picture Ray's face as they'd stood against the gate that night and she recalls just how he made her feel. Alive. Not dead, not ignored. That she might actually be good company.

But it's no use. The fact remains Ray is not a Witness and he's not right for her. She has to put a stop to this fantastical idea. To go down this path would ruin her and her good reputation as a faithful baptised Witness. Perhaps it was already too late. Simply having the desire is as bad as the action, that's what they said. She can't win. But then the tiniest flicker of what could be a solution is beginning to form in the far left-hand side of her brain, it comes out of nowhere and gathers strength very quickly. Perhaps, maybe, if she was bold enough she could make it play out at the meeting the following night.

*

Alan is sitting two rows in front of her with his family. During the first half of the meeting he is on the microphones and passing it to those that raise their hand. He flicks and stretches the cable up and down the aisle as he walks, doing such a good job. She attempts to catch his eye but he's not responding. Outside, when the meeting has finished Jess sees Alan standing with his friend Grant talking under the floodlight in the car park. She won't approach him while Grant's there so waits until he moves off.

She saunters towards him.

"Alan, hi."

"Hey Jess, how are you? Did you enjoy the assembly? You went to Norwich didn't you?" Good start! He was talking to her! Actually talking!

"Yeh, it was good. You?"

"Twickenham again."

An awkward silence falls between them, clearly not going to be filled by Alan. She sees him shuffle from one foot to the other and he looks as if he can't wait for her to go away. Should she do what she's got planned?

Her heart starts beating faster as her nerves try to get in the way. She'll just have to go for it. What's the worst that could happen?

"Alan, I was thinking. Would you like to go somewhere with me, like on a date or something? We could go for a walk in the park?"

She heard the words as if they were coming from someone else's mouth. She can't quite believe she is doing this. There is a moment when she thinks Alan is going to laugh. His feet suddenly stop moving and he looks up at her face, his eyebrows raise then fall into a deep frown and he almost imperceptibly shakes his head. He doesn't say a word. He walks away. He just walks away!

What on earth was she thinking? She's just made a complete fool of herself and now Alan will go round telling everyone what she's done. She'll be a laughing stock in the congregation when word gets out, be labelled as 'bad association' for trying to lure a faithful baptised brother into wrongdoing. It's always the female that does wrong; Bathsheba, Eve, Saphira in the Bible all took the blame, Jess remembers.

A relationship is not wrong is it? How do couples actually manage to get together? And if the boy isn't going to make the first move, well… What's the matter with them? And what exactly has a girl got to do around here to get noticed?

It doesn't take long. By the time Jess is ready to leave the Hall and walk down to the bus stop with Marianne two of her friends, Kate and Nicky, are standing together looking directly at her. She knows from their pointed gaze they've already been told and the smirks on their faces linger as Jess walks by.

*

This is her chance, maybe the only one she'll ever get. She has to take it with both hands otherwise she'll be stuck here with her mum forever. She can't afford to think too far into the future in case she bottles out. Right now is the only thing that matters. The monotony of her life will eventually drive her mad, she can feel it, and where would that leave her? Firmly stuck on the shelf, that's where. One good thing was she still had her job delivering the brochure. She'd worked out how much her commission would be after the next delivery and, adding it to the money she had put aside, she could see there was enough for a coach ticket back to Norwich.

*

The next evening while Marianne is out at the group preparing for Sunday's *Watchtower* Jess calls 192 – Directory Enquiries. Heart thumping like a rabbit's back foot she dials the number for the clubhouse at Golden Sands campsite, Lea Malling.

Someone, a female, answers and Jess nervously explains: "There should be a boy in there right now and I need to speak to him. His name is Ray. Please could you get him for me?" A crackling sound followed by a thump is what Jess hears as the phone is dropped onto the counter. A few moments pass and she hears footsteps getting louder as the handset is picked up.

"Hi," he says curiously.

"Hi, Ray it's Jess. I said I'd call you, didn't I?"

"Jess, er yeh." He sounds bemused.

"I'm buying my ticket tomorrow so I'll be with you on Saturday. Can you meet me at the station in

77

Norwich? I'll call you again tomorrow night to tell you what time. OK? You OK Ray?"

"God Jess. Er yeh, talk to you tomorrow."

They both hang up.

She's done it. There's no going back now.

*

The following day bus number 365 takes her into town, straight into the coach station where she purchases a single ticket for eighteen pounds fifty to Norwich, changing at Peterborough.

The small pile of clothes and things is ready to throw in a bag just before she leaves.

The note to her mum is short:

I'm leaving.
Please don't try to find me.
I will be safe.
I love you.

Her thoughts and plans stretch as far as getting on the coach. No further. It doesn't enter her head that Ray might not be there at the other end. He will be expecting to have sex with her, she doesn't think too hard about that right now, and she certainly doesn't plan for it. She will be committing fornication and she hasn't considered the consequences of that with regard to being a baptised Jehovah's Witness. She just needs to go. Get away from the town, from Mum, from Alan, from the boredom.

She's right in line for being disfellowshipped. Running down that hill, straight for it, not looking behind. To be disfellowshipped is the result of not being repentant enough, not the actual sin. That's what they say anyway.

*

Jess knows what it means to be disfellowshipped. In practical terms it's an overnight ban on communication with a person who has been deemed by the Elders as unrepentant. They are the ones that decide. Disfellowshipping is not exactly common and reserved for baptised Witnesses who have committed a serious sinful act. It's supposed to be a final resort, when all other forms of encouragement and correction have failed. And it's all scripturally based, of course.

The list of offences is long and includes many things worldly people do every day, things that are deemed acceptable, normal and sometimes necessary by non-Witnesses: anyone repeatedly receiving someone else's blood, having sex with someone outside of marriage, engaging in homosexuality, smoking, associating with someone who is disfellowshipped, attending another church, artificial insemination and surrogate motherhood, lying, swearing, dating a person not legally divorced, celebrating Christmas, oral sex and gambling.

It's totally necessary. It keeps the congregation clean and free from bad influences. JWs have to be seen to be different to the churches who just allow anyone in. But ultimately it's a loving provision designed to teach the offender a lesson and draw them back to Jehovah. That's how the literature describes the practice anyway. However, in Jess's experience the reality is far different.

*

At one Thursday night meeting in her old congregation down south, Jess's world was shaken when a Brother whom she regarded as very strong in the faith had become weak, she hadn't seen him at many meetings then realised he'd stopped going completely, although his wife and children still went. Following several months of no sight of him the announcement was made that the brother was 'no longer one of Jehovah's Witnesses'. This was the official wording when someone was disfellowshipped.

No reason was actually announced for his being disfellowshipped, it never was, not in so many words, but the talk that was given after the announcement was all about marriage vows and loyalty between marriage partners. Sneaky Elders. They claimed to be trustworthy and to keep people's private affairs private but they had ways of getting round that if it was seen as benefitting the congregation in some way.

Jess recalled that when she heard his name from the platform the atmosphere in the Hall changed to one of sudden seriousness. It was like a cold grey cloud had settled all around, dulling the sound. People were frowning at each other, looking questioningly, as if asking, 'What's going on? Wonder what he's been up to?' Jess took it all in but didn't really understand what had happened. She'd heard the 'D' word before but didn't know of anyone locally who it had happened to. Later on Marianne explained to her:

"Well, David has certainly shown his true colours, hasn't he? He's done something very bad against the congregation and even worse, against Jehovah. He'll regret it," Marianne said, tutting and shaking her head.

"How could he?" She continued, angrily, as if it was personally against her, "he's deliberately turned his back on everything, his friends, his family, his wife and children. He's got no appreciation for what Jehovah has done for him and bang goes his hope of being saved at Armageddon. It's a terrible shame but, you know, 'the truth will out' as they say."

"So, won't he be going to meetings anymore? Isn't he allowed? Has he been kicked out?" Jess enquired, trying to make sense of it.

"Well, he's sort of been kicked out and yes, he can go to the meetings if he wants to but if he turns up we're not to talk to him, not even a 'hello'. If we're friendly with him it would show him that his sin is not really that serious, but it is, and he needs to learn a lesson. It's a loving thing, to be disfellowshipped, it's not a punishment. Let's hope he comes back."

"So, what about if we see David and Sue down the shops? Can we speak to him then? Just not at the meetings?"

"No, dear," Marianne continued. "Unless he comes back and is reinstated into the congregation we are not to speak to him. Otherwise we could be disfellowshipped ourselves. We wouldn't want that would we?"

It seemed so harsh to Jess and she was struggling to understand how cutting someone off could be a loving thing. Was this a case of 'tough love'? She'd heard that phrase before when her older brothers were being discussed.

Time passed and David started attending meetings, just Sundays at first, then Thursday nights. He wouldn't be allowed to go to the Tuesday group as it was held in someone's home. Sat in the back row as instructed by the Elders, he slumped in the seat but tried to look alert, like he belonged. Sue and the two little ones sat alongside him. Some people decided not to speak to her either. The whole family was 'infected' and it was a line many people were not prepared to cross. Jess had noticed what was going on.

"But Sue's not disfellowshipped. Why are people ignoring her as well?" Jess wanted an answer.

"This is what happens, Jess. It not only disrupts the life of the disfellowshipped person but affects their whole family. He did wrong but the Elders felt he wasn't repentant. It's as simple as that. He knew this is what would happen – he did have a choice."

Something didn't ring true with Jess, young as she was things needed to make sense to her. David was not a 'gross sinner' as the scripture described people who must be put out of the congregation and shunned. He was a nice man, funny. He loved his kids, his family and they adored him. How could he suddenly turn against everything?

Poor Sue. That obviously wasn't a nice thing to happen to her. But on top of that she began to see less and less of her friends as they could no longer go to her house. The children lost their playmates and invitations to any events stopped completely.

Jess would turn in her seat at the start of each meeting to see if he was there. She didn't dare smile at him in case she was seen by an Elder, but she wanted to. She presumed he really must have been sorry, deep down. He would have apologised to Sue, that's what was important. Perhaps the Elders were being too hard on him. *It must be awful to sit there with no one talking to him, totally rejected.* He didn't look very happy, in fact he looked grey and empty, but that was understandable if all his friends had turned their backs on him.

But Jess could not understand why it had to be quite so harsh. And she certainly did not believe Jesus would have treated David this way. She'd always been taught that Jesus was kind and loving, understanding and generous, ready to forgive. He mixed with people who made mistakes and ended up hurting themselves all the time but he didn't reject them. He welcomed them back. And they wanted to come back to him. This was the Jesus Jess had been learning about and getting to know all her life. He just wouldn't do this to anyone. This can't be right.

Jess wasn't sure how much time had passed but David was eventually reinstated as a reward for his consistent meeting attendance. That's all they could judge him on, he wasn't allowed to do anything else. No ministry, no answering at the *Watchtower*, he had to conduct himself as though he was invisible where the Organisation was concerned.

The night it was announced Jess wanted to shout out, 'Yes!' or clap or something to show how pleased she was for David and his whole family. But clapping was not allowed. No, for an undetermined period of time, David's spiritual progress would be observed, monitored, and he would have to prove himself to the Elders. His weekly Bible study with one of the Elders and getting back out on the ministry would help him to rebuild his faith. So he was welcomed back with a few handshakes and a large amount of caution.

David changed after he came back. He wasn't funny anymore. He looked like he'd been kicked in the stomach.

*

In the coach station Jess can see the bus in the second bay and hear its engine running. Showing the driver her ticket she settles into her seat about halfway down and it suddenly dawns on her that this is the first journey she's been on where she hasn't brought along a pile of magazines. Ministry-minded all the time, as everyone is encouraged to be, she had always taken a few mags to leave on the seat or to place in a phone box or on a table somewhere. You never know who might pick them up. One of the articles inside might just be what a person needed that day and Jess was happy to be a part of helping anyone who was worried about the state of the world. But today she'd left her ministry bag at home.

*

Jess had no fear travelling on her own. That had been knocked out of her from an early age. As a small child during the week she'd been put on the local bus and sent to infants' school in town about five miles away. Once off the bus she needed to cross a main road to get into the playground and on the way home it was two main roads. But Jess never wanted to go alone. She wanted Mummy to go with her but despite all her begging and tears Marianne refused to get dressed and make the journey with her. Her advice had been, "If you get stuck or need help, ask a woman." With a parting cuddle from Mummy at the front door, head buried into her fluffy dressing gown, she had to dry her tears and make the lonely journey till she was six and a half years old and had left the school.

*

It's a dull day with drizzly rain blurring the view from the coach window. The flat scenery she'd watched only a week or so ago in Bodger's Lodge hadn't changed and some of the turnings the coach takes are familiar. The spongy seats on the Eastern Counties coach are far more comfortable than the ones in the camper and there's a lap tray that pulls down. *Handy*.

Changing coaches at Peterborough doesn't take that long, just a twenty-minute wait which gives her a chance to go to the loo and stretch her legs. The further into the Fens the coach goes the more the landscape changes as the clusters of villages become more sparse. Each one finishes abruptly and is neighboured by sprawling orchards of red and green apples, the abundance of which makes for a beautiful panorama, like a picture in a children's book. The driver has the radio on and above the drone of the heavy engine Jess can hear a song she'd heard before. The dreamy voice of Nik Kershaw rings true to her as he explains that life is getting harder. It's getting harder just keeping her life and her soul together. And, yes, she's sick of fighting even though she knows she should. Nik knows.

And yes, Nik, wouldn't it be good if we could actually wish ourselves away? Yes, indeed, she thinks as she realises that's exactly what she's doing. She's making it happen.

*

I'm really going to miss Sophie. Hope Mum will take care of her properly. Alan won't miss her – he won't even notice she's gone. Mum won't miss her, or maybe she will, just a bit. Who knows? She's such a closed book. Cassie will. She pulls the notebook and pen from her bag and sets about explaining things to Cassie. But then, pausing with the pen ready to fly, she realises that anything she tells her is likely to be repeated or the letter shown to her parents then the game would be over. Someone would likely turn up at the campsite and haul her back home. Then there would no doubt be a meeting with the Elders after Marianne had told them she'd run away. The gossip would make its way around the congregation like wildfire and she'd be 'marked' as a bad association, someone to avoid. No. She can't tell Cassie anything. She can't tell anyone anything. She's completely alone in this.

*

A bit peckish now she's glad she'd packed something to eat – a couple of sausage rolls and a bag of crisps. That will keep her going till half five when the coach is due to arrive in Norwich. She'd picked that arrival time so that Ray could still do a day's work then meet her afterwards. In her purse is about three pounds, enough to get some food over the next couple of days.

The driver had slung her bag in the storage compartment under the coach along with everyone else's. Whenever Jess bought any clothes they were purchased with appropriateness for meetings, ministry or assemblies in mind: no skirts too short, no tops too low, no trendy items that would show she was a slave to the world's fashions. She didn't possess many sports or leisure clothes made for relaxing in, there was just her jeans and a few T-shirts so that's all she packed.

A few hair accessories some toiletries and a second pair of pumps had been stuffed in the bag. Her clothes just wouldn't impress Ray, she knows that. They're boring, unimaginative and do not bring out her assets at all. As much as she loves the red dress she bought for the assembly, she had chosen not to bring it. She'd bought that in the hope of catching Alan's eye but he hadn't even been at that assembly.

*

Jess is used to travelling by coach. At about twelve or thirteen years of age she and Marianne occasionally took the coach down to London to spend the day at a museum or Regent's Park or Covent Garden, or do a walk-past of places where her mum had worked in the fifties.

Marianne was proud of her past jobs. She had worked as an office temp, secretary, shorthand typist for several prestigious national and international firms. She was intelligent, diligent, a loyal employee and her letters of recommendation glowed with compliments. She took them out and reread them sometimes when she was feeling low to be reminded of happier times.

Jess was able to see a different side to her mum on those days: she smiled and looked completely at home in the city.

Those coach journeys to London took around three hours and always felt like six, stopping at remote villages where there was precisely no one waiting. Once off the coach they got swept along crowded pavements onto a bus, the conductor taking their fare, turning the handle to issue two tickets. These Jess would add to her collection at home or stick them in her scrapbook as a reminder of their day out together. Jess was so proud of her mum who appeared to remember her way round on the Tube and buses extremely well.

Ding! ding! and they jumped off into the throngs and the mystery tour would begin again, Jess half walking, half running and not knowing where they were

87

heading. But it didn't matter, Marianne knew. The point was she was with her mum who was happy for the day, away from home, out in the fresh air, in the company of all kinds of people and seeing crazy, wonderful sights.

Their walk would take them through grassy squares surrounding a central monument of someone important adorned with smatterings of bird mess. Past tall glassy buildings with suited personnel whizzing through the revolving door, newspapers under arms.

It wasn't easy navigating the narrow pavements with others coming from the opposite direction. Each had to turn sideways at some point especially when walking beneath scaffolding erected for the big clean-up operation. London's soot and industrial filth had built up over the decades and coated the buildings making them matte black, adding to the drabness of a winter's day. The facades on some buildings were almost completely obscured by a spider's web of metal poles hiding the now sparklingly clean bricks laid down a hundred years ago. Dark, ill-defined stonework gave way to a pleasing sharpness and rich terracotta tones as each section was completed.

They descended steep, slippery staircases with thin handrails down into the Underground, along shiny tiled tunnels displaying framed posters advertising Genesis' Invisible Touch Tour at Wembley Stadium. There were 'No Smoking' signs everywhere, on the trains, on the bins, on the escalator walls but on one particular journey Jess saw the glow of a discarded cigarette, its owner lost in the crowd.

Unfamiliar tunes from lone musicians would make their way through the twists and turns of the

Underground, fading to nothing as the doors closed on the train.

Jess thought it weird that no one spoke on the Tube. Maybe it wasn't allowed for some reason so she didn't attempt it, and Marianne looked comfortable enough with that too. Jess left her to sit there in silence, looking at her own reflection in the window, lost in her memories.

The quiet gave Jess the chance to take in her surroundings. The vast array of colour always struck her; people dressed in weird clothes with choices of fabrics that really did not complement each other in her opinion. Tartan, chains, safety pins holding things up *or was that just for decoration?* Jess wondered. Fishnet tights with biker boots, long delicate lace gloves, longline jackets with the biggest shoulder pads she'd ever seen. And the hair! Mohicans of differing heights framed boys' and girls' faces their eyes heavy with black liner.

Poverty was visible throughout the day: a bundle of knitted fabric curled up in a doorway with cardboard underneath. So still. *Is that person alive?* she wondered as she dropped coins in their dirty jam jar. Charity is never mentioned at the meetings. Passing on the Kingdom Message being the only charitable act encouraged and talked about, Jess had never given poor people much thought.

She saw shocking pinks, the brightest greens, leather with studs and fake animal fur collars. It was fantastic!! She loved the hustle and bustle of people in a hurry. Groups of teenagers hung about in doorways, she loved the painted brickwork, friends shouting at each other across the street, the strange aromas from restaurants and cafés as they turned each corner. Music played as they passed shops, none of it she recognised, or would be allowed to buy. But it was all wonderful and Jess just loved being there. She felt alive.

This was London – anyone could wear anything. And do anything.

On another occasion Jess and Marianne travelled all the way out to Southend to visit Peter and his new wife. That really was a never-ending journey and Jess vowed she'd never do it again, not there and back in the same day anyway. They arrived about three in the afternoon, had some lunch and fell asleep only to have to get moving again by five. It was too far. While there she had a chat with Peter and made plans to repeat the journey on her own during the school holidays.

She was lucky she ever arrived…

Chapter Seven

The trip to Peter's in Southend back in 1982 got her on the X49 coach down to Marylebone one afternoon. It was half term and a break from her oppressive routine would do her good. It would be worth going all that distance for some time away. There would still be meetings to go to but no ministry if she didn't want to. Peter was much more relaxed about the whole Witness thing and Jess was looking forward to chilling out, maybe going to the cinema or getting a takeaway. And of course there was the beach. In reality she wasn't fussed if they didn't do anything, just a change of scenery would be nice.

Off the coach she felt the need to orientate herself and 'get her London head on' as she called it. Familiar to her now after several trips, Gino's café on the corner outside Marylebone station was a well-established and cheerful place. Frequented by regulars as well as travellers passing through it was a warm and friendly café to eat in. The autumn sun had disappeared and the sky was just beginning to darken. As Jess looked at her watch she decided there was just enough time for a snack before catching the bus out to Southend. Fried egg on toast was her favourite so that's what she ordered. She washed it down with a quick slurp of weak tea, paid the bill and moved on.

The next part of the journey took her by foot along Marylebone Road to Baker Street Tube station. Images of Sherlock Holmes greeted her around each corner on the way down the stairs to the platform. As she sat waiting with her two carrier bags close to her legs she felt so comfortable, as if she belonged there. *I love London*, she thought to herself, and smiled at the man sitting next to her. Jess always wanted to linger in the city, not just pass through it.

The Tube was taking its time but Jess wasn't worried. She knew exactly where she was heading – the bus stop outside Kings Cross station and a little walk to the left. She eventually arrived at Kings Cross after an announced delay with the Tube and an apology for the inconvenience. Up ahead through the dusk she could see the bus stop sign.

Yep, that's the one, she thought, and confidently headed straight for it. And waited. The sky was dark now and the street lights glowed an even orange up and down the street. She was anxious to get on the bus and snuggle down for the long journey out to Southend. An hour and a quarter later she was still waiting. She moved from foot to foot with impatience. The thing was, she hadn't investigated what time the bus would be leaving, she had just decided to get there and wait for the next one to come along. Eight o'clock came, half past eight and still no sign of her bus.

The volume of people was thinning and some of the cafés opposite were cleaning up ready to close. The temperature was dropping and Jess pulled her coat around her neck. She wasn't worried. She had no plan if the bus didn't come. But it would come. This is London, buses run all through the night. She just wished it would hurry up. Suddenly she was conscious of a presence at her side.

The man was very tall, of slim build and had a walking stick. Not so much an aid for walking, more like a cane. He was wearing a beige mac. He came and stood right next to her and she realised he'd been standing near for quite some time.

"The bus you're waiting for won't be leaving for another forty minutes. It's the last one. But it starts its journey at the depot just around the corner," he informed her.

"Thank you," Jess stuttered. Her throat was dry in the night air.

In a firm tone he continued: "This is no place for a young girl to be out on her own in the dark. Anything could happen." He looked her straight in the face and instructed: "Follow me. I'll put you on the bus where you'll be safe."

With that he was off, mac flapping, strutting down the road, and strangely not even using his cane. Jess hesitated for a millisecond and then decided to follow him. Her thought process, as quick as lightning, was that if he was no good he wouldn't have just walked off, he would have walked by her side as if to lure her away. So she followed him. Down the street into the beginning of a residential area. *Where is he leading me? Should I turn back?* She hesitated for a second, halting mid-stride. But something made her continue.

Sure enough, up ahead there was the bus and a number of others all parked behind each other. Drivers and conductors were hanging about, kicking invisible things on the ground, smoking and chatting. Jess saw the tall man speed up and approach one of the drivers, saying something. They both looked back at her and she heard a swoosh as the doors of her bus opened.

She arrived at Southend station at five to midnight where Peter was waiting with a scowl on his face.

*

She was safe, and with her spiritual education she put the experience down to an angel watching over her. She'd been taught that God used angels for jobs like that and there was no doubt in her mind that he'd stepped in. Once she'd grown up and understood what a dangerous situation she'd been in that night she wondered why her mum had allowed her to travel through such an area, at night and on her own. Marianne had worked near King's Cross and knew it was a rough spot. The whole experience, which she relayed to Peter during her stay, strengthened her faith somewhat and made her feel that she was never actually alone. Not really.

*

The coach hits a bump in the road and brings her back to reality with a start. Can she talk to God now? She'd done wrong already back at the campsite by talking to Ray so often and going down to the beach with him and his brother. Although she didn't like to think about it too deeply she must be causing Marianne a big headache back home. She didn't want to upset her, it wasn't personal. *Oh, Mum.* How can she pray to God, her Heavenly Father and explain what she was up to, knowing how wrong it is? He knows better than her how this is going to go and if he could speak directly to her she'd be getting a right telling off. So, no, she doesn't feel she can pray at this moment. Maybe there are times after all when she really is completely and utterly alone.

The time is five twenty and the sun is shining, and through the windows on the coach the view of the countryside is now obscured by tall buildings in the city centre. It's store closing time and the bus station up ahead is busy with shoppers laden with bags and children. They glance around for the right bay and join the queue for their bus home. As the coach pulls into the yellow marked bay Jess sees patches of diesel from previous parkings and smells the headache-inducing odour of the fuel seeping through the driver's window.

She stands up before the bus has stopped, stretching and bending trying to see if she can spot Ray anywhere. She has arrived a little ahead of schedule so isn't that worried when she can't see him. Not particularly in a rush to get off the bus she helps a woman who is struggling with her luggage and her crying child and lifts the little one down off the high step and onto the paved area away from the other vehicles. The woman thanks her and she moves back to the side of the coach to wait for her bag to be unloaded. All the while, her head is bobbing left and right but there's no sign of Ray. She's not worried, just excited to see him. It's real now. She's here. She's left home and she's back in Norwich!

Twenty minutes have passed. She sits on the bench where he will be able to see her. *Which end will he approach from?* She isn't exactly sure. Forty-five. Needing to stretch her legs she takes a slow-paced walk from one end of the row of bays to the other. She times it on her watch. It takes precisely one minute and seventeen seconds. There are still no thoughts in her head about what to do should he not turn up. With just three pounds in her purse she wouldn't be able to get back home. But she completely trusts that he will be there. She just needs to wait.

Suddenly the straw-coloured hat she sees at the other end is a head above all others and is coming this way. It must be Ray. A few bodies sway in front of her as she moves towards it and then she sees his smile. An awkward hug and a peck on the lips later and her bag is in his hand and he's leading the way to the local bus which would take them out to the coast.

"I didn't really think you'd come," he admits, "you're crazy, you know that?"

"But you're here aren't you, so you must have," she points out through a smile that won't relax.

"You hungry?" Ray asks as they near the end of the journey. "We can get something to eat in the clubhouse."

"Starving!"

It has been a long day and all she wants to do is have a bite to eat and crash in… in what? In Ray's small tent. Dane would be there too. She hadn't considered if there would be room for her. Over burgers Ray updates Jess on how his work has been going and the mundane things since he's last seen her but she's not really taking it in. The tiredness swoops over her suddenly and a long but stifled yawn tells Ray it's time to head over to the tent.

Across the table he lays his hand on top of hers and wraps his fingers underneath, and with a gentle tug she stands.

They leave the clubhouse and this time, for the first time, walk hand in hand through the campsite. The warmth of his large hand is reassuring and comforting, and his grip is neither too loose nor too tight, it's just right. Neither speak. They just walk, picking up the pace the nearer they get to the tent. There's no going back.

Dane is curled up inside reading a copy of *Smash Hits* by torchlight.

"Hey Jessie, love. You're back then," he says, not moving.

Ahead of her Ray kneels inside the tent. He nods to Dane then nods towards the tent door and the action accompanied by a hitchhiker's thumb makes the message loud and clear.

*

It wasn't what she had expected. But she hadn't exactly had time to imagine how her first experience of sex would go. She hoped it would be with Alan and it was easy to picture herself in all sorts of situations with him, but Ray? Her focus for the last two weeks had not been what they were going to get up to but more about simply escaping, of not being caught halfway there and dragged back. Whatever she had to endure along the way was just a necessary part of it. 'A means to an end' they called it.

But it wasn't as calculated as it sounds: she did like Ray and he made her feel wanted, admired and worth something. Her impression of him had been correct right from the start: he was responsible and trustworthy, he'd shown that last night on the production from his pocket of a packet of condoms. She'd let him sort himself out down there, not interested herself in the mechanics or the sight of it. The thought of there not being a provision for birth control had not, at any point, entered her head. The night could have gone in a completely different direction, with an unwanted result. What would she have done then? Her knowledge of such things was scant and unclear as no birds and bees discussions had ever taken place between mother and daughter. She was just very lucky Ray was who he was.

It felt as if it happened in slow motion. Its significance as far away from her mind as it could possibly be. Is this what innocence is? Or ignorance? Overnight Jess had passed from being a child to a woman. Look what he'd done to her! This young, good-looking man, Ray, had singularly made her feel as if she had the right to breathe, that she now had a place on the planet. A fully-fledged member of the adult human race and she had the pelvic aches to prove it.

*

The following morning as she lies there, a smile spreads across her face even before she opens her eyes. The smell of the canvas is heavy and heady and she knows the heat outside is rising. A cool, cleansing shower is calling her. The note Ray had written before he left for work and stuffed in her left flip-flop is to the point, but ends nicely:

"Off to work. Back around 5.30. Hope you don't get bored today. Last night was awesome! See you later. X."

She decides it must be time to make her way over to the shower and toilet block situated at the end of the row. Pulling on the oversized jumper Ray had worn last night as the temperature had dropped, she crawls out of the tent. On all fours she raises her head to a new day, blinking as her eyes adjust to the brightness. The sun's up and the sky is clear and blue, so very blue on this, the first day of her new life. She's got no idea of the time.

Others around are carrying armfuls of plates and cutlery, mugs and saucepans, trying not to drop them before reaching their tents. No one looks at her but she holds her head up and her back straight as she remembers her new status in the world. Dreading to think what a state she must look with her hair resembling a bird's nest, the scuttle along the gravel path is as fast as she can make it and the safety of the shower cubicle is so welcoming. She leans against the wall as the shower head douses her in a million lukewarm diamond droplets and lowers her head to look down the length of her body. These breasts have been touched by someone else now, these hips, these thighs, and in between, and there was no going back. The bubbles that she rinses off slink towards the drain hole and disappear carrying with them their mingled sweat and saliva. Wrapped in only a towel she returns to the tent to dress and think about the day ahead. She's starving!

*

Everything on the laminated menu at the clubhouse looks highly appealing – she's ravenous – and the pictures of the different permutations of a full English breakfast in vivid colours sets her mouth watering. But there isn't enough money for that so she orders fried eggs on toast. There's a red phone box on the corner by the shop and from the window Jess can see the door isn't quite closed. The call must be made at some point: she doesn't hate her mum, she loves her, and should really let her know she's safe. But not today.

*

Ray has been so good to her. He hasn't questioned her

once about her actions; not about Maureen's warning name-call on that first night by the pool table, not about being called back from the beach by Cassie and her dad, not about this large group of people she was with and where they went each day. He doesn't ask why she's come back and isn't aware of the kind of life she's been living and has managed to get away from. He's so laid back and accepting of her. *What does it matter that he's not one of Jehovah's Witnesses? Surely what matters is how a person treats others.* If her mum was to meet him she'd really like him; his gentleness and good manners and consideration. He'll be such a good son-in-law to her.

*

Although she'd just had a shower the thought of the beach just over the bridge is too strong so Jess heads towards it, humming a tune. The tide is just coming back in but still a long way out so it takes a while to get to where it's deep enough to swim. The sea is cool and refreshing and sandy underfoot. A gentle breaststroke takes Jess further out and the silence strikes her as she turns and floats on her back, raising her stinging eyes to the blue sky. "Push your bottom up," she can hear her sister Diane saying as the subtle waves lift her, pull and push her. She's completely under their command, completely relaxed. *Where are you, Daddy? Karen, Jackie, Diane? Where have you gone? And why haven't you been in touch for so long?* The feel of the water always takes her back to her family.

There are things she wants to do with her new life; buy some new normal clothes, not ones that shouted 'Jehovah's Witness on the ministry' (she needs a job), take driving lessons, find Dad and her sisters, move back to the south coast where she belongs, have a different hairstyle, something a bit wild (perhaps one of the many styles and colours Madonna or Cyndi Lauper has), bring Sophie and the kittens to live with her. A new start. She was free at last! No more ministry, no more meetings, study, preparation for the *Watchtower*. Forget those stuffy barn dances, she could go to discos and dance till the early hours, watch *Top of the Pops* on a Thursday night, drink undiluted beer if she wanted to.

The possibilities strike her as she lies there bobbing in the sea and she closes her eyes and wallows in the thought of all that has suddenly opened up to her. It had happened overnight, literally. *Why didn't I leave before now? Too busy with those stupid exams, had to finish those really.* But she could have left back in May, done what Ray and Dane were doing and worked her way back down south in bars, restaurants or fruit picking. *Why hadn't I thought of that?*

But she is here, and decidedly from now on, her own woman.

*

Ray and Dane are back at teatime and both starving after a hot day's picking in the sun, so it's something with chips at the clubhouse. Dane, usually chatty is rather quiet, Jess notices, and when they've all finished eating he announces he's making his way back to the tent for a sleep.

"What's the matter with him?" she asks Ray. Maybe the heat is getting to him.

"Oh, he's all right, just being Dane. Tired probably." He brushes it off. "Jess, shall we go for a little walk? There's a lane that comes out near a river at the other end of the site. It's got all kinds of birds there. I fancy looking at something that's not a strawberry."

The walk takes no more than ten minutes. Not a word is spoken as they wander along the grassy path and Jess feels a prickling of curiosity at the cause of this silence. His arm around her shoulder calms her though, there's nothing to worry about, he likes her, and they're together. Next to the river is a wooden bench where they sit side by side. Ray draws her to him and she snuggles into his warmth. She could stay like that forever, safe and hidden from the wicked world, shielded with affection – a different way to rules and constant reminders.

"Jess? What exactly are you doing here? Tell me honestly. Why did you decide to come back?" he asks, searching her face for clues. He slides round in the seat to face her, making her look him in the eyes. "Have you run away from home? Does your mum know you're here?"

Oh God, he might not have been asking her any of these questions up to now but he'd certainly been wondering. There's no getting past it, she needs to give him an explanation, it's only fair. She takes a deep breath and starts to lay out her whole life before him. There's no spin in particular, just the facts and how it all makes her feel – she's not after his sympathy, just his friendship. He listens without interrupting, without questioning or judging.

But fair's fair, Jess hadn't heard his story, the reason why he and his brother were down here on the Norfolk coast when they live in Oldham. If she was honest, his position was yet another thing she hadn't even considered, being so focussed on her own problems. After her enquiry, Ray then takes his turn to tell Jess his side of things.

"But now we have a problem, Jess." Ray turns a corner in the conversation. Jess can feel a tension in his voice but prompts him to continue. "The picking season finishes the day after tomorrow. I've no idea what me and Dane are going to do, let alone you. Us two lads camping in our tent is fine, we can stop where we want and go in any direction the work takes us, but having you with us, Jess… I can't see how it'll work."

She listens, taking in the seriousness of what he is saying but her thoughts are scrambling around trying to find a solution within the next three seconds. It wasn't happening. The silence falls again. Ray sighs and sits back in the seat and repositions his arm around her shoulder.

"What did you expect to happen once you got down here? How did you plan to survive? You haven't brought any money with you, have you?"

Actually, no, she hadn't thought anything through at all. It's a complete mess. She'd put these boys in an awkward position by dumping herself on their goodwill and now she'd be a burden they didn't want.

"I'm sorry, Jess. It's been really nice to have you here and I do really like you, but I think you're going to have to go home."

Chapter Eight

"No, Ray, I can't go home. I don't belong there, don't make me go back, please. I can work, I'll try anything. I'm a fast learner. Let me go to the field with you tomorrow and the next day and I'll show you how hard I can work." She was breathless in her attempt to convince him not to dump her.

"I don't know, Jess, it's a really tough day out there. I don't want you getting sunburnt and feeling like I do at the end of the day, aching like hell."

And then it happens again. An idea just drops into her head like a rock onto sand. Exactly the same as that day on the beach when she turned around and told Ray she was coming back. It comes out of nowhere, from the sky, from God? The devil? A solution is on her lips that is just so right she stumbles over the words and can't get them out quick enough.

"Kathy and Greg, yes that's it, let's go. Let's go now, come on. They'll have us, there's loads of work down there. We can stay together and get a place. That's it, Ray, come on we need to pack up."

"Hang on, Jess, what are you going on about? Slow down. Start again and tell me what you mean."

She takes a breathe and explains: "Kathy and Greg are friends of mine in Eastbourne. Kathy's like my second mum, Ray. She wouldn't turn us away, I mean, she'll be cross with me for running away and all that, and she'd probably guess that we've been up to no good but, it's worth a try."

Ray listens and doesn't comment.

"Ray?"

"Is she a Witness?"

"Yeh, the whole family is, but they're, you know, a lot more laid back than my mum. They'd love you, they'd welcome you into the family, I know they would, that's just what they're like. Please Ray, we can get work down there no problem. Let's do it."

*

Not yet forty Kathy had eight children – four from her first marriage and four with Greg, the eldest twin girls, Nerys and Misha, being the same age as Jess. She should have been born twenty years earlier, then she could have taken her kids to festivals in the 60s, dressed them in crochet and watched them as they danced barefoot to The Mamas and The Papas. She fed them on hunks of bread and cheese. There was molasses in the wooden cupboard – not sugar – brown rice, wheat spaghetti, garlic (lots of garlic). She offered Jess a garlic sandwich once when she'd had a sore throat. As soon as Kathy had left the kitchen she lobbed it onto the compost heap outside. No doubt the chickens finished it off. There was a range of herbal teas in the old biscuit tin, which Marianne would always try when visiting, with Kathy sitting in expectation of her verdict. The enticing smell of a dense rich fruitcake baking in the double oven would permeate the house and would never last that long once on the cooling rack.

Kathy was the one who cut the kids' hair which, for the four girls, amounted to an inch off their fringe before term started. For the boys, well, the least said about their haircuts the better.

"No thanks, Auntie Kathy, Mum's taking me to the hairdresser after school on Monday," came the reply following an offer of a quick trim.

Kathy included Jess with all her own kids, unquestioningly. She fed her, she tucked her up in bed when she came for a sleepover and passed her hand-me-downs from her girls. She had got to know Marianne very well, they spent a lot of time together while all the kids were at school and Greg at work at the post office. Their softly spoken conversations blended from one subject to the next with silent thinking time in between as they watched the toddlers play on the grass.

Kathy's hair was long and wavy, a rich brown and in a bad light showed the faintest appearance of a silver streak. She often wore a tie-dyed triangular scarf to keep her long locks back, knotted at the nape of her neck. Her skirts, multicoloured, patchwork and or gingham, flowed around her as she moved through the house wafting the smell of patchouli in her wake. Kathy never hurried. She moved at the pace of waves on a calm day and a quiet hum accompanied her as she worked through the chores.

She wasn't a jewellery wearer in particular, maybe a wedding ring or a watch and occasionally a beaded or a daisy bracelet made by one of the younger ones. These she treasured and when a replacement came along she would secure the current gift in her special box. Jess had made her an assortment of necklaces from items she'd found round about and as she grew her gifts showed off her new skills of knitting and crocheting. With babies coming along in quick succession Jess was never short of ideas for gifts really.

The house at the edge of town suited the family

well. It was just off one of the main roads north, one side of which were large turn-of-the-century houses with incredibly long front gardens, the other side large open spaces. Being surrounded by beautiful countryside foraging became a big part of the family's frequent country walks. Baskets for the apples, margarine tubs for blackberries and once the baby's potty had to serve as a container for the plums. Treasures spread out on the kitchen table later would get Kathy and the girls thinking what they should make with them this time. Jams and compotes, fruit buns, apple crumble, plum chutney – they could have opened a little shop with the amount of goods they made.

Their homelife was truly the stuff of *The Waltons*. That's what Kathy was aiming for. Very much an accepted matriarchal arrangement Greg seemed completely at ease with it all. He knew where he stood and what his expected role was, the same with the kids. It all seemed to run smoothly enough with little bumps along the way, many of which could be turned into a humorous episode to be regaled for years to come.

The rolling deep green Sussex Downs were viewable from the front bedroom windows, clusters of houses just visible in the distance. Their walks would bring them closer to the flint structures so the details could be seen. The grey and white fist-sized rocks, quarried from the hills' insides, sat in straight rows and were often framed by traditional orange oblong bricks set in a herringbone pattern. The colours worked beautifully together and the buildings looked so solid, they would stand for thousands of years to come. Adorned with foliage in a million shades of green, fragrant roses, tall swaying hollyhocks and bold sunflowers a summer's afternoon was good for the soul and spirit in a way that nothing else was. Kathy and Marianne felt themselves blessed to able to bathe in this level of beauty laying right on their doorsteps.

At dusk a campfire and toffee apples in the allotment at the back of the house brought the neighbours' children along and then, as the darkness descended, a telling of a few of Greg's spooky tales would see them scurrying back to the safety of their respective homes.

Living in one three-bedroom 1950s terraced property was proving to be too small as the family was growing fast so the purchase of number five next door was necessary. The houses were a mirror of each other, the second kitchen being for the laundry, second lounge for Greg's aging mother with her TV and commode, and the second bathroom being a home to more than one grass snake over the years found curled up beneath a towel. Greg was the one who brought animals home, much more often than the kids. There was usually something lurking in a corner somewhere, waiting to make the little ones jump, later to be brought into their bedroom for a closer inspection and a house made for it – a hedgehog or a stick insect.

Bedroom-wise the purchase meant the kids could spread out a bit more, each having to share with only one other sibling instead of two or any visitors that happened to be staying. When Jess slept over she invariably ended up topping and tailing with one of the girls.

Kathy and Greg's room at the front of the house above the main living room (the warmest due to the open fire below) contained a rather creaky four-poster bed. In beautiful, shiny, dark wood it was adorned with antique lace drapes and a huge colourful, crocheted bedspread. Above the bed and stretching the whole length of the wooden underside a mirror had been attached which, to the eldest son Jonah's disgust, was there for a purpose and not just for his mum to make sure she looked decent before getting out of bed.

He told the story one night whilst all the older kids were having a midnight feast on the landing, the babies and toddlers fast asleep in the other house. A regular occurrence on a Friday night Kathy turned a blind eye at the weekends and provided them with a tray of goodies – real goodies like chocolate and crisps, not health snacks.

One night in order to escape a promised good hiding from Greg for nearly throwing little Anise into the nettles and making her scream Jonah found himself under their bed. He wouldn't have thrown her in really, he was just mucking about but that was enough for a punishment. Jess knew him quite well and viewed Jonah as a little brother, only two years between them. She knew he would never have been that cruel.

So there he was amongst the cobwebs, fluff and odd rabbit droppings for what seemed like hours until the door was thrown open and in stumbled Kathy and Greg, huffing and moaning and breathing heavily. He could see their feet edging closer to the bed as he pulled himself further under. Next thing they were under the covers and exuding grunts, sighs, moans and whimpers. Jonah inserted appropriately placed balks in the telling of the story and whispers of 'yuk!' and 'ew, gross!' were exchanged. Eyes wide, another fistful of Wotsits went in

Jess's mouth.

The whole bed shook with such ferocity that Jonah was sure the mirror would come crashing down at any moment. Did it? No, but he had to stay there for what felt like hours till they were finished and had fallen asleep before he dare move a muscle. Through sniggers and giggles the kids all thought the whole thing was thoroughly disgusting and sympathised with him for having suffered such an ordeal. Poor, poor Jonah. He had an education that night.

Over the years many cats, dogs, birds, chickens, ducks, rabbits and even a stuffed badger were all part of the family and every member was treasured. There was always wood for the fire, a pan of water on the stove for a hot wash, a bun in the oven – yes, Kathy was constantly pregnant for several years it seemed. But the thing that defined the family was that they were Witnesses. It was their focus in life and affected every aspect of it. From exclusions from assemblies and Religious Education at school to getting ready for Saturday morning ministry, like Jess, the children knew nothing different and, at the time, didn't complain.

More often than not one of the children had a cold or had picked up nits from someone, but the rest of the family would be seen by the neighbours all piling into Greg's Rover to attend the meetings at the Kingdom Hall. In an aging congregation these were the only other children and the two families had become very close. Jess bonded with Nerys especially well and these were the only ones who knew how Jess felt about things.

Kathy and the family's way of life seemed to attract visitors, and once they came they didn't want to leave. It seemed nearly every time Jess went to the house there would be someone new staying there. Teenagers who'd fallen off the track somewhat, just lost their way a little, and whose parents could see no redeeming features in them sent them packing off to Kathy's in the hope she'd sort them out. From day one they would receive a good meal surrounded by kids their own age. They would be taken on long walks, very long walks, where the most natural thing to do and, perhaps the only thing to do, was to talk. Walk and talk, walk and talk. Kathy knew what she was doing when she got them out of bed at five in the morning with a cup of milk and a biscuit announcing: "Put your jumper on, we're going for a little walk." Everyone would go, even the nit-infested toddlers would be piled onto or under the pram, handed a banana and be bounced along for a few miles regardless of the weather.

Of course, these unhappy, neglected-feeling youngsters would benefit from some 'spiritual food' too so, given no choice, they were sat down at the old oak table once or twice a week with either Greg on his own or both Kathy and Greg. A Bible study would consist of an hour-long question and answer session using one of the Witness study books. Here was a chance for them to speak, to hear their own voice, for their brain to form actual words and offer more than a grunt. They were listened to and given individual attention for just a short while. No wonder they didn't want to leave.

*

Since moving away from Eastbourne when she was twelve Jess was missing the family almost as much as she was missing her own Dad and sisters. In the new congregation Jess made friends with Cassie on day one and she had become a good friend. A few of the others in the congregation were pleasant enough to be around for a short while, but their company always had to include something spiritual and was dressed up as 'fun'.

The small gatherings held in each other's homes, which were regular enough, had a bring-and-share food arrangement. The background music was only ever the Kingdom Melodies (available on record and now cassette!) and the game played most often was, 'In my ministry bag I've got…' One person would start off, saying something like 'a Bible' and the following person had to add an item each time until the list was far too long to remember. At other times a portion of a Bible story would be enacted (great for the younger kids) and a quick discussion of one of the articles in the magazines on nature or the universe would end the evening.

But that wasn't a fun evening in Jess's book. To her, and to Kathy and Greg's family, fun meant running through the woods, climbing trees, playing in the park till they saw the first stars appear, squirting water from empty washing-up bottles and generally going home filthy with mud, dirt, leaves in her hair and a huge smile on her face.

*

And so, Jess finds herself on another long coach journey, but this time she's not alone.

Lea Malling to Norwich, Norwich to Victoria, Victoria to Eastbourne, Eastbourne to Langney on the eastern edge of town. As soon as they'd taken their seats at Norwich Ray bends his long legs in the way a contortionist would have been proud of, not caring what he looks like. His head finds a hollow in Jess's lap and he intends to spend the journey asleep, clearly. The driver, as he comes along doing a final check on tickets and making sure all large bags are in the hold, looks down at him and smiles, probably wondering how on earth he got into such a position. Jess pushes his fringe back off his face and notices a faint display of freckles over his nose that she hadn't spotted before. As for Dane… well, poor Dane has decided he can't carry on the adventure alone. What fun would that be? He's making his way back up the country to Oldham having assured his parents that he'll find work soon enough and would help out financially.

*

Ray perks up when they hit the outskirts of London. The juddering of the stop/starts of the coach woke him up. He's hungry but they haven't brought anything to eat so he'll just have to wait. The hour in between coaches at Victoria would give them plenty of time to get something.

London. They must be nearly there. None of the streets they pass through look familiar to Jess, and it still takes another fifty minutes to get through the city to Victoria coach station.

She recalls one time when she and Marianne had visited her brothers' dad, Lemuel, in Finsbury Park. For the sake of her boys Marianne had reconnected with him some time after Ben had left. Nothing romantic, he wasn't a Witness. Lemuel loved Jess, often slipped her a tenner as she was leaving. He knew of Marianne's religion and their discussions in the back room of his flat worked their way around to biblical topics.

One particular conversation included why Witnesses did not accept blood transfusions or eat black pudding. Jess watched his face as he listened to Marianne's reasoning and her well-formed arguments. But she couldn't get him to understand her determination to avoid taking blood at all costs. His cooking skills were to die for though, especially his gravy. He usually made a full roast when they visited with all the trimmings and one time Marianne asked him for the recipe for his delicious gravy. Back home she tried it out several times but it didn't taste quite the same. She was convinced he put blood in it just to annoy her. She asked him about it once and he just smiled…

*

Ray seems distant. At a very busy Victoria coach station they lean against an advertising board and watch the people walking by. They eat their sandwiches and drink their tea in silence. Jess wonders if Ray's regretting his decision to head south. A mother hurries past with a small case in one hand and drags her child with the other, tickets in her mouth. She frantically searches the signs overhead and as the child moans for the toilet they stumble up the steps onto their coach bound for Worthing. Jess wonders how well that journey's going to go…

*

The last time Jess had been in Eastbourne it wasn't for long enough. The two-week Easter break the year before had seen Nerys and Jess invited out with young ones from other congregations along the coast to ice skating in Hastings, bowling in Brighton, pizzas in Seaford and a chilly picnic on the Downs. Spring along the seafront was welcomed in by the shock of colour in Eastbourne's sweeping manicured Carpet Gardens. A walk down one side of the pier and back up the other had taken all her spending money between ice creams and the machines in the arcade. It had been a fantastic couple of weeks, great to be so busy and to be with people who knew how to have proper fun.

Going to the meetings whilst away seemed like an interruption but there was no choice, all the kids went, no arguments. The sea in early spring was still cold so she made no attempt at a paddle. Jess made her mind up to come back in the summer and spend whole days on the beach like she used to with her sisters. Eastbourne was her home, where she belonged, the last place she had lived with her complete family and a strong memory was evoked around each corner, making her want to weep. She still missed them terribly.

*

The bus from Eastbourne town centre out to Langney takes twenty-five minutes and the house is another walk of the same length. The main road was once a country lane but now is fast-changing as the town expands. Halfway down on the left is an old farmhouse made huge with ugly modern extensions and is now a busy Beefeater restaurant. On the right lies the foundations for a new housing estate, once an open field where the fair used to be held.

Kathy and Greg live past the restaurant and down a lane on the right-hand side. She can see the turning up ahead. Nearly there. She just knows that Kathy will welcome them in, there won't be a problem. All they need is a base for a while until they get jobs and can afford a place of their own. There isn't a question of Ray liking Kathy and Greg – everyone does.

Jess pushes the bell on number four and hears footsteps beyond the front door. Nerys stands there in silence for a few seconds, then as recognition strikes, her face broadens into the biggest smile. Arms outstretched she shouts:

"Jeeeeessssss!" and grabs Jess in a tight embrace which turns into little jumps at the end. They hug and jump, look at each other, then hug and jump again, turning in a circle. It was so lovely to see Nerys again.

"Where have you been? Mum!!" she calls franticly. "Jess, we've been worried sick about you. Where did you go?! Mum!! They've been looking everywhere for you."

Kathy walks through the door of the lounge into the hallway, wondering what had caused such urgency in Nerys's voice. As Kathy and Jess stand there facing each other the events of the past two weeks unexpectedly and without warning, come into the sharpest focus and the planet slips on its axis. The oceans swoosh over the edges and the forests are flattened by an unrelenting wind. Jess can feel the ceiling coming down on her as her legs buckle beneath her and she hits the floor.

*

Was it Ray saying her name that brought her round? Perhaps it was the familiar smell of the house – baking bread mixed with spices and burning wood. When she opens her eyes all she can see is the sky. She had been lain on one of the kids' beds at the back of the house overlooking the fields and can feel the bobbles of the crocheted throw on her cheek.

"Ray, would you make Jess a cup of tea please, Nerys will show you where everything is," Kathy says.

Kind as he is, Ray asks if she wants one too, this stranger in a stranger's house. He's fitting in already.

"Now Jess, how's your head?"

"OK, I think," she says as she feels the back of it and pulls herself up the bed to sit up. "Did I pass out, Kathy?"

"Yes, you did. You need to rest for a while. I'll bring you something to eat and check on you later."

Kathy leaves her to herself for a while, giving her a last look of concern as she pulls the door to.

The tea is good. The banana sandwich is good. Being here is good. What had just happened? Jess looks around her. The double-bell alarm clock on the bedside table says seven-thirty. Next to it lays a *Watchtower* and a Bible and a small hand mirror. Jess picks it up and cautiously takes a look at herself, struggling to meet her own eyes.

There they are, full of guilt. In that moment she has never felt so ugly.

What. Have. You. Done? Her own voice accuses her.

She throws the mirror to the end of the bed and covers her ugly face with her hands, digging her nails into her forehead. Then the tears come. In torrents. And they don't stop. Her sniffs and moans can be heard downstairs and Kathy goes up the wooden staircase to be by her side, wordlessly taking her in her arms and rocking her to the rhythm of her sobs.

Kathy waits patiently till Jess's breathing settles into a regular pattern, till her sniffles stop and she asks

117

for a tissue. She whispers, "I've called your mum to let her know you're here and you're safe. You probably don't want to hear this but you need to know that she's been devastated, not knowing where you were." Kathy takes Jess's face in her hands. "Your brothers have been all round London looking for you in hostels. That's where they presumed you'd gone. We've all been worried sick, Jess." They hug and feeling as if Jess is about to start sobbing again Kathy tells her that her dad's been contacted as well.

Jess sits with a sullen face and her hands half over her ears. She doesn't want to hear these words, the trouble and worry she's caused. Hostels in London? As much as she loved the city, it would never be her first choice to escape to. Her brothers obviously don't know her that well.

But strangely Kathy said her dad had been contacted. *But Mum doesn't know where he lives so how could she contact him? Has she known all this time?* she wonders. Jess has no idea what the reaction would have been, she didn't know him anymore. But it's true, Marianne doesn't deserve this trouble. How could she do this to her? Her nerves are bad enough, her depression doesn't really give her any peace, she doesn't need anything more to deal with. The guilt is piling up in Jess's head, thick sheets of heavy slate laid down upon her heart and as the conversation goes on it increases to an unbearable weight. She feels sick and puts her hands on her stomach.

Kathy only asks one question about Ray:

"Are you 'together'?"

Jess knows what she means and has to tell the

truth. "Yes, we are."

Chapter Nine

And there she was. A fornicator. A baptised Jehovah's Witness that has been clawed away by the devil. Lured by her own desires to sin against her family, her God, her friends. God would be so angry with her behaviour and the devil would be laughing his head off. Belly laughing. Another one in the pot. She'd been a pushover for him, walked straight into this situation without a thought for where it was leading, without a care for her own standing and reputation. She must truly be an evil person, just like everyone else out there in the world. After all that God has done for her throughout her life. What had she wanted? An adventure? Just something to do? Had she done it for attention?

It wasn't a personal vendetta against anyone. There was no one that she disliked so much she would cause such trouble and hurt for them. Neither had it been a burning passion for Ray that took her down this path. She didn't love him – she didn't even know him! She had no answers. No explanations for herself or anyone else. If a gun was pointed at her head she would have precisely nothing to say in her defense and the trigger would be pulled. She still can't bring herself to talk to her mum on the phone. Hearing her voice would make her want to go home and a big part of her wasn't ready for that, not least because she knew she would have to face a conversation with the Elders.

*

Over the next two days Jess and Ray settle in and not

only are they given beds in separate rooms but in separate houses, Ray in number four and Jess with the girls in number five.

On the third day Kathy sits Ray down and informs him that he will be having a Bible study with Greg. It is not a request. Without having to put it into words Kathy makes it clear that the study is a condition of his staying there and Ray submits to this arrangement and thus his spiritual education begins. Greg works through the study book at a steady pace, taking it in turns to read the paragraph, then Greg asks the question printed at the foot of the page and then it's over to Ray to give the correct answer from what has just been read. There's no room for reasoning or deep questioning. The correct, Christian way is spelled out in black and white right there in front of him.

Familiar with all of the study books Jess knows Ray will be discussing subjects he's probably never considered before – why the world is so bad, why God doesn't step in and put it all right. He'd given Jess no hint as to what his thoughts were about God, whether or not he had any beliefs, and he never got back to her with accusations about what she'd got him into. She considers he might actually be finding it quite interesting.

*

One afternoon just before tea Greg gathers Jess and Ray and asks them to sit down at the table. He doesn't often speak other than to give instructions or make announcements– 'kids, get in the car' 'pick up those rabbit droppings' 'I'm going to bed'. He leaves the real talking to Kathy except when he is conducting a family Bible study, so for him to do this means he has something important to say.

"Glad you're safe, Jess. You know we can't really have you to stay too long? What's your plan? They're looking for staff at the Beefeater."

Short and sweet was Greg. To the point.

*

The following day the two of them take a walk up to the Beefeater restaurant in the hope that any possible jobs would still be available. Originally a farmhouse on the ancient farm which was mentioned in the Doomsday Book, the building had been extended over the years, the most recent addition a two-storey structure on the back giving a large seating area suitable for events.

The manager Mark and his wife are interested when they hear of their request for work. Wanting to talk in private he leads them through a tiny wooden door off the main seating area and up a short flight of narrow, winding steps, Ray ducking all the way. The office is through another small door and in a room barely big enough to fit in a desk let alone any chairs. A tiny framed window, it's ornate catch painted to death, looks out on the hedged garden below with scattered chairs awaiting customers.

Mark asks each of them a few questions about previous experience and their availability and nods his head as he listens. He writes something on a piece of paper and circles it and, trying not to make it obvious, Jess strains to see but it's impossible, his writing is atrocious. After explaining the roles of barman for Ray and waitress for Jess they are asked to wait downstairs by the bar while things are discussed and invited to get a complimentary drink at the bar.

"You've done this before, Ray. Do you think I can do the work?" Jess is a bit nervous about what she'll be expected to do.

"Yeh, of course. It's easy. Just do what you're asked and be polite to people. Hard on your feet standing up for hours but you'll get used to it. It'll be easier than strawberry picking." Ray smiles at her as she turns her head to survey the huge expanse of tables and chairs over in the restaurant area.

They see Mark duck back through the door wearing a smile and watch him head behind the bar and pour himself a small Coke. As he beckons they all move over to a table in the corner and Mark spreads out two copies of the contract for them both to sign.

"We're happy to take you on for now and see how things go. Ray, can you start tomorrow evening at six? Jessica, we need you for lunches tomorrow so could you be here for ten? I'll sort out a uniform for you from the cupboard, might find one that will do you while we order your size. How does that sound?"

They looked questioningly at each other then declare, "Yeh, that's great," nodding their heads, chuffed that this has been so easy.

"That's good then. Pay is weekly in cash and you'll need to bring your National Insurance number. We'll see you tomorrow."

*

Jess is convinced she can see God's hand in this one, wondering why he is still providing for such a despicable sinner who had rejected him in the worse possible way. But maybe it wasn't her he was helping. Ray didn't know God's standards and so he wouldn't be angry with him. And Jess knew God wouldn't see Kathy and Greg out of pocket for doing a good deed. They had unquestioningly taken in two sinners who were in need, compromising their own position as faithful, upstanding Christians, so God would see them right. She really feels the odd one out and completely undeserving of any help.

*

On entering the restaurant at the start of her first shift, after being shown where the kitchen is and where to store her bag, Jess is handed a folded uniform. In the full-length mirror in the toilet she admires her reflection and turns from side to side to check how she looks.

The red pinafore has black and yellow lines with a central motif. It doesn't fit too bad really, maybe a little long, but the ruff on the white too-big collar of the blouse is touching her ear lobe and making her itch. It'll have to do for now. Hopefully next week she'll have one that fits. And yes, she does look like a Beefeater at the Tower of London. Once, and once only, she walked the eight minutes to work along the main road getting strange looks from passers-by and hoots from drivers. Someone shouted something about going to a fancy-dress party. After that she took her uniform in her bag and got changed once she'd arrived.

During her first break Jess has a chance to look around and take in the features of such an old building. Of all the subjects at school she had enjoyed history the most and architecture in particular.

The lowest ceilings are in the oldest part naturally, and the dark wooden beams run through the length of the lounge area. Thick sturdy pillars, positioned at the most inappropriate points (Jess thinks as she rushes through with plates and glasses), sport an assortment of horse brasses and horseshoes on all four sides. Intimate seating behind partitions alternates with open areas furnished with big family tables. On each one stands a small ceramic vase with sweet peas and some greenery. The curved beams in the walls create natural spaces for pictures and country scenes hang at eye level all around. Orange bricks combine with earthy grout and the prominent pillar by the bar has been worn shiny by a million hands as people swiped around it to face the bar. Behind the copper surface of the bar a mirrored wall gives the impression of a magnificently stocked bar and the optics stand to attention ready to be squeezed.

It was a comfortable place to be, homely and welcoming, not unlike Kathy's house, and Jess felt at ease straight away.

They have really landed on their feet. Having a job is the key to all else and this one (and they only needed one job each) has miraculously fallen in their laps. Jess can't quite believe their luck – although luck was not a word she liked to use as it was connected with false gods. She'd been taught that the people in the Bible who had rejected God preferred to put all their hopes in the God of Good Luck for anything they needed.

*

There had always been encouragement to search out the origins of common phrases and customs that the world used. More often than not each one has a sinister beginning dating back to ancient Egypt or Babylon, Christians who had turned apostate or from demonic practices. Though her mind was young, Jess wondered why some things were strictly forbidden and others fully accepted, and yet others were left as a matter of conscience. And when that was the case it was advised that if the subject or action offended someone *else's* conscience then it's better not to do it.

Always put Jehovah first, she'd been told, and true happiness comes from putting oneself last. A popular motto drawn on homemade bookmarks and given as gifts was 'J. O. Y.– Jehovah Others Yourself'. The list of questionable customs was long and included: wedding rings, calendars, attending a fireworks display on 5th November, hitting a pinata, clinking glasses and saying 'Cheers', throwing soil into the grave of a diseased person, celebrating the new year, wedding cakes, body piercings, tattoos, beards, make-up – so many areas to disagree on. It was a minefield and so easy to upset a fellow Witness. The judgmental looks and comments would come flying so quickly that sometimes it was easier not to do whatever it was. Jess often felt quite paralysed.

*

Kathy doesn't ask if Jess wants to attend the meetings, for which she is grateful. The Kingdom Hall is the last place she wants to be. There is nothing like a quiet, sombre, serious atmosphere to bring any emotions to the surface. She just knows she would spend the whole meeting fighting back tears. Thankfully Jess is left alone which means she has a little time to stop and breathe, to gather her thoughts and to get in touch with her feelings. That is the bit she doesn't like. It's just too painful and the progression of her thoughts stretches way too far into the future. It scares her.

The thought of facing her mum, the Elders, Cassie,

and the rest of the congregation is so overwhelming she struggles to keep from sobbing to herself each time they surface. *Had it been foolish to open up to Kathy?* But really, she hadn't. All she'd said was 'yes' when Kathy had asked if she and Ray were 'together'. She hadn't confessed anything in so many words. But she knows it means that Kathy is now under obligation to inform Marianne and that she strongly suspects Jess has committed fornication.

It doesn't matter about Ray. If she keeps her head down, works hard and plays ball by living the Witness life back down here maybe it would just fizzle out. Maybe it's possible to just brush this all under the carpet and move forward with her life and make it how she wants it to be. But Kathy has her own way of reminding everyone what is set before them – life or death. That's what it boils down to and when Katherine Hamnett designed her CHOOSE LIFE T-shirt made popular by Wham! she may not have imagined it would be used as an anti-sin-against-God advertisement. Kathy wore it around the house at least once a week, a silent but powerful warning message to all in the household.

*

A few shifts in and she's getting the hang of the work; laying the precise number of prawns on top of the glass bowl of salad, twirling the cone so the ice cream falls into the shape of a turd. There isn't too much nonsense from awkward customers and she is always polite and helpful which gets noticed by the other staff. The job had been called 'waitress' but there isn't much waitressing as it turns out: it's more behind the scenes work, just as valuable but with less chance of getting any

127

tips.

But now more comfortable in her better fitting uniform Jess flits about between the restaurant floor and the kitchen with confidence and the determination to improve – maybe one day she would be asked to serve at table. Her wage of one pound twenty-six per hour isn't a lot but means she can pay her way and have a little left over. She doesn't care what Ray does with his money but was pleased when she caught sight of him handing over some notes to Greg.

Most of her shifts are daytime starting at ten and finishing after lunches are over about three, but occasionally she is asked to do an evening shift. She really does not relish the thought of walking past those spooky houses along the main road at midnight on her own, even though it's only a short walk.

Jess remembered years ago walking back home in the dark on many nights when she and her mum and Peter had visited the family. Late in the evening after the small kids were in bed they all sat by the roaring fire and Greg told spooky stories about residents in those old houses along the main road: spiritualists that held seances and the reports of visitors not being able to open the door to leave. One time a Witness had called on one of the houses and offered to show the householder a scripture about how God disapproved of fortune tellers. When they looked down the pages of the Bible had gone blank. After listening to these stories Jess, Peter and Marianne had had to take the long walk back home in the midnight darkness past those very houses. Jess would grip her mum's hand extra tight and try to hurry her along.

Yes, the demons were very active along that road and Jess now wonders if those people are still there, still holding their seances and communing with the devil.

*

On what turns out to be their final shared shift Jess and Ray make the foot-aching walk home through a fierce westerly wind. It had turned up unannounced and displaced anything that wasn't strapped down. Young branches snapped off in their prime lay in the road, their now starving leaves fluttering for help. A lid from a metal dustbin clatters against a fence untethered and would soon be pushed off the edge to wheel its way to another garden.

Unprepared for such drama Jess pulls a thin cardigan around her shoulders; she hadn't thought to bring a jacket when she'd packed her bag to leave for Norwich. Taking the first brave step outside the restaurant Ray puts his arm around her shoulders and with heads down they battle their way out of the car park and start off down the road towards home. Something's not right. His touch feels alien and unwelcome. She wants him to get away from her, doesn't want to be anywhere near him. Using the wind as an excuse she shrugs his arm off her shoulder and pulls her cardigan tighter around her and starts running. *Got to get out of this blasted wind.* She doesn't want to hurt his feelings but the truth is he is the reason she's feeling so awful at the moment. He has unwittingly ruined her life and he doesn't even know it. It's Ray that has made her realise what a terrible person she really is. Ray's fault that she's in this damn mess.

Ray, who are you? What am I doing here with

129

you? I wish you would just clear off back to where you came from, she can't help thinking.

He catches up with her and his subsequent attempt to hold her hand gets him nowhere. Arriving at the front door he pauses before putting the key in. He's obviously been thinking about things too.

"Jess, what are we doing here? We need to talk and work out a plan. Come to my room and we'll talk, yeh?"

Disgusted though she feels, it needs to be done and she needs to be grown up about it.

"OK, I'll make a cuppa and bring it up."

*

It's late and everyone is in bed, the house in darkness. Creeping through the house and up the stairs Jess has to manoeuvre around Pebbles, the family red setter, as she lays on her blanket hopeful that a door will open, any door, so she can sleep on a nice soft bed. She places the mugs on the table and sits herself on the bed beside Ray, but not too close. He shuffles up next to her and the moment his arm goes around her shoulder she freezes.

"What's the plan then, Jess? I don't feel we can stay long here. Kathy and Greg are your friends, not mine, and they've been so good to let us crash here while we get sorted." He sighs. "Have you managed to save any money?"

"Not really, I've given Kathy some board and I had to buy a few bits, toiletries and stuff, so there's not much left."

His arm tightens at the same time as Jess tries to lean away from him.

"Be nice, a place of our own. Wouldn't be able to afford much just yet but in time maybe a flat or something? Perhaps we should look around for other digs and not impose on Kathy any longer. Cosy, just me and you," he says wistfully. "A double room in town by the sea."

His cool fingertips gently bring her face up to meet his and he places his lips on hers. A little peck, that's OK. But he clearly wants more as his mouth is searching for hers backed by a fast-growing passion and urgency. Jess pulls away and shrugs his arm off her, turning her face away from his confused gaze.

"Ray, I don't want this."

"What d'you mean, you don't want this?"

"I think I've made a terrible mistake. We shouldn't have come here." A whine enters her voice and she tries to control it. "I shouldn't have gone to you, in Lea Malling. It was wrong. I don't know why I did it, Ray. I really don't know."

Ray sighs and she feels his body slump where he sits. He takes a few gulps of his tea. Jess does the same as if the answer can be found in the swirl of the remaining tea leaves somehow. He plonks his mug down on the table and looks her in the eyes.

"You mean to say after all we've been through you've changed your mind? Changed your mind about being with me, after all I've sacrificed for you? And what about Dane?" His voice is rising and Jess shushes him with a flap of her hand, indicating the rest of the household is sleeping. "He had to change all his plans too because of you. We were getting along just fine, Jess. For God's sake!"

He drank more tea, a deep scowl on his face and Jess shrinks away from him as the terrible feeling she's really let him down sinks in. What a mess she has made. Not knowing what else to say to him she gets up to leave. As she heads through the bedroom door, she turns to look at him; dejected, rejected, he won't look back at her. Through the partition door into the other part of the joined houses Jess sneaks into her room and curls up on the bed fully clothed. How can any of this be fixed? What can she do to make it right, to undo any part of it, to rewind to the first days of the assembly and behave as a proper Jehovah's Witness should? Nothing right now, at this moment, at one o'clock in the morning.

For the first time for many weeks she prays. With her head in her hands she begs for help to put things right. She hasn't got the answer but she knows and fully trusts that God has, so she pleads for his direction and guidance before falling into a very uneasy sleep.

*

The following day brings sunshine and the last remnants of that strong abusive wind last night. On waking, Jess remembers the words she and Ray exchanged and hopes she won't bump into him today. She thinks he's working a lunchtime shift so stays out of his way till she's sure he's left the house. Tuesday night is the Book Study meeting. It's the one that takes place in someone's house. One hour. Thankfully she's been allowed to miss the other meetings at the Hall but this one is at the house and she needs to show willing really. A small group of Witnesses who live nearby attend.

She's not sure if she can stomach it. It will mean facing all those old faces that hadn't seen her for four years since she'd moved north. There will be hugs and kisses and people asking how she is and saying how lovely it is to see her again. If they knew what she'd been up to they would have a very different opinion of her. It's a deception that, once discovered, would never be forgiven, or forgotten. Jess knows how it works. She'll just have to put her best Witness head on and keep smiling for now.

The brothers and sisters start arriving at seven even though the meeting doesn't start till half past. The chairs for the adults had been set out during the day in a circle around the room and cushions thrown on the floor for the children.

The format: a designated brother of good standing reads the paragraph from the study book, the Elder conductor asks the set question and waits while hands rise to give the correct answer. There's no free discussion and no sincere questions, it's simply the material in the paragraph and the accompanying scriptures being thrashed out, reworded, regurgitated. Just like Ray's study with Greg. Back home Jess's nerves often prevented her from answering up even though there was pressure to do so. It was pitched as all part of her responsibilities as a Christian and was an outward display of the condition of her faith, the same for everybody present. There are no answers from Jess tonight.

After successfully getting through the niceties before the meeting starts Jess finds herself a spot on the floor near Nerys's feet, places her borrowed book and Bible in her lap and waits patiently for the meeting to be over, nodding and smiling in all the right places.

She steals a glance at Ray who has managed to get a chair somehow, to find him looking completely absorbed. He follows the book and is trying to locate the scriptures in the Bible as they are read out. A flutter of pride and hope passes through her at the possibility of Ray progressing in the Truth. What a story that would make!!

"So, Ray, how did you first hear about the Truth?" people would ask!

She didn't hate him, and he had the right to be told about Armageddon too just like everyone else out there. To be given the chance to get to know God and start to live a Christian life.

Kathy and Greg's eight children are spread out on the floor cross-legged at first, later to be lolling against each other and trying not to nod off as the cosiness in the room increases. In amongst the children Pebbles lies stretched out across several laps. She really is a stunning looking dog, and so friendly. Her silkie long coat the colour of a copper kettle has subtle waves in it and the shine looks as if she's been to the hairdresser. Kathy had been known to wash Pebbles with a natural henna product from time to time so maybe that's why.

Comfortable in the surroundings, everyone is relaxed and in the swing by the fourth paragraph. Suddenly, one of the older ones shuffles on her seat and looks enquiringly at the sister to her left, then the brother on her right. She sniffs. And sniffs a second time. Tight-lipped she continues listening to the conductor but the smell is too strong necessitating a hand over her nose and mouth. Others can smell it too now and as the foulest odour makes its way around the room a shuffling breaks out and with a loud whisper of "disgusting…" from the old lady, Pebbles is roughly manoeuvred out of the room by Greg and all the windows thrown open. The blast of cold air soon dispels the miasma and things settle down again, apart from the uncontrollable sniggering children.

A little while later the same odour is doing a second round but Pebbles is safely out in the garden. It's Jonah that Greg grabs by the ear and flings out into the hallway. Poor Pebbles always gets the blame.

Several people stay after the meeting is finished and as some leave Jess notices it's the oldies who hang around in the hope of a cup of tea and a biscuit. *Nothing changes,* she thinks. The smaller children scatter to the four corners of the house, the teens gather round the oak table in the kitchen and suddenly there's noise and chatter and laughter in the house. The back door is opened, Pebbles bounds back in, wondering why he'd been slung out there in the first place, followed by the cats and the rabbits. The meetings are so tense and so serious, it's as if everyone can breathe again the moment the final prayer is said. Tea is welcomed and the biscuits disappear.

*

"Phone!" someone shouts from the hallway as the double ring bounces off the tiled floor.

"I'll get it," shouts someone else.

There's just enough tea left for another small one, Jess thinks, as she brings the huge pot back through to the kitchen. Used tea-dribbled cups and mugs are piling up on the top and she flinches at the clink of spoons on metal as they are thrown into the sink.

"Jess, it's for you." The long telephone cable reaches around the doorway to where Jess stands.

"It's your mum."

Chapter Ten

The curly cable stretches across the tiled floor and under the bathroom door and Jess, sitting on the toilet, takes a deep breath before speaking. She needs some privacy for this call.

"Mum."

"Hello dear, we haven't spoken for so long I wanted to hear how you are."

Marianne's voice is under perfect control. It isn't like her to let her emotions take centre stage. Unknown to anyone she'd been out of her mind with worry when she'd picked up Jess's note and for the following few nights she could not sleep wondering where her daughter was, who she was with, what she was doing. Every waking moment Jess was on her mind and her concentration on the simplest of tasks was impossible.

There was no one she could turn to in the congregation, she hadn't bonded with any of the other sisters. It wasn't through lack of trying but she felt so different from them, and they didn't understand the way she changed from one week to the next when another bout of depression kicked in. So they kept their distance and she put them all in a box, closed the lid and left them there, labelling them as uncaring and unchristian.

Peter was the first one she called, but thinking about it, if Jess had gone there he would have phoned immediately. Peter then got in touch with his brothers and they told Marianne of their plan to search amongst the London hostels. They knew the coach from home came into Marylebone so began their search there. The Blue Dog, The Eagle, and The Dell held no clues as to her whereabouts so their search widened. She could be anywhere. Needle in a haystack.

She needed to speak to Kathy, her dear friend who she missed very much. The phone call to Kathy was short, asking her to ring if she heard anything from Jess. Following her promise to call Kathy offered words of encouragement:

"Marianne, listen, you have to look after yourself, you know. Try and get some sleep. Jess is a strong girl and she's not stupid. She'll be safe wherever she is. She wouldn't purposely put herself in danger, would she? No. So come on. I'm sure we'll hear from her soon. We'll all be praying for her and for you."

When she'd later received the call from Kathy to say Jess had turned up she let it all out and howled down the line.

*

Considering the range of emotions Marianne has been through in the last few weeks, on the phone she holds it together and, for Jess's benefit, is being remarkably calm.

"I'm OK, Mum. How are you?"

"Never mind about me, I hear you've got a job now, at the Beefeater. I hope you're paying your way down there." Practicalities are high on her priority list.

"Yeh, I am. It's a good job, I like it." There is a long pause before Marianne mentions Ray.

"He sounds a nice boy, Jess. I'd like to meet him one day. I've been thinking, maybe we can get a council exchange back down that way. Would you like that?" Jess didn't answer. "Anyway, something to think about. You know, I didn't know what to think when I found your note. Didn't have a clue where you would go. So I called your dad. I had to. I thought maybe you'd found his address amongst my papers and headed there."

The tension is palpable: "What did he say, Mum?"

"He wants you to give him a ring, I'll give you his number."

A few more words are exchanged between them devoid of any angle, any accusations or anger, just factual and emotionless. Jess is grateful for that but speaking to her mum again after all that had happened, after all the worry she's undoubtedly caused her, drives a spear through her heart.

*

Dad? Daddy? Ben? What should she call him when she rings? She had to steel herself for either a good telling off or to hear heartfelt relief in her father's voice. It could go either way. Most of all she just wanted to hear his voice. Her dad's voice. Nine years on for a heavy smoker it would have changed no doubt, but it didn't matter. Would he hear a difference in her voice since she was seven? Would he be able to hear that she was a woman now, not a little girl?

Down the phone he hardly gives her a chance to speak.

"What d'you think you're playing at? Have you got money for a ticket to Uxbridge? Get your arse on the train and ring me when you get there. I'll pick you up from the station."

Wow! That was my dad! She really doesn't care

how he is with her, just that they are now in touch. That's all that matters. They have so much to catch up on; all these years of being apart means he knows nothing of her schooling, her friends, how active she is in the religion. She can't wait to sit down with him and tell him all about her life. He'll be so proud of her.

On the move again. Her final shift tonight then; six till close, another late one. She'll have to grab hold of the manager and explain that she's really sorry but she'll be leaving; there's a family emergency and she has to go up to London tomorrow. It's kind of true.

And what about Ray? Things are cooling off rapidly between them and this will just accelerate it, hopefully finish it completely. Her feelings for him are gone, apart from the tiniest bit of sympathy as she imagined telling him she's dumping him. He'll survive. He's got a job, a place to sleep, and he's with a good family. And he'll be baptised and pioneering before long no doubt so he'll make lots of friends too. She has to think ahead now and leave the past behind.

*

Ray isn't in the least surprised as Jess explains she's leaving. He knew how she'd been feeling about him, about how they'd ended up. Knew it couldn't last. It had been fun though, an adventure really, and had opened up a whole new world for him – the Jehovah's Witness world. He'd not heard of the religion before and to him a lot of it made sense. He wished her well and as they hugged for the last time they reassured each other that there were no hard feelings, not really.

"Maybe we'll bump into each other again one day?" says Ray.

"Yeh, maybe at Norwich assembly!" calls Jess as she walks up the stairs to her room.

Uniform in her bag, Jess sets off for her final shift at the Beefeater. The restaurant is quite busy tonight for midweek, lots of families in, lots of noise. Mark had put some background music on but it's drowned out by the voices, chatter, laughter, a bit of an argument in the far corner.

"Mark, can I have a word please?" There's no right time to walk out of a job.

She explains her position and Mark is very good about it, confident he can get a replacement soon enough. She assures him she will return her uniform in the post and he promised to send her wages on if she gives him a forwarding address. All sorted.

The evening is passing smoothly, a tiny part of Jess regretting having to leave, but she needs to see her dad. There are some regulars whose faces she recognises now, mid-weekers, like the people on the table by the window. She's guessing it's mother and son. Perhaps they don't live together and this is where they meet each week to have a catch up. Maybe they do live together and they're out to celebrate something. They have happy faces and at times are so deep in conversation they don't notice when the waitress is standing at the table.

The mother looks well dressed in her casual trousers, a short sleeved floral top and medium heels. A ginger touch to her hair, Jess wondered if that's what is called strawberry blonde. When she smiles her whole face lights up, a characteristic that her son shares – two beaming stars shining by the window as the darkness descends outside. The son looks to be in his early twenties, tall with dark hair and piercing brown eyes and his strong but not unpleasant aftershave surrounds him in an invisible cloud as he contemplates the menu. Last week he'd caught Jess's eye to ask for some more gravy. He'd looked at her name badge and said, "Thanks, Jessica." This week he'd said "hello" on his way in. Jess was enjoying the feeling of being noticed and gave these customers extra attentive service wherever she could.

As she stands with her back to the kitchen surveying the floor for any customers who might need assistance, her eyes are drawn to the front door where two people have just entered. She recognises them: a couple of Witnesses from the Book Study the other night. She wills them not to see her, not to talk to her. It's the last thing she wants, to have to put on the Kingdom Smile for them and be upbeat, happy and so very Christian. To have to be someone else for a few minutes, with them not knowing who and what she really is, a fornicator without a care for anyone else but herself, someone who has rejected Jehovah and all that he's done for her. Someone who has to go home at some point and face her mother who she had deceived and disappointed, face the prospect of a serious meeting with the Elders about her appalling behaviour…

Her head is suddenly spinning and she needs some air quickly.

Arms outstretched and slamming through the doors Jess heads for one of the benches on the lawn, staggering as she reaches for support. She can feel her chest tightening and her throat closing as she steadies herself holding the table. She can't breathe; gasping for air she can take it in but not exhale and her lungs are filling and filling and they're going to burst. Her ears are ringing loud and she can hear the sea pounding the rocks in her head. She tries to make fists with her tingling hands but her fingers are now set in strange immovable shapes. The leaden feeling in her legs is pulling her towards the ground, and she has no control over her body. She can't breathe, can't breathe, can't… and everything goes black.

Will, the customer with his mum, happens to exit the restaurant just as her legs give way and she fell onto the soft grass. He had stepped outside to meet his brother, Duncan, due to arrive soon for the family celebratory meal. A reason to celebrate indeed, he had recently qualified as a doctor and had returned from Manchester University to be with his family for a while before his busy life began. Will rushes over to her, checks her breathing and puts her into the recovery position. As a First Aider with St John Ambulance he is familiar with such occurrences and knows exactly what to do.

"Hello, can you hear me?" His hand on her back is the first thing she feels. "Jessica? Can you hear me?"

As she comes round she sees the deep green of the grass and a pair of denimed knees.

"Let's sit you up. Jessica, can you hear me?"

He is doing things to her, feeling her wrist, her forehead and looking into her eyes.

"Are you hurting anywhere? Mum, can you help me?" His mum, Esther, had come outside to see where he'd got to. Esther is a nurse at the District Hospital in town and when Jess is coherent enough and describes all that she remembers happening they all agree she'd had a panic attack and had lost consciousness.

Esther takes charge: "Let's get her inside."

Once Mark has been informed he tells Jess she needs to get herself home, never mind about the rest of her shift. He fetches her belongings and hands them to Esther who offers to drive Jess up the road to her house. Will motions to Duncan to stay put and get some drinks in while he's waiting. Dopey and extremely tired she feels no fear at getting into a stranger's car and in a flash Esther is helping her out at the other end. It really is only a two-minute drive away. When Kathy opens the door on a tear- and mascara-stained face and two complete strangers she wonders what on earth has happened.

"Sounds like she had a panic attack. She lost consciousness for one minute, thirty seconds," explains Esther, accurate as ever. "I suggest she goes to bed and takes it easy for a while. Jessica, here's my phone number. I'd like you to ring me tomorrow to let me know how you are."

*

A good night's sleep does her the world of good and Jess wakes up feeling refreshed and headache-free. At breakfast Jess explains to Kathy the gist of her phone call with her dad and tells her of her plans to head up to London to stay with him. She can see Kathy's expression of doubt fall across her face and is relieved when the cause is not what she thinks it is: travelling on her own after an event like last night is a bit unwise so she takes Kathy's advice to leave it another day. She'd thought for a moment Kathy was going to talk her out of going as she remembers Dad and Kathy having had words in the past. About the Truth, of course. Dad had

144

said young couples need to live together before marriage these days, which was instantly dismissed as the devil's opinion. It's a good suggestion of Kathy's to wait as the extra time gives Jess the chance to think things through.

Her head starts to throb after a morning of deep thought about her position right now, so she takes a couple of aspirin from Kathy's medical box. She had to dig deep to find anything recognisable amongst all the natural remedies with strange unpronounceable names: black cohosh, bromaline, saw palmetto. *What are all these things for?* wondered Jess. *Perhaps Kathy is really a witch and she uses these to make up her potions! That wouldn't go down too well in the congregation.*

Esther and Will had been fantastic. Two people she'd never met before had helped her, gathered her belongings, explained what had happened to the manager and had driven her home. They were lovely people, very kind and caring. She digs out Esther's number from her purse and gives her a call to let her know she is feeling very much better and to thank her and Will for their kindness.

"I'm so glad you're feeling better, Jessica. It would be a good idea to go to your doctor to let him know what happened. He'll give you some breathing exercises that you can do if that ever happens again. I hope you can have a restful day today, you're not working are you?"

"Thank you, Esther, no, I've actually finished my job, that was my last night. I'm going up to London tomorrow to stay with my dad." She feels the urge to tell this kind lady the whole story, right from the start. She comes across as very understanding and a good listener, but Jess decides against it. There is no point – they will never meet again.

"Well, be safe and have a nice time. Oh… oh, wait. Will wants to have a word."

"Hi, Jessica, glad to hear you're feeling better today. I'm at Mum's picking up some lenses for an event tonight."

"Hi Will, lenses?"

"Yeh, I'm a photographer, freelance. My work takes me to some strange places, I'm doing a shoot at the lighthouse tonight. Listen, look after yourself, yeh?"

How kind these people are, thinks Jess as she puts the phone down.

*

The house is empty. Everyone is out, kids at school, Greg at work, Kathy on the ministry. It's just Jess and all the animals. In the garden as Jess admires Kathy's planting skills, that of 'just stick it in the ground and see how it grows', she can feel the sun is starting to lose its intensity. In early September that's to be expected, and she can just make out one or two leaves on the trees starting to turn. The long-haired black cat, Bubbles, jumps up onto her lap and nudges her head against her chin.

She wonders how Sophie and the kittens are. They'll be so much bigger now. Probably climbing the fence and exploring the neighbourhood. A little walk around the park opposite the house and a go on the rope swing hanging from the big oak tree makes her think back. Back to the days when her life was simpler, when she and Marianne and Peter lived in Eastbourne. Yes, there were meetings to go to and ministry to do, *Watchtowers* to study and magazines and books to read but the intensity wasn't there like it is now. She used to laugh a lot more often, there were many more people in her life it seemed. Why had the Truth changed so much since moving north?

She thinks about her mum and can see that under her own steam, in her own space, Marianne has the intensity of a laser beam where the Truth is concerned. If she didn't have her frequent down times she would wear herself out completely with the pressure of having to perform, to prove the level of her faith, to herself if not to others. That pressure impacts on Jess's life which was fine when she was little but is too much to deal with now she's getting older. In contrast, she can see that in Kathy's and Greg's lives the Truth touches every aspect and yet at the same time they seem to find a balance. She wishes her mum could be more relaxed about it all, it would make it so much more enjoyable. The Truth was the right way to live – undoubtedly – but Jess was sure it wasn't supposed to be such a burden.

*

Jess has plenty of time to pack her things away in her bag. The weather is changing and she needs to get some warmer clothes somehow. She says goodbye to Bubbles, to Pebbles, the rabbits, the stuffed badger, the chickens, the snake now curled up on the landing under a cushion, giving them all a kiss – except the badger. In her mind she is ready to go, to leave this episode behind, Ray, the Beefeater, her sinful behaviour, and move on to better times. A good night's sleep and a hearty breakfast and she would be off to see her daddy.

*

After taking the train to Victoria and then the Tube she

feels very nervous as she waits outside Uxbridge Tube station, the last stop on the Metropolitan line. The sweeping curve of the art deco frontage means it's possible to see a long way either side and the wide paved area is busy with travelers going in and out with bags, briefcases, suitcases and pushchairs. There are a few memories that had stuck with Jess even though she had been only five years old when the family left Uxbridge: the memory of her nursery, held at St John's Church hall, was a strong one in particular and had been reinforced over the years as she looked many times at the photos of herself on the climbing frame. Colham Manor infants' school: being taken out of the class when the others were making Christmas decorations. The Kingdom Hall: technically in Hayes, and some of the nice people that used to come round to the house to study with Mum. But Uxbridge doesn't hold a special place in her heart as Eastbourne does. It was too far in the distant past and a bit hazy.

Where is Dad? She'd rung him to say she'd arrived so he should be here soon. As a man of small stature approached she didn't recognise him till he was up close. He was tiny, that was her first impression. No taller than her. And still smoking. He saunters up, sticks his fag in his mouth and they hug, smoke curling round her head.

"Alright, love? Good journey?"

"Hi Dad, yes it's pretty straightforward from Victoria." Jess can't take her eyes off him. She hadn't seen him in nine years and right now all she wants to do is hug him again and not let go. He grabs her bag and shoots off towards the car park. Not wanting to lose him in the crowded town centre, she hops and skips after him trying to keep up.

His flat is a rented property near Merriman's Corner with a parade of shops close by. Two bedrooms, a lounge, kitchen and bathroom are more than enough for his needs and the front of the block faces south, nice in the summer through the huge windows. Walking through the front door, Ben gives straight forward instructions: "I'm working during the day so you'll have to amuse yourself somehow. There's the TV and the stereo in the front room, I'm sure you can work out how to use them. Make yourself comfortable. I've made up your room, it's a bit basic but you'll be all right."

It all feels a bit strange, being here with a man who is, in effect, a stranger. There's nothing about him that Jess can remember except his glasses. He always wore black-rimmed glasses that had made a permanent red mark either side of his nose. Having lived away from London for so long now, she notices his accent, not officially Cockney but similar, rough. He doesn't comment on hers. In fact, he doesn't say anything about how she's changed, how tall she's got, how long her hair is. Nothing. *Guess he's just pleased to have me here and those things don't matter.*

"Thanks, Dad. Shall I make a cuppa?"

"Yeh, go on then. You can tell me what you've been up to, what's got into you, running away like that." She dumps her bag in the spare room before she puts the kettle on. He's right, it is basic with just a bed, a chest of drawers and a chair but what else would she really need? The two of them sit at the kitchen table and, pushing yesterday's newspaper to one side along with the rather full ashtray, she sets his mug of tea down. Starting to feel a little more comfortable in her dad's presence she begins to relay her story. Just the facts. If he wants to know how she actually feels about things, he'll have to ask.

*

Over the next few days the conversations roll out between them. Ben doesn't want to talk about his life, now he just wants to hear about his daughter's. He wants reassurance that his decision to leave back then had been the right one and that Jess hasn't been adversely affected by it. He flinches as Jess tells him of the repeated dream she had about him turning up at school saying he's come back. He accepts that she would have had some kind of reaction and that's regrettable but, long term, he hopes she has turned out to be a balanced individual, capable of making her own decisions. He would only find out if he takes the time to get to know her, but life is so busy.

Ben doesn't like some of the questions Jess asks but he needs to answer them, for his sake and hers. The big one – why did you leave? – makes him take a deep breath before answering as truthfully as he can. He tiptoes around trying not to run Marianne down too much, trying not to hurt Jess's feelings about her mum. He describes Marianne's obsession with the religion, the effect her behaviour was having on his girls and the endless pushing for him to go to the meetings and have a Bible study. He just couldn't take it anymore.

None of this comes as a surprise to Jess. She knows how her mum can be. She tries to explain to Ben that Marianne just wanted to shield all the children from a wicked world full of violence and immorality and that was not a bad thing, surely? Ben doesn't accept his daughter's reasoning and says there were better ways of doing that without it involving religion.

"But Jess, do you actually believe all that rubbish? Armageddon and demons and paradise and living forever and all that shit? Why don't you take a look at what other people believe? The world is full of all kinds of people who believe different things."

"But that's just it, Dad. They believe in things they haven't learned the origins of, they spend their time carrying on traditions and rituals that are pagan and that God doesn't approve of. He says so in the Bible, I can show you if you like."

Ben throws his hands up as if in defense. "No, Jess, none of that please. All I'm saying is you need to think about your future and do some exploring before you make decisions, before you set your heart on something. You're young, you've got time. How would you like to stop here for a while, get yourself a job and see how it goes."

"Stay here? With you, Dad?" How fast things are changing.

All of a sudden she has a choice. To stay with her dad who she hadn't seen in nine years, live back in her birth town, maybe get in touch with her sisters and make up for lost time – so much lost time. Where were Karen, Jackie and Diane? What had they been doing all these years? Ben explains they all live near each other in Ashford. Karen trained to be a nurse and lives with her girlfriend Suzie, Diane is a teacher in a primary school and Jackie runs her own beauty therapy business.

So much has happened! Jess can't take it all in and sits mulling over this news about her sisters, her family.

She wants to learn everything about them – what their hobbies are, where they've been going on holiday since those camping days, do they have boyfriends or perhaps they're all married. Karen, though, is a lesbian and therefore not one to be mixing with. Jess will need to gently warn her that if she carries on disobeying God's commands then she will be in line for destruction at Armageddon. But all in good time. She wants to get to know them first.

The girls are too far away to visit this time but if she came to stay again they could travel over to Ashford to see them. The first thing she thought about when she pictured Diane was going swimming with her. It's not surprising she went into teaching, she just had that natural way about her. Not only had she taught Jess how to swim but also how to rub flour and margarine together using fingertips only, not palms, and how to knit. She pictured a photo she'd seen of her splashing through the waves with Diane and Jackie in her red swimming costume with the white skirt around it. She loved that thing. *Wonder what happened to it?* she thought.

She pictures herself living this close to London. It would be easy to get work there, maybe find an interesting role in a theatre or a museum or at the Tower of London. She could study and become a London Guide, work in an office overlooking the Thames, anything was possible. No more thoughts of pioneering and trying to survive on a part-time wage. This could actually work.

Hope is growing in her as she ponders the possibilities. There is a whole world out there that maybe she could explore. Being able to truly relax Jess feels the memories of her sinful behaviour starting to melt from her mind, and the seriousness of an act that was viewed as common in the world is fading more and more as each day passes. It's as if her steps are lighter without such a great burden pushing down on her shoulders.

*

The rest of her stay is spent taking walks through her old neighbourhood. Her school still bears the colourful mural on the outside wall and through the bushes she spots the trampoline frame in a former neighbour's back garden. It's been eleven years since the family had moved away but it all looks much the same, maybe a couple of front doors have been painted including the one on their old house (Jess is quite sharp on the condition of front doors) and the chip shop she used to go to with Peter has become a Chinese takeaway.

Her wanderings are spent in deep thought. Good, positive thoughts with no guilt or fear attached. A yearning to have her family back together, yes, but on the whole she looks forward to the future.

While Ben is at work *Spandau Ballet* keeps her company and strangely for a man of fifty Ben has their *True* album. He must like the funky tones of the title track. Jess plays it over and over and eventually records it onto a blank cassette she finds in the cabinet. There's also some Roberta Flack and some reggae in there too. Ben's speakers are set in the corners of the room and the sound is fantastically rich. She turns the volume up, hoping the walls are thick and the neighbours won't complain. She can actually hear each instrument, the stereo sound bouncing from one speaker to the other. It's magnificent.

*

As the days go by Ben's entire record collection has been exhausted and there's nowhere else she needs to walk. Her thoughts turn inward and she's drawn back to the present and the cloud that hangs ominously above her head. She does a mental run through of all that has happened since Norwich assembly, from start to finish, asking herself some important questions. Why *did* she decide to leave home? How could she have done what she's done having been brought up with such a high standard of morals? No answers come, though.

She remembers the many conversations with Ray from the very first time at the pool table to the last one where they said goodbye. He was OK, was Ray, and now she feels sorry for having, in effect, used him. But it wasn't planned. It just happened. She thought of Kathy, how she'd taken in her and Ray unquestioningly when they turned up on their doorstep unannounced. Talking on the phone to her mum and how she hadn't been cross with her, just practical. The job she'd just walked into at the Beefeater which had provided her with a means to pay her way and buy what she needed and get the train up to Dad's. God definitely had a hand in that one.

She was still hopeful that God loved her, he had after all put her in touch with her dad again, that was a real blessing. She could stay. Should she stay? Would she truly be able to put this episode behind her so completely that it wouldn't rise up again and drag her back? Her conscience had been Bible-trained almost from birth. Confession was good for the soul (that's the one thing Catholics had got right). Talk it through, get it sorted out, rebuild damaged relationships and learn to trust herself again. That was the way to deal with regrets. Clear the path. Then, and only then, would she be able to move forward and be happy.

Yes. What was she thinking! How could she possibly just leave it and hope it would all go away? She had to do it. She had to go back home, ease her conscience, confess her sins to the Elders and then she'd be free to come back to her dad's and built a new life.

*

The evening of the sixth day at Ben's Jess asks if she could use the phone.

"I need to ring Mum. I need to go back home, dad."

Ben doesn't ask why, or even try persuade her to stay, just looks a little disappointed. Arrangements are made with Marianne and the following weekend Ben drives Jess the hundred or so miles back up the M1 towards home. Towards Mum. After coming in for a quick cuppa his goodbye kiss comes with a promise to keep in touch whatever happened; wherever Jess found herself, she was always welcome at his.

As she watches her dad walk down the path away from her she feels a prickling behind her eyes and wants to call him back, fearing she will never see him again. The door is open for them now though and she resolves not to leave it too long before she goes back down to see him. Her dad is back in her life. And he still loves her. She can't quite believe it.

Marianne closes the front door on Ben and turns to look at Jess. Unsure of what her mum might be thinking Jess cautiously holds her arms out to her. *Will she be OK*

155

with me or am I in for a lecture? But as Marianne steps forward Jess knows everything is going to be OK. They hold each other tight and stand in a silent, surprisingly warm, embrace for a few moments.

Nothing is said and as Jess heaves a big sigh and releases herself from Marianne's hold, she realises she needs to make a start and get on with the practical things. She heads up to her bedroom to unpack and sort out her washing. In her nervous state before she'd left she'd pulled open all the drawers trying to decide what to take with her to Norwich and had made a large mess. The bed was left unmade, the covers thrown back over a pile of books she'd been sorting through. On the floor lay the warm jacket she wished she had taken with her. Now it all needs sorting, cleaning and reorganising. Like the rest of her life.

Chapter Eleven

"Sophie! Here, Soph!"

Jess calls the cat, anxious to see her little furry friend. When there's no sign of her she has a quick look in the other rooms upstairs but she isn't there. *Probably curled up on a windowsill somewhere behind a curtain,* Jess thinks, as she continues with her jobs. A pile of clothes in her arms Jess cautiously makes her way downstairs and lets the tap run for a while till it's really hot. Washing powder in the sink and a swoosh around with her hands and it's ready.

"Sophie," she calls again and heads towards the back door. *She must be in the garden,* she thinks, but there's no sign of her.

She'd kept Ray's oversized jumper – that would take a long spin in the new spinner Marianne had got from the catalogue. They'd been through three spinners in the last three years and had fun watching it dance around the kitchen as the speed picked up. The calf-length skirt and high-neck blouse she'd worn at the Book Study. Her work uniform needs to be washed and spun separately as she knows the red runs. She'd found that out at Kathy's when Jonah's socks and PE top had come out pink.

Standing at the kitchen sink pummeling, squeezing and kneading the fabrics Jess gets lost in the music coming from the radio and finds herself bobbing along to 'Dance Hall Days' by *Wang Chung*. A great beat.

Very catchy.

Her Christian training pops into her head and she tells herself that there isn't a lot of music that's acceptable these days. It's full of innuendo or outright filth and promotes drugs and sex and a bad attitude towards authority. Stevie Wonder is safe, Cliff Richard and maybe a few others but on the whole it's best not to listen to the music of today. All these performers are being influenced by the devil when choosing their lyrics, the heavy sexual beat and rhythmic patterns and we don't want to allow that kind of wickedness into our houses. With some records, as she was told from the platform, if they were played backwards, the lyrics were giving praise to the devil. Some time ago Jess and many others in the congregation got rid of their entire record collections just in case. How well they are protected in the Truth!

Jess turns the volume up.

*

It's Wednesday. Nothing is said between Jess and her mum about the past few weeks. Neither attempts to bring it up. The meeting is tomorrow night and she really doesn't want to think about going. She knows the first one will be the hardest – her guilt will be written all over her face. But she just needs to get it over with. Anyway, it'll be good to see Cassie again, she'll sit with her if Marianne's not going.

As the day progresses into evening Jess's head is starting to ache.

"If it's a migraine you need to go to bed, Jess," Marianne informs her.

"It's just a headache, Mum, it's OK. I'll go for a

walk, get some fresh air. Oh, where's Sophie? She's not upstairs. Is she out the back?" Jess hasn't seen or heard the little mews of the kittens either. "Where are the kittens?"

As Marianne stands in front of the black and white portable TV trying to find BBC2 she shouts over her shoulder: "They're gone. Rehomed. One of the sisters in Market Harborough congregation. They were too much for me while you were away, Jess. I couldn't manage with them under my feet all the time, letting them in and out, clearing up after them. I thought she'd have just Sophie and one of the kittens but was happy to take them all, I couldn't believe it."

A lead weight drops on Jess's heart in that moment. She loves Sophie, she is her cat and the kittens are hers too. She had been the one that prepared a box in the spare bedroom for the birth of the kittens, she'd watched over them as Sophie nurtured them, saw them growing and getting stronger. Listened to their tiny cries and smelled the milkiness in their pure new fur. All this time they'd been part of the family and Marianne had just given them away. How could she!

Perhaps she can get them back somehow, and as she visualises picking up the phone to the sister and asking for them back her cheeks are suddenly wet with tears. Forget the walk. She stomps off up the stairs to the comfort of her room and slams the door. *Thanks, Mum.*

Burying her head in the pillow with another one held on her head Jess just wants to disappear. Her emotions are all over the place, swinging from relief and happiness at being back home with her mum to a feeling of fear and trepidation about her spiritual future, to elation at having seen her dad again. The turmoil of recent times is buzzing around in her head and snapshots of conversations with her dad, with Kathy, loom into focus then fade to be replaced by a memories of a cool swim in the sea, the sound of the tent zip, the ins and outs of her first sexual experience, the smell of coach diesel and the noisy engine, diners calling her over to the table to ask for more wine, the sweet smell of strawberries.

Nerys, Pebbles, Mark, Will, Esther, Jonah farty-pants, Greg's demons and a train ride to London. It swirls and heaves, subsides and attacks her from all sides and her tears turn to sobs and her sobs increase on the intake and she's in a full-blown panic attack again. Unable to call her mum for help she makes her way through it, powerless to stop its progression. Her chest aches with lungs about to burst and as she looks down at her tingling, tightly scrunched hands everything goes blank.

*

She has no idea of the time when she wakes up but there's a cup of tea on her bedside cabinet. She feels it. It's stone cold. Next to the tea is a pair of the latest magazines.

The front covers are speaking directly to her:

'Remain Without Spot From the World' the *Watchtower*.

'How Can I win My Parents' Respect?' the *Awake*.

Each word is a stab in the chest.

She hasn't read any magazines for a long time and resolves to pull herself together and think positively. Perhaps it would do her good to read some good upbuilding information. Scriptures directly from God's Word – the only reliable source these days.

Marianne knocks on the door.

"That must have been some headache, you've been asleep for hours."

"What time is it?"

"Nearly eight. You look rough, Jess."

Marianne sits on the edge of Jess's bed and pauses before quietly saying: "You know you can talk to me if you want to. I am your mother. If you want to get anything off your chest, I'm a good listener."

She pauses again.

"If anything has happened that you wish hadn't…" she implores with her head. "Has anything happened…?"

Jess takes a breath and Marianne listens in silence as she makes her confession about Ray. It has to come out somehow, sometime. Giving the facts at her own pace Jess feels herself relax just enough to describe how she felt throughout it all. She talks about the time she collapsed on arriving at Kathy's, how she felt at being present at the Book Study, her panic attack at work and how those people helped her. Her thoughts about her wrongdoing and how she wonders if Jehovah is actually still helping her or has turned away from such a sinner.

"You know, that was the best decision you could have made, to go down to Eastbourne, to Kathy. Look what's happened now – Ray is studying the Bible! I can definitely see Jehovah has been directing things."

Jess continues to talk about how she felt meeting her dad again. Fear of coming back home to face the music. There aren't any gasps of horror, any shocked expressions on Marianne's face. Nothing. With exhalations as the words tumble out of her mouth into the open air, Jess's body relaxes and for a moment, the chat with her mum feels comforting. Like two girls talking about boys although Jess doesn't go into any great detail about that night in the tent. They actually laugh together.

"In a tent! Of all the places to lose your virginity!"

"Where did you lose yours, Mum?"

"In the back of a cowshed!"

That's the first time she's seen her mum laugh or even smile for such a long time. But the laughter is short-lived as a few seconds later a more serious tone falls upon the conversation. A pigeon lands in the tree outside her window and looks in cocking his head as if he wants to hear some juicy gossip.

"You know I'm going to have to tell the Elders, don't you?"

"Yeh I know. I want to get it out in the open anyway, then I can put it behind me and get back to normal."

"You seem to get on best with Kevin, do you want him to choose the other two for your Judicial Committee?"

"I suppose so."

After a quick prayer downstairs Marianne makes the phone call to Kevin. He knows what to do, and another two phone calls later by Kevin and a Judicial Committee is formed: a group of three Elders, one being the Presiding Overseer, Kevin, the one who supervises the other Elders. Kevin Choi had worked with Jess on the ministry many times and had got to know her. He was the one who had noticed her improvements and the efforts she was making towards baptism, and was one of the Elders that went through a portion of the baptism questions with her. He was quite old school, and a stickler for the rules, she thought, but at least everyone knew where they stood with him.

A return call comes to inform Marianne that a meeting is set up for Friday evening at the Kingdom Hall. That's the first and most difficult step over, Jess thinks. Now she just needs to get her head in the right place to get to the meeting tomorrow night.

Sitting on her dressing table stool, she forces herself to look in her own eyes. What can she see there? A sixteen-year-old girl, woman now, who, yes, has done wrong. That's a fact. She can't undo what's been done. Does her mum still love her? Yes. Will she forgive her? Yes, she can see she's sorry and wants to move on. Who is aware of what she'd been up to? She doesn't know. Probably no one at the moment. She'll have to go into that Hall with her head held high, put all this to the back of her mind and concentrate on the talks. And pray, of course. Pray that she can get through it without any kind of panic attack or tears.

*

The following evening Marianne holds Jess's hand on the bus and doesn't leave her side for the whole meeting. She's being really good about it all. Cassie comes running up to Jess and throws her arms about her. It was so, so good to see her again. They catch up with general news and arrange a sleepover at Cassie's at the weekend. Then they'd have loads of time for a proper conversation. Cassie gently asks where Jess has been but is not surprised when Jess says, "I'll tell you later."

Alan was there, he gave a riveting five-minute talk on idolatry. That's his first number four talk – usually he only does the number two Bible reading talk which is reading aloud a long passage of scripture and making one or two comments at the end. He's obviously making progress. Good for him, Jess thinks, but beyond that her feelings for Alan are dead. Maybe they would be rekindled in the future but for now Jess has too much on her mind and must prioritise her interests. The Truth must come first and foremost now, above everything else.

That night Jess sleeps better than she has for a long time. A dreamless peaceful, deep sleep, and wakes refreshed and determined to get through this day and to feel just as peaceful by the end of it. She knows she is going to get a good spiritual telling off followed by lots of encouragement from the scriptures. She'll be shown passages where characters in the Bible who committed similar acts and worse, King David for one, went on to be fully forgiven by God. She'll be told how generous Jehovah is in that he puts the repentant sinners' acts as far away as East is from West.

It'll all be OK.

*

The following evening Jess looks at her watch and announces that the bus leaves for town in fifteen minutes.

"I'm as ready as I'll ever be, Mum."

"I'm sorry, Jess, but you'll need to go by yourself, I'm not feeling too good. I need to rest. But don't worry about anything, just explain things to the

Elders just the same as you did to me. They'll understand. One of the Elders will probably give you a lift home. Have you got your Bible?"

The light was starting to fade and it would be dark by the time she arrived at the Hall. She doesn't like the idea of travelling at night on her own, not after learning about the danger she'd been in at Kings Cross that time. Bag in hand she takes a deep breath and leaves the house not knowing that a major turning point in her life is on the horizon. That her development as a teenager, as a human being, a young woman, would be interrupted, stunted, irreversibly.

*

It's seven twenty-five and the Kingdom Hall is in darkness as she walks up the driveway. Three cars are in the gloomy tree-lined car park, the fallen leaves providing a light layer of yellows and browns over the tarmac. The Elders must be inside already and as she gets nearer, the strip of light visible under the main door guides her feet. It's cold and damp in there, and there's a smell of stale bodies and dead flowers and as she walks through the inner door to the main hall it intensifies. The burning smell of the three-bar electric heater hints at which of the side rooms they're in.

Jess pushes the door open.

"Come in, Jess. Take a seat," comes the emotionless invitation from Kevin. The seats are set out in a row of three for the Elders with one single chair opposite for Jess. Bob, Jess's Book Study conductor, sits on the left. Bob is a gentle short hairy man with a high voice. A plodder, dependable, and sees the good in people before anything else.

Kevin sits in the middle. Chris, the most outspoken of the trio, takes his seat on the right. He always shows an interest in many of the young ones, especially the lads, and gives them support when they seem to be struggling.

Kevin gets up and closes the door so the room can warm up. Jess is extremely nervous and the sight of the three Elders all looking directly at her makes her want to run straight out that door. *This must be what it feels like to be in court, with a judge and a jury*, Jess thinks. But there are no others here, no one to speak up in Jess's defense, to give a character witness or to explain any mitigating circumstances. She is completely on her own.

"So, first of all let's say a prayer and ask for Jehovah's guidance on the proceedings tonight," announces Kevin. It was standard practice; before meals, before bed, before meetings, before studying. Before everything. Say a prayer.

Following some niceties and introductions although everybody knows everyone else, Kevin leads the meeting by explaining that Marianne had told him Jess had unfortunately committed a serious sin recently.

"Is that correct, Jess?"

"Yes."

"Sadly, these things do happen but what matters is our attitude to what we've done. Jehovah says he will forgive us our sins if we are repentant. Are you repentant? Have you approached Jehovah in prayer and poured your heart out to him?"

"Yes, I have," she answered truthfully. One of the other Elders, Bob, started flicking through the pages of the Bible, searching for an appropriate scripture to share.

Kevin continued: "So, as I understand, you ran away from home, without your mum's knowledge or approval, to a campsite on the Norfolk coast. You met up with a boy you'd met there previously while staying for the assembly. Is this correct?"

"Yes." Jess shuffles in her seat, feeling the heat rising.

"What happened then?"

"We had something to eat and had a chat... and then we went back to his tent."

"I know this is difficult, but in your own words can you explain what happened," Kevin continues.

"We committed fornication." That's what happened. That's it. What more do they want?

"Who made the first move? Was it the boy or was it you?"

"Er, we both just moved together." Jess's hands hold each other as her nerves start to jumble about.

"Presumably, some kissing was involved. Who tried to kiss who first?"

The shuffling of Bible pages stops and Bob and Chris are looking directly at Jess in silence.

"Both of us." Jess frowns.

Chris took over the questioning.

"And did you remove his clothes first or did he remove them himself? Did you take your own underwear off? You see, Jess, we're just trying to build up an accurate picture here, it's important."

"I... I don't remember exactly." Her cheeks are burning now and she's really feeling the heat. The questions are coming thick and fast with no time in between to consider her answers or to remember the precise order of things. Why are all these details so important anyway?

"He must have been aroused, did you help him to get aroused by touching his penis? Did he touch your vagina? And what about birth control? Presumably you don't take the contraceptive pill so what provision was made for that and who arranged it?"

"Condoms," she says quickly.

"Who bought them? Did you? Did you plan to have sex with him? When did you buy them? When you arrived there or before you left?" All said with such gentle control.

"No… no!" She can't think. Needs some water.

Chris continues.

"We need to ask you, Jess, did he bring you to orgasm? Did he help you or did you get there by yourself?"

This was beyond a joke, so embarrassing! How can they sit here and ask such personal questions? She doesn't know where to put her face so covers it with both hands and refuses to talk anymore. The questions continue but she can't hear them, won't hear them, won't listen. She needs a break.

"Can I get some water please?" she blurts out.

"Yes," the rather red-faced Kevin says, "let's all have some water. I'll turn the heater off too." He's sweating. She can smell him.

Jess gets up and rushes out to the kitchen area, leans against the sink and splashes water on her face from the cold tap. There's a pint glass in the top cupboard and she glugs not one but two full glasses down her neck. This is too much. Why isn't her mum here? She wouldn't allow all these questions, perhaps they wouldn't have even attempted to ask them if she was here. She thinks about taking in a tray with a jug and three glasses. It would be the kind, Christian thing to do but, no, they can get their own water.

*

When Jess walks back into the room the three are sitting waiting for her with Bibles open.

"We now need to establish what happened after, Jess. So what happened immediately following the act? In your own time."

Jess sits back, giving herself time to think. They will get her answer when she is ready.

"We went to sleep."

"In the same tent? In the same sleeping bag?"

"Yes."

"And what did you do the next day?"

"I stayed around the campsite and Ray went to work picking fruit."

"And that night? Did you do it again? Did you use condoms again? Did you have an orgasm?"

Here we go again. "We slept, that's all."

"Right. Right," said Kevin, looking as if he was setting it all in place.

"Does anyone else have any more questions? Bob, Chris?" He looks left and right at the other two questioningly. There was nothing else.

"So, Jess, obviously the three of us need to discuss things between us, we will pray again for Jehovah to guide us to make the right decision following your behaviour. So can you just wait out there in the main hall until we call you back in."

This is procedure. Jess had heard from others what happens during a Judicial Committee meeting. One of the teenagers had been in trouble back in the summer for getting out of his mind drunk one night and making a fool of himself in the neighbourhood. His behaviour would bring reproach on Jehovah's name and was unacceptable. He was given a public reproof, a telling off from the platform to the whole congregation, and restrictions placed upon him. No more passing round the mic or leading a group in prayer until he had accepted the seriousness of what he'd done. Thereafter he was viewed as 'bad association' as the scripture said. Even after his restrictions had been lifted several months later, though he was supposed to have paid the price in full, he was viewed with caution for ever after.

The main hall feels chilly and damp. It's strange seeing it empty and dark when it's usually filled with colour and joyful chatter. Just as Jess is thinking they're taking a long time, she hears voices. No distinct words, just noise and the volume rises briefly. They're arguing! It settles back down and before long the door opens and she's invited back in. She takes her seat, crosses her arms, and waits for someone to speak.

Kevin, sitting in the middle, invites Jess to get her Bible out and turn to Genesis chapter thirty-nine. The account of Potiphar's wife trying to seduce Joseph was familiar and she knows where this is going. She had tried to get him into bed but he had immediately fled leaving his cloak behind in his hurry to leave.

"So you see, Jess, Joseph fled. He didn't stay and go through with such a wrong act. He left. Immediately. He couldn't bring himself to sin against God not after all that he'd done for him. What should you have done, even up to the point of getting into this boy's tent?"

"I should have left. I know that."

"And what should you have done after you had gone ahead and committed the act?"

"I should have left straight away. But I couldn't. I didn't have any money and it was the middle of the night!"

"Did you *want* to leave? If you had really wanted to Jehovah would have made a way out for you, you know that. Instead what happened was, not only did you not leave the next day, you stayed with him for several days, in fact weeks longer, travelling on together to the south coast, yes, a nice romantic little adventure wasn't it?"

Their faces were like stone. It's true, they were right. These spiritual police had investigated and found her guilty of this spiritual crime. Now she was awaiting her sentence. And the words that would change her life forever bounded through the walls, up through the carpet tiles on the floor, disembodied words that she heard coming at her through a tunnel, vague but deadly and murderous:

"Having considered all that you've told us, it's quite clear you are not truly repentant and because of that we have decided to disfellowship you."

Chapter Twelve

She can't feel her feet. It's like she's gliding along the carpet as she makes her way out of the room, out of the Kingdom Hall and down the sloping drive to the main road. A faint offer of a lift home reaches her ears from behind but is swiftly rejected by an angry wave and a shrug of her shoulders. In total shock at such an outcome her ears are buzzing and she can't quite take it in although she knows it's the worst thing that could possibly have happened.

I'm dead.

If Armageddon comes tomorrow I'm a gonner.

Why did they disfellowship me? It's not like I denied it ever happened. I've never tried to hide what I did, to myself, to Kathy, to Mum to Dad, to Jehovah. Yes, it took me a while to get back home but when I did I confessed quickly. So what's the problem? Where's the forgiveness?

She can't make any sense of it.

But her confession is clearly not what is important to these Elders. It doesn't warrant any level of leniency from them. The cold hard facts remains: she had not fled the scene *immediately* therefore she was not truly repentant.

Jess has the right to appeal the decision within seven days but that is in case any new evidence coming to light. There is no point – everything has been confessed, exposed and explained. They asked enough personal questions which she answered truthfully, and there's nothing more to add. The Elders have made their decision and it won't be changed.

But deep down, in a heart that has been trained since early childhood and moulded unquestioningly Jess feels it must be right; the Elders are appointed by Holy Spirit, led by God, and don't get things like this wrong.

Do they?

*

Jess's feet turn off the road that goes straight into town where she would usually get the bus home. Not really knowing where she's going her instinct is to get help, she can't be alone right now in such a distraught state. The tears are stuck behind her eyes as she turns a corner and nearly bumps into someone. She follows the little alleyways into the estate where Cassie lives and bangs on her friend's door with furious fists. Cassie herself answers.

"Jess! Come in, what are you doing here so late? It's almost nine." As she speaks she can see Jess's face crumbling and knows something is very wrong.

"Oh Cassie! Cassie!" is all Jess can summon as she shakes her head and lowers her eyes. Her face is now wet with tears, released all at once and running down her chin in rivulets. Under strict instructions from Kevin Choi not to tell anyone about the result of this evening's meeting her lips are sealed. She raises her head and looks directly into Cassie's eyes willing her to read her thoughts instead.

"Come in, come in, Jess, whatever's the matter?"

The girls hug where they stand and Cassie's tight arms around her are the only thing keeping her up. Jess's legs have almost gone to jelly and all she wants to do it lie down.

The girls climb the stairs hand in hand, Jess shaking all the while.

"What's happened, Jess? What is it? Is your mum all right?" asks Cassie with strained concern in her voice.

Jess straightens herself up as she sits on the bed and wipes her face with her sleeve. She takes a deep breath and states: "My mum's fine. Listen to me carefully. I'm really sorry, Cassie, I can't come to sleep over at the weekend as we planned. I can't tell you what's happened so please don't ask me, and... I... I..." Jess can't continue. She puts her face in her hands and just sits there, not crying, not talking, just taking deep breaths in through her nose and out through her mouth, trying to control her emotions. She doesn't want to have a panic attack. It's embarrassing.

Cassie tells her friend to stay there and goes downstairs to make her a cup of tea. In the lounge Cassie's parents are watching the TV but had heard the banging on the door and anxious voices, then footsteps on the stairs.

"What's all that racket, Cassie?" calls her dad from the front room.

Waiting for the kettle to boil Cassie puts her head round the door and explains what she can: "Dad. It's Jess. She's really upset."

"Jess? What's she doing round so late? What's happened?" he enquires.

"I don't know, she can't tell me, but she looks pretty awful. I'm taking her a cuppa. Can we give her a lift home in a while?"

"Oh, right. Well, she'll be OK. Whatever it is will sort itself out. It always does. Tell her not to worry too much."

"Thanks, Dad," she says as the kettle starts to sing. When Cassie enters the room Jess is lying down on her bed sobbing into the pillow.

"I'm sorry, Cassie, I'm sorry, I'm really sorry."

"Ssshh, come on now, drink up and we'll take you home."

*

The drive home in Bodger's Lodge (because the car is in the garage) is made in silence with the girls sitting on the bouncy sprung seats in the front hand in hand. Jess does not let go. She swings between feeling angry one moment then like she's been stabbed in the heart the next. The chorus of 'Karma Chameleon' starts playing on the radio and is just too cheerful. She wants to reach out and turn the damn thing off but she clamps her hands over her ears instead. She's just been murdered and Boy George doesn't even care!

As they turn the corner into her road the thought of now going inside to tell her mum what's happened fills her with dread. She will be horrified. She knows how her mum has reacted when hearing about others that have been disfellowshipped and how she has treated them, sticking rigidly to the rules.

But maybe with Jess, being her daughter, she will try and make the Elders see they've got it wrong. She could make them see that she's really been through a turbulent time what with everything and that it just took a little while for her emotions to settle down. Maybe her mum will stand up for her.

*

The uncomfortable but necessary conversation begins. Marianne keeps pushing Jess for the result, the decision, not the whole story from the beginning, not all the questions she was asked. She wants to know the outcome. She reasons that at the most it will be a private reproof – a meeting in the back room with those three Elders and a spiritual admonishment. A loving and encouraging discussion on how she can rebuild her relationship with Jehovah and how they can help her to do that. She'll be offered a weekly Bible study to build her up, probably with one of the mature sisters, and be encouraged to go out on the ministry a bit more. *Yes, that's what would have happened. A spiritual slap on the wrist at the most,* Marianne concludes.

She does not expect to hear that her daughter has been disfellowshipped. Such a nasty word, 'disfellowshipped'. She doesn't say anything when Jess says that word. Her mind whirs in different directions all at once. She thinks back to David and how he came out of the experience a different man, of others that she'd heard of. The talks about how to deal with a disfellowshipped family member and reminders of not to look for excuses to be with them.

No! This can't be right! Jess is a young girl, foolish and headstrong but still… Perhaps she shouldn't have let her get baptised so young. If she hadn't taken that official stand of dedicating her life it would not have been possible for them to disfellowship her. The same as if a person isn't married, they can't get a divorce. Maybe it was all her fault?

Marianne is not one to turn to drink during stressful times but right now she needs a small brandy. Standing at the cabinet she pours herself a small amount and looks over at Jess. Slumped in the chair she's as white as a sheet, looking at the Bible on the table but not focusing, just staring. She takes a second tumbler and pours another for Jess; she looks like she needs one too.

"Do you want anything to eat?" enquires Marianne not really knowing what else to say. This isn't the time to reassure her daughter that everything would be alright. She couldn't promise that.

"No, I'm going to bed."

"You need to say your prayers tonight, Jess," came the unnecessary reminder.

Downstairs the TV is playing the BBC News at Ten and as Marianne reaches out to turn the set off the news item reminds her of something she's completely forgotten about: the broadcaster's voice announces: "O level and CSE exams are to be abolished and replaced by a new examination for sixteen-year-olds, in the biggest exam shake-up for over ten years."

Jess's exam results are sitting in an unopened envelope in the sideboard! They'd arrived in mid-Aug when she was away and Marianne had slipped the envelope in the drawer and thought nothing more of it. She'll give it to her tomorrow. It'll give her something else to think about.

Sitting alone with her thoughts Marianne tries to make sense of it all. Jess's behaviour itself had come as a surprise to her. She thought she was happy enough. There are plenty of kids in the congregation her age, she sees them regularly on the ministry and at meetings, she had her little job. Her exams she'd found hard, that was true, but she got through them. What had made her so unhappy that she felt she had to run away from home? The family split had happened years ago, it wasn't like it was recent, and Jess had adjusted to that the same as everyone else. No, Marianne couldn't really put her finger on why Jess had rebelled. And to run straight into the arms of a worldly boy! What was she thinking? Had she not been listening at the meetings and taken in all the advice about immorality and to keep separate from the world? Clearly not. She couldn't work it out.

Then she'd remembered the behaviour of some of the other young ones over the summer when Jess was away. The story went that there had been a gathering in one of the Brothers' gardens where he had allowed alcohol. As expected it had turned into an evening of drunken behaviour, loud unchristian music and lewd dancing into the small hours and some of the neighbours had complained. She'd also heard that Alan had been caught smoking. The general opinion was that they had all turned into rebellious teenagers at the same time and had been goading each other, their spirituality evidently taking a backseat. Marianne wonders if this has featured in the Elders' decision.

*

The next morning Jess awakens to a bright but chilly autumn day, the sun shining through the gap in the curtains. She rolls over in bed ready for a few more minutes before getting up then remembers the events of the night before. Her heart sinks in her chest and she pulls the covers over her face. A tentative knock on the door is followed by Marianne entering with a cup of tea

178

and some toast on a tray. She sits on the bed next to her.

"How are you? Did you sleep alright?"

"Think so." Jess sits up and takes a slurp of her tea and looks directly into her mum's eyes. "Oh, Mum," comes her first words of realisation. Then the tears start. Wails and breathy sobs fill the room as Marianne takes her in her arms and holds her tight. She strokes her messy hair and waits for the right moment to talk to her.

At a break in her crying Marianne says ponderously, "You know, Jess, I've been trying to work out why they've taken such a serious step and disfellowshipped you, and d'you know what I think?"

"It's because of my behaviour, Mum, that's all it is. I've been so bad and now I'm being punished. Jehovah directed them so it must be right."

"No, Jess. In my view your sin does not warrant such severe discipline. While you were away there were some incidents amongst the young ones, Alan and his friends, and their behaviour was no better than those in the world. Even indecency was mentioned. I think the Elders have made an example of you."

"What, to show what would happen to them if they carry on like that? They'd end up being disfellowshipped?" says Jess trying to understand what her mum was getting at.

"Exactly. And I fear there is no point in appealing the decision. Their minds are made up." Her Irish Catholic background fitted well with her view of the authority of the Elders. What they say must be accepted whether it's right or wrong. No one argues with the Elders.

A confused Jess asks the question: "So, does that

make me a good example or a bad example?"

Marianne is unable to answer.

*

The next few days are hard for Jess having so little to occupy her mind while she waits for the Thursday night meeting, the night she will officially be cast out. She could do with having Sophie around right now, listening to her purrs and playing with the kittens. She has given up her catalogue job, it's something she can't cope with at the moment but the supervisor, who proved to be very understanding after Marianne told her Jess had run away, said she could pick it up again anytime. The slow progression of the week towards Thursday makes her feel sick and she just wishes it was over.

Trying to get her head round to a spiritual viewpoint, she wonders what Jehovah actually thinks about her situation. She comes to no conclusion, she doesn't profess to know God's thoughts, but resolves to keep the line of communication with him open. He's all she's got now. Her prayers are full of requests for strength to get through this time as difficult as it will undoubtedly be. She is determined to be as spiritual as she can in her new status, even with all the restrictions she will be under, and to make her way back into the arms of the congregation as soon as possible. She is looking forward, not back and once she had put the announcement into its rightful place in her mind, that of just something to sit through, she feels a lot stronger and better able to cope.

*

Thursday arrives and, as supportive as Marianne has been so far she feels that to attend and hear the announcement that her daughter is disfellowshipped is just too much to bear. This is probably the time when Jess needs her most but despite prayers for the strength to go she just can't do it. There would be looks and comments and commiserations after the meeting from people who have never been that friendly to her before and she doesn't think she can deal with it. No, she doesn't want the attention and she hates hypocrisy.

Jess doesn't need to go. The Elders will understand that of all the upcoming meetings she could be excused from this one without them thinking too bad of her.

*

But Jess goes. Alone. She feels she must make a good impression, start as she means to go on and show the Elders she's serious about coming back. She walks extra slow from the bus stop in town, head down, not waving at those that pass her in their cars. She takes a seat on the back row, where she will be expected to sit, just as the first song is getting underway. No one talks to her, but it's time to shush anyway. She can see Cassie sitting in between her parents, level with her row on the other side of the Hall. She doesn't want to catch her eye. It would make her crumble into a snivelling mess. The two friends will not be allowed to speak again until Jess is reinstated, whenever that will be. It could take months, years. It all depends on Jess's progress and behaviour. *I'm so sorry, Cassie*, she thinks, *I would undo it all if I could. I'll miss you so much.*

The first half of the meeting ends with another song immediately following which the Chairman declares that Kevin Choi has an important announcement to make. As he makes his way up the

181

steps to the podium Jess sees everyone perk up, eager to know what he's going to say.

In a practiced monotone with all the seriousness of a High Court judge passing sentence he declares: "Jessica Dalton has been disfellowshipped for conduct unbecoming a Christian." That's it. He leaves the platform and a hush descends. Heads turn towards each other questioningly, frowns are exchanged, while others bow and shake their heads. Jess hears the rustle of a tissue and a nose being blown nearby. Looking over at Cassie, she can see her tears falling as her mum whispers something to her. The two of them stand and make their way to the back of the Hall, probably heading to the ladies' room for a bit of privacy. She feels the breeze her friend makes as she walks behind her, she hears a discreet sob and cringes in her seat, biting her lip to stop herself crying.

The worst bit's over. Jess sits through the rest of the meeting, which is comprised of a talk on how to answer the question 'How Do We Respond When Asked Why Jehovah's Witnesses Do Not Vote?' and then comes the expected giveaway talk.

When a disfellowshipping announcement is made no reason is given and technically no one is supposed to know except the three Elders that formed the Judicial Committee. But the talk entitled, 'Your Virginity – a Precious Gift' says it all. Jess sits there listening to the Brother talking about her, without naming her, and how rebellious and unthankful she's been. He tells the congregation how much shame is brought on the congregation when one of its members sins in such a way and how such an act can never be undone.

Jess wants to disappear, run right out of that building and never go back. She is being publicly shamed in front of her friends and associates. How will she ever be able to raise her head again? She stays glued to her seat, determined not to bring any more attention to herself by getting up and walking out.

*

As soon as the final song and prayer are over Jess leaves swiftly and walks the twenty minutes to the bus station in town. It's 9.55 by the time she gets there and the dark pillared concrete structure is deserted. Situated beneath the shopping area the station is a cold, damp unwelcoming place, and Jess looks around fitfully as she stands with her back against a cold tiled wall. There are dark patches that never dry, of diesel, spilled drinks and, in some corners, urine. The ticket office where she'd bought her coach tickets for Norwich stands closed and in darkness, the posters in the window offering discounted day trips to Skegness. A few drunk men stagger down the slope towards her guffawing, puffing on their cigarettes and thankfully head over to the other side to catch a different bus. Hers arrives after a fifteen-minute wait and as she boards the empty vehicle she breathes a sigh of relief that tonight is finally over.

*

The realisation of Jess's new status sinks in over the following days.

She can't see or speak to Peter, her big brother who's always been there for her. Can't go and stay with him and his wife in Southend, can't talk to him on the phone.

Cassie, her good friend for the last several years

since moving to the Midlands will be a stranger to her now. No more sitting together at meetings, no more sleepovers. No more going into town on a Saturday afternoon to buy make-up or records. The young ones in the congregation will shun her. Many of them live on the same estate and it's common to bump into them while out and about.

Her mum, only because Jess lives in the same house, can mix with her but nothing spiritual is allowed – no studying, no preparation for meetings together, no spiritual discussions, no prayer.

Marianne is obliged to tell Kathy, Greg and family so there are no visits from them or trips down to Eastbourne to stay.

If she bumps into anyone from other congregations that may not know she's been disfellowshipped she must tell them quickly and move on.

If she gets ill and needs to go to hospital no one can visit her except Marianne. If she dies no one can go to her funeral except Marianne. No one is allowed to pray for her. If Armageddon comes while she is disfellowshipped God will kill her.

The fact that she has been obedient all these years and has not made friends of any worldly people means that now Jess is completely alone. She has absolutely no one in her life she can talk to. Not one person. Her dad, who she was thrilled to be back in touch with, is classed as bad association as he is an outsider. He had the chance to learn about Jehovah and find out what the Truth was all about many years ago but he rejected it. He would be a bad influence on Jess so it wouldn't be a good idea to get in touch again, although she wants to so much.

She has no idea how hard things will get over the coming months, how much her mental health will suffer, how her physical health will be affected long into the future by the stress of her unnatural life, a life imposed upon her by three men who say they are chosen and directed by God.

An imprisonment of sorts, a cruelly restrictive existence that could continue for years and years. If Jess doesn't make her way back and stays in a disfellowshipped state nothing will change. In five, ten, twenty years' time Peter, Cassie, Nerys would still not be talking to her.

It was in her power to change it, and only by doing what was expected of her: go to the Thursday night meeting, go to the Sunday meeting. These are the only signs of progress visible to the Elders and the rest of the congregation. She has to do it. Has to be seen at every single meeting. Otherwise there is no hope for her.

*Jess makes a schedule for herself and tries to stick to it. She needs a routine. There are things she can do at home to keep herself occupied and build her spiritual strength. God will see her trying and appreciate her efforts even if the Elders don't.

Monday: Go through the Daily text for that date. Pre-study the material for the Tuesday night group meeting (even though she is not allowed to attend as it is in a private home).

Tuesday: Daily text. Stay at home while Marianne goes to the group meeting and make her a cup of tea when she gets back.

Wednesday: Daily text. Pre-study for the Thursday

night meeting – read the allotted portion of the Bible that will be covered, look up the cited scriptures that people will use within their talks.

Thursday: Daily text. Go to the meeting regardless of whether Marianne goes or not.

Friday: Daily text. Free evening so some personal study on an unfamiliar subject (Jess has chosen Ancestor Worship).

Saturday: Daily text.

Sunday: Daily text. Go to the meeting regardless of whether Marianne goes or not.

*

Jess needs to get a job.

Having had no guidance on how she can use her skills or even what her skills are Jess has little clue what she wants to do, or can do, workwise. The unemployment figures are still high in the area, after the closure of the steelworks four years ago, and scouring the job section in the local newspaper every Thursday shows the limited options available for someone like Jess. Just out of school, and only having… O levels!! She suddenly realises she hasn't had her results!

"Mum!" she calls. "Did my exam results arrive?"

"Yes. They're in the top drawer. They came while you were away. With all that's been going on I forgot to tell you, sorry," says Marianne distractedly as she picks up her knitting needles.

Tearing open the envelope bearing her name she unfolds the slips of computer paper and searches for her grades.

"How did you do?" enquires Marianne, checking her knitting pattern for the next instruction.

"Yeh, not bad, four O levels. I got Office Practice, English Lit, English Language and Maths. Happy with those." It was a miracle considering the amount of time she'd been absent from school over the last two years.

*

During that time some days she had felt so down that she would simply not go to school. Leaving the house at the right time she knew she would be deceiving her mum but she couldn't face being trapped at school all day, having to concentrate on worthless subjects and mix with bad people. She would walk and walk all day not eating anything and return home at the appropriate time to a highly suspicious Marianne.

"Why, Jess? Why?!"

"I don't know."

"You know you have to go to school. It's the law. What is it that makes you decide not to go to your registration class? Has someone upset you? Are you being bullied?"

Jess didn't have the words, she didn't know why. All she knew was she couldn't cope with the school day and all that it entailed. After several high volume discussions with her mum who was making no headway whatsoever with Jess, the truancy officer was called and a meeting was held with Jess and Marianne.

How could Jess explain how she felt? How could a truant officer possibly understand what was going through her mind on a daily basis? That school was pointless. Marianne was no better at understanding and, regardless how Jess felt, she still had to go to school. So what was the point in discussing it? The few girls she hung out with in between lessons started to edge away from her because they didn't know why she was away so often. She felt so different to everyone.

*

Through the darkest clouds of her depression Marianne could see her daughter struggling. Some days when she came home from school she looked quite fretful and others exhausted. Maybe the pressure from her teachers was getting to her. Marianne could see she needed to pay her more attention, ask her what's going on in her head. Perhaps she would benefit from a personal weekly Bible study with one of the more mature sisters in the congregation. The last thing she wanted was for her to end up like herself, depressed most of the time and not coping. Yes, she would speak to one of the Elders and arrange that, and a trip to the doctor wouldn't do her any harm either. Perhaps he would put Jess on the same antidepressants as her?

*

Jess had almost laughed when Marianne suggested it. *How on earth can I explain my life to the doctor? He would never be able to understand.*

Thinking about it she wondered if her mum was right. Antidepressants wouldn't change anything but perhaps they would make her relax a bit and help her not to be quite so anxious at school. But conscious of going down the same route as Marianne, Jess didn't want to start taking pills. She didn't want to become reliant on them, a slave to them for the rest of her life. She struggled through the remaining time at secondary school, through her worthless exams and limped along, very much alone and completely unmotivated, to the finishing line.

The weeks roll by and by the end of November Jess is feeling the increasing boredom of her empty days getting to her. She hasn't had a conversation with anyone except Marianne for weeks now. Her self-imposed spiritual routine is a real struggle and it feels like she's wading through mud.

She needs to find work. For her own sanity. She needs to fill her days so well that she won't have time to think too deeply about her situation. Application after application produces nothing, not even a 'thanks, but no thanks' but she keeps at it. Eventually after seeing an advert in the window of a pub restaurant nearby she decides to apply with her CV and a carefully worded covering letter. After all, she has experience having worked at the Beefeater in Eastbourne so maybe she's in with a chance.

About a week later a phone call comes with an offer of an interview. *This could really change things,* she thinks. In a phone call later that day Jess was informed the interview went well and asked if she could start the following Wednesday. Her regular hours would be Wednesday to Saturday from ten in the morning till three to cover lunches.

Yes! thinks Jess, *I can work during the day and I can still do my studying and I won't have to miss any meetings. It's perfect! This must mean Jehovah is still looking out for me.* She had really enjoyed working in the Beefeater, the best thing about it being interacting with the customers. *This means I can have contact with people, maybe have a laugh, but still play by the rules. Maybe I could work my way up to waitress and not be*

189

behind the scenes so much. They said I would need to help out in the bar now and again but I don't mind that at all, as long as someone shows me where everything is and how to serve measures and pull pints. This is great!

"Mum! I've got a job!" She couldn't wait to tell her mum.

"That's great, Jess, where is it, what will you be doing?" asks Marianne picking up on her daughter's excitement.

"At the Spread Eagle down the road. I'll be technically waitressing and helping out sometimes behind the bar. It's perfect, the hours are just right, they fit in with my routines and I won't need to miss any meetings. I can't believe it. It couldn't be better!"

Marianne falls silent.

"Mum, what is it?" enquires Jess, following her mum's face as she turns her head away. "Am I too young? Sixteen-year-olds are allowed to work in restaurants, aren't they? I worked at the Beefeater."

"Yes, they are, dear. But you know…" Marianne struggles to find the right words. She doesn't want to burst her daughter's bubble but has to be straight with her. "…If the Elders hear that you've started working in a pub you'll never be reinstated."

The sting of the words made Jess flinch.

"What's the matter with working in a pub? That's not wrong. I wouldn't be doing anything unchristian," says Jess with a whine in her voice.

"It's just that a pub is a very worldly place and it would say something about you if you were to feel comfortable about working in such a place. It's hard, but you've got to be squeaky clean right now. Don't give the

Elders anything to make them think bad of you, to make them think you're not serious about going back into the Truth."

She has to admit, her mum is probably right. Her bubble has indeed been burst and the strait jacket she feels she's wrapped in becomes even tighter.

Chapter Thirteen

Winter is fast approaching and according to the weather report on the radio snow is expected. Jess has never experienced proper snow prior to living up here. It never settled in Eastbourne – too much salt in the air and the town was somewhat protected by the Downs. It's exciting in a way, time to dig out boots and hats and scarves and gloves. But the house is so cold. Marianne's social security payment means the heating gets put on only when absolutely necessary and often Jess wakes up to see her breath forming a cloud in front of her.

Empty days spread out like a desert scene. There is nothing to look forward to.

*

"Mum, I'm going to decorate my room," Jess announces. She has to make an effort and get her head into something positive and productive. A pot of paint doesn't cost too much and if she put it on sparingly it should cover the whole room. It would be easy enough to paint over the small bubbled Anaglypta wallpaper already on the walls. A soft peachy colour, warming and comforting, a colour that reminds Jess of an August sunset, a gift from a loving God. Jess moves all her furniture into the spare room, rolls up the large rug and sets about carefully cutting in around the edges and corners. The filling in takes forever with a four-inch brush but she has plenty of time. Radio on, window open a bit to let the fumes out Jess gets into a rhythm of painting in large squares on the walls and soon enough the room is complete. It looks good. Jess is pleased with her efforts and is quite proud of herself, a feeling she hasn't had for a long time.

"Well done," remarks Marianne after an invitation to see the finished project. She checked her cutting in around the window and above the skirting boards. *Very good,* she thought. She'd taught her daughter well. After Ben left it fell to Marianne to do any repairs, electrics, fixing. She didn't know the first thing about wiring a plug or putting up a shelf, changing the lock on the back door or fixing a leak under the sink so she had to learn. Books from the library and some guidance from Mr Laughton the old man next door got her through most of the time and whatever job she did she involved Peter and Jess, even if they just watched. Decorating was a nice job with a pleasing result and Marianne was always happy to start on the next room.

*

Another night or two in the spare room just to make sure all the fumes had dissipated and then Jess could move her bed and chest of drawers back in.

A trip to the shops on the estate takes her down the main road and as she approaches a bend something catches her eye. She walks faster and peers in between the parked cars to see a scruffy-looking tabby cat wandering around in the middle of the road. It doesn't seem to know where it was going, walking clockwise then turning round and coming back, then it walks in a few circles anticlockwise, then clockwise again. It's all over the place. She crouches down on the path and with gentle calls of "here, puss," Jess tries to catch its attention. Its fixed stare made her think it's responding to her but it walks straight past her to begin another circle. *This is not right,* thinks Jess, *there's something very wrong with this cat.* At top speed she runs home to fetch the cat basket and runs back to the cat who is still there about to walk in front of a cyclist. He swerves to avoid it and Jess manages to get a hold of it and place it in the basket. Its stare does not change and it still tries to walk even in the confines of the basket.

"Poor thing, probably been hit by a car or something," remarks Marianne when Jess shows her. It's a male cat and looks like it needs a good meal. They check him over for signs of injury and don't find anything. Jess sets him up in her empty room with a bowl of fish flavoured cat food. There was a tin left over in the cupboard from when Sophie was here. He sniffs at it, does a circle and then eats a small amount, circles, miaows and circles in the opposite direction. Jess sits on the floor and puts the blanket on her lap. The cat allows itself to be stroked as Jess tries to settle him down. *He must be exhausted continually walking,* she thinks. Her gentle strokes and head scratches produce a warm purr and Jess can feel him start to relax, but that fixed stare does not change. *Perhaps he'll be better after a night in the warm with some good food and some fuss,* Jess muses, *he's got no collar on so maybe we can keep him. It would be so good to have a cat again.*

The night passes with the cat safe and comfortable in Jess's room. He's got everything he needs: food, litter tray, water and a bed. She thinks about Sophie and the kittens, grown now and probably each with a new owner. Of all the cats the family had cared for over the years Sophie had been her favourite and she still misses her and feels resentment that Marianne got rid of her. It feels like part of her punishment.

Morning arrives and Jess can't wait to see how the cat is doing. Wrapping herself in her dressing gown she slowly opens the door to her newly decorated room and the foul smell suddenly hits her. It's a mixture of crap and fish and it makes her balk and cover her nose. As she peers into the room she can see the cat, wide-eyed and still walking in circles. The floorboards are covered in a million little shitty footprints that look like chocolate mousse. There is crap up the walls, on the windowsill and on the back of the door. In between the slats on the cupboard door the colour sits and stinks. The wallpaper has been scratched in each corner and the lower half of the whole room looks like a motorbike has driven past at speed through a muddy puddle. *What has this cat been doing all night?* wonders Jess, as she starts to think about the clear-up operation. She will need to redecorate that's for sure.

Marianne makes an appointment to take the cat to the vet later that day who concludes he must have received a serious bang on the head resulting in some form of brain injury. He is sadly beyond help. They leave him with the vet to deal with and return home to clean Jess's room, the windows thrown wide open. It was a shame the cat was so damaged as Jess could have done with a pet. From then on she keeps a look out for any more strays.

*

As forecast the snow arrives the following day, thick and brilliant white. Overnight a good five inches had been dumped in the area and the view from Jess's window shows very little human activity. One set of footprints leads from next door's front porch along the side of the house to their garage and the snow had been shovelled off their front path. There are no car tracks, no other hints of life out there. It's like the world is on hold, asleep, tucked up under a blanket of sparkles and the shapes lie there waiting and dreaming of change.

Jess reads through her Daily Text and looks up the cited scriptures. Today's text is about enduring under tribulation and persevering in prayer and the application is when faithful brothers and sisters find it hard to continue to treat a disfellowshipped relative in the way they have learned – to cut them off. The suggestion is that it will make a person's relationship with Jehovah stronger if they obey his direction in this regard. The text reads: "Does this mean that we should not have strong love for our relatives? Of course not! But our strongest love should be for Jehovah." (1)

Can't argue with that, thinks Jess. Jehovah must come first and no matter how isolated she is feeling there are other people who are finding it a challenge to treat her this way. Peter and Cassie in particular and everyone she's ever spoken to at the Hall or worked with on the ministry. Every one of them is being obedient by shunning her – such faith! Are they considering their relationship with Jehovah? Or is it that they don't want to be caught talking to her and risk being disfellowshipped themselves? Maybe a mixture of both. Perhaps she is easy to ignore. It's all very complex and Jess feels like her brain is twisting in her skull thinking about the technicalities as well as the spiritual side of it.

Jess's meeting attendance is almost one hundred per cent, missing only one Thursday night meeting when there was a bus drivers' strike. As tough as it is nothing prevents her from getting there and Marianne's attendance is quite irrelevant, she doesn't need her mum to hold her hand every time, although sometimes that would be nice. Jess is going under her own steam and wonders if Jehovah is pleased with her. Ultimately, that's why she'd doing this, to please Jehovah so that one day he will prompt the Elders to accept her back in the congregation.

Another Sunday morning meeting has just finished and Jess mumbles her "Amen" along with the other eighty or so brothers and sisters and turns around to pack her books away in her bag. She pulls her coat off the back of the chair, being too embarrassed to hang it up in the cloakroom where everyone else puts theirs. It's icy out there, cold and miserable, the grey skies have assumed this colour for the last two weeks with not a sliver of blue in sight. The morning frosts don't thaw and layer upon layer of glassy ice settles upon the pathways, slowing the country down to the pace of a tortoise.

Head down Jess makes her way out of the Kingdom Hall with scarf wrapped around her neck and hat firmly on and covering her ears. She doesn't own any boots and the soles of her shoes are completely inappropriate for this type of weather. Every step she takes is agonisingly careful. Her first steps on the slope go well and so does the first two steps down leading to the drive and her confidence makes her lift her head and think about the direction she's going in. But all of a sudden she goes right over and lands on her back with her leg twisted under her body.

Dazed, her eyes make out the top of a leafless tree and she shakes her head as she sits herself up. But the pain in her foot has her gasping in agony and looking down she sees it's swelling fast. There are voices approaching from behind but, unable to hear what they are saying, Jess clutches her leg and moans into the pain as she waits for footsteps of help to arrive at her side. The crunches in the ice are level with her now but they don't stop, the feet keep walking. There are people stepping past her on both sides as she sits there in obvious trouble. No one helps her to stand up, no one even looks at her, they just carry on walking. A child holding her mum's hand stops and says: "Mummy, Jessica has fallen over. She's crying, Mummy." But she's swiftly pulled along and away to their waiting car.

She has to get herself up. Shuffling her bum across to the wall she leans against it and breathes deeply as the pain increases. Still her old friends walk past her, looking away. She manages to raise herself up and take a first tentative step, still on the ice. Her foot is so painful but she must get home somehow. There's a twenty-minute walk to the bus station and Jess hasn't a clue how she's going to make it. But there's no choice, she just has to get on with it and as cars exit the car park Jess hobbles towards the main road into town. It takes her an hour to get there and she makes a mental note of the seven families that passed her on the way.

The weather is miserable.

Jess is miserable.

But a little ray of hope is about to come her way.

*

A few weeks later all Jess's efforts to find work are rewarded when she is offered a full-time position at one of the units on the huge industrial estate. The business is eyewear and the company well established, being founded in 1876, and they make glasses for the high street as well as for royalty and celebrities. Full-time hours are not what Jess has ever had in mind as her goal has always been to work part-time and pioneer but, well, that is out of the question for now. There is no reason not to take the job. It means being up early to catch the factory bus at seven thirty. Work starts at eight and finishes at four thirty. The bus home takes longer for some reason though it's the same journey in reverse with the same people getting off. Home by five thirty after walking from the bus stop back through the estate. The days seem endless and although there are lots of people milling around Jess's job is in one of the small lens rooms in which there are only two other people. Her job is to select the right lenses and put them with the frame and the customer's order sheet in the wooden box. The box then goes through to the next room where they are tinted, if required, and fitted into the frame.

At lunchtime in the canteen Jess enjoys seeing and hearing the life behind the factory noise and gets chatting to a couple of the other young girls there.

One Monday morning Morag, who works in the frame room, comes tottering over to the table with her tray of square sausage and chips and sits herself down between Jess and another girl, Rhona, who works next to her. Both of them have long blonde hair and from behind no one can tell them apart. When they stand up though, their identities are clear. Heels are not allowed on the factory floor but for some reason Morag flouts the rules and gets away with it.

"How come you don't get your pay docked for wearing those shoes, Morag? You doing favours for someone, hen?" Rhona asks, laughing, showing her Scottish roots.

"Hey, haud yer wheesht." Morag's use of Scottish words was more frequent and sometimes Jess couldn't understand what she was saying. "They've never pulled me up for it so I'll carry on till they do. Anyway, what happened to you Saturday night, I looked around and you were nowhere 'e be seen."

"Didn't like the music so I went down to the first floor. Gary was there – get this – wi'out Sharon!" says Rhona, prompting a gasp of disbelief from Morag.

"Did you actually, I mean, did you *actually* get off wi' him?" The juiciest bit of gossip was coming her way…

"Aye, I did! Knew they wouldn't last long. We're going out next Saturday to that new club in Northampton."

"You bitch!" teases Morag, and their conversation moves from night clubs to new clothes, to a pair of shoes that Morag got from the catalogue that are too big and does Rhona want to try them on. As Jess listens to their foul language and immoral talk she winces on hearing the 'F' word, thrown in on occasion. It's so alien to her and sounds like shattering glass. They are such a worldly pair of girls, so brazen. It's true, all that she hears from the platform about the ways of the world has been displayed at this table in the last ten minutes. But a tiny bit of her is a little envious of the freedom those girls have to choose how they want to spend their weekends.

Veronica, who works in the postal room at the end of the line, is a little older than Jess and quieter and she finds she's quite drawn to her. They snatch a few words while on their tea break and chat about the latest films at the cinema and bands they like. Although she struggles to summon up some band names Jess feels normal for a short while, she has someone to talk to at last, and she's not being judged, avoided or ignored.

It's exactly what she is craving and she wishes she could spend more time in Veronica's company. But the switch in her head is flicked as she remembers all she's learned about mixing with worldly people. Veronica doesn't love Jehovah. She doesn't even know Jehovah. She has worldly traits and tendencies that Witnesses don't have and her values are not the same. Spending more time with her than is absolutely necessary would be a bad move. All her efforts to make it back into the congregation would be wasted because she will draw her away and she would have to stay in this stifling hold for the rest of her life.

Veronica asks Jess what she is doing for Christmas this year. The most dreaded question for a Witness.

Any time she thinks of Christmas an image of a theatre gathers at the edge of her consciousness. She remembers her little-girl-self on the stage standing with several others, all in a row. She'd been selected from the audience to go up and shake hands with Jack standing triumphant next to his beanstalk. It was exciting to be up there knowing there were lots of people looking at her, she was wearing her new blue dress (purchased for the upcoming Circuit Assembly in January). She remembered gently swaying to show off the full skirt while the boy next to her was speaking. The adult came to her and asked the same question of them all:

"And what's your name, then?"

"Jessica."

"Hello, Jessica. I bet you get called Jess all the time, don't you? Tell us then, Jess, what did Santa bring you for Christmas?"

Her honest reply came. She could say nothing else; there was nothing to elaborate on.

"Nothing."

The audience released a collective "Aaaahhh," in sympathy. They might not have believed she was telling the truth, maybe they thought this little girl was a bit nervous and didn't want to speak. It must have been the first time Jess felt embarrassment and so it stuck in her memory, to be resurrected each and every December. The same emotion exerted itself each January too when her classmates reeled off a list of their new toys, bikes, dolls, books and the wonderful parties they'd been to. Those that knew her didn't ask her what she got anymore, they knew what the answer would be and could see on her face it embarrassed her; she was so different to them.

And that question is even more embarrassing not to mention complicated right now for Jess.

How can she possibly answer?

*

The new year begins with fireworks from random gardens on the estate and Jess stays up to see them from her bedroom window. They're so beautiful. Loud shouts from happy, probably drunk, neighbours walking past are completely acceptable, unlike on any other night of the year.

It signals a new beginning, new ideas and hopes, it encourages forward-thinking and firmer resolves and for Jess the hope that this year will see her being reinstated. She will see Peter again, perhaps travel down and stay for a few days. She can't wait for her exchange of letters with Nerys to resume and sleepovers at Cassie's. She even thinks about the barn dances and yearns to be with everyone she knows again. She's so anxious to get back to normal.

*

It's good to have a proper wage coming in. She pays Marianne her board and has money for some new clothes. Her creative side is teased out by the magazine she has started buying – *Prima*. It's full of wonderful ideas for making gifts and practical items, recipes, ideas for home decorating, and following the instructions in the latest edition Jess learns the basics of crochet.

For an unknown reason Esther and Will from Eastbourne pop into her head. She wonders how they are and considers getting in touch again. Just a quick chat on the phone wouldn't be so wrong. While Marianne is at the Tuesday Book Study she digs out Esther's number and dials. Esther is thrilled to hear from her and listens as she describes her new job, about Sophie having moved and things being a little quiet at the moment. Jess can picture her smiling at the other end.

"And did you have a nice Christmas? What did you do?"

There's that question again…

"Oh, it was quiet, you know. What did you and Will do?"

Esther recounted how they spent the week with family and friends at each other's houses, cooking, washing up, drinking and watching all the old Christmas films. They ate far too much and went for long walks along the seafront with the dogs, being battered by the fierce winds. There had been no snow down there. She had spent New Year's Eve at home as she just wanted to go to bed and Will went to a party at his friend's in Brighton. That all sounds very normal, thinks Jess. Being with family. Being with friends. Having fun together. She misses that so much.

Her heart is aching with the emptiness. It's getting heavier and heavier as the weeks and months go by and she wishes she could take it out and put it in a cardboard box so it's not so much of a burden to carry around. *What point is there in having a heart if you can't use it, if you have no one to show affection to, if there's no one to express your feelings to? No one to laugh or cry with?*

*

What worldly people refer to as Easter is approaching and along with it, Jess's birthday. She always thinks of it, even though she has never celebrated it. 'It's just another day,' is the standard returned phrase. Birthdays are not observed and have a macabre association in the Bible with John the Baptist having his head chopped off on one such occasion. Anyway, it's wrong to elicit such attention when all honour should be going to God. It's not something Jess misses because she's never done it and she agrees with the sound reasoning behind it. She wants to please Jehovah and if he disapproves of birthdays then that's fine with her.

This time of the year, however, the Witnesses observe the last evening meal Jesus spent with his disciples – the Last Supper. It's the only thing they celebrate in the whole Christian calendar and for Jess it's a special occasion, one of serious contemplation and meditation on how Jesus gave his life for us. This Memorial would be the toughest one Jess has been to yet.

Every Witness knows this meeting is absolutely vital to attend, there are no excuses including illness. The bread and wine are passed around but no one partakes unless they are sure they are going to heaven when they die. The Elders says that only 144,000 will go to heaven to rule as kings with Jesus and right now there are only about 8,000 left alive, all of them Jehovah's Witnesses.

*

Jess recalls that a few years ago one of the brothers was in hospital at the time of the Memorial and, suppressing a snigger, asked her mum how he was supposed to get to the Kingdom Hall if he was in a coma.

"One of the Elders will take the emblems to him and read the passage and say a prayer I suppose."

"But he can't hear anything!" Jess was flabbergasted that this would actually be done.

"Well, Jess, they say the last thing to go is the hearing so perhaps he can hear and understand what's going on. When he comes out of his coma he'll be so grateful to the Elder for including him, won't he?"

Jess figured it really must be that important.

This year the Memorial happens to fall on Jess's birthday and from somewhere unknown, maybe from someone at work, she has caught a nasty dose of the flu. She'd had many colds before but this is something different. In bed for five days with a raging temperature, little appetite and feeling very low she just wants to cry. Her eyes are stinging with heat and it feels as if every pathway in her head is blocked and is backing up like traffic hitting roadworks. Her body aches like she's never known and with the passing of the days a different part of her body is under attack each morning when she wakes.

Honey and lemon, a couple of aspirin and sleep is the prescribed remedy from Marianne who provides a chilly version of a bedside manner. 'Just get through it,' is her way of dealing with illness and, 'don't expect any sympathy.' Practical care is all that's necessary in her view and although she checks on her daughter from time to time she largely leaves her alone to sweat it out.

The day of the Memorial arrives and Jess, still feeling very rough on the sixth day of her illness, knows she has to summon up the energy from somewhere to get to the Hall. With her head pounding she asks God to give her the strength she needs. She simply must go tonight no matter how bad she's feeling. There no excuse whatsoever for missing the Memorial of Christ's death. If she didn't attend the Elders would notice and it would go against her for sure.

Late afternoon she hears Marianne's feet on the stairs bringing with her a bowl of thin homemade soup. Having no desire for food Jess forces herself to eat some of it and surprisingly it perks her up a bit. It's time to make a move. This is the last thing she feels like doing – dragging herself out of bed and having a bath when her skin is on fire.

The early spring sun has been shining all day but it's still nippy out there and Jess wishes that just for once she could pull on a pair of trousers instead of having to wear a skirt and tights, but they are not allowed. Women must look like women and men, men. She bundles herself up in layers of her warmest clothes not caring what she looks like. She just wants to go back to bed and curl up with Chubbers, her pink long-haired stuffed toy cat.

She feels terrible and is sure her temperature is raised. Through shivers and sweats she and Marianne make the bus journey to the Kingdom Hall. A woman already seated watches as they stumble down the bus to find seats and looks at Jess's sickly face. She listens to her hacking cough and gives a sympathetic smile before turning her head away against the germs.

From Jess's right-hand side the silver platter of bread and crystal glass of red wine are handed to her by Marianne, and she then passes them to the person on her left, trying not to cough and splutter. As soon as they are safely in the next person's hands she barks into a tissue as discretely as possible and hears her own chest rattle with the effort.

At the end of the row stands Alan, dressed extra smart in what looks like a new suit and with his hands behind his back as if standing to attention. *He's obviously doing well,* thinks Jess, *making spiritual progress after nearly slipping up back in the summer.*

One of the Elders must have noticed his efforts – he's never been given such privileges before. Handling the emblems is an honour usually reserved for upright, commendable Brothers. Oh well, she thinks, *good for him.*

As he waits for the emblems to reach him he catches Jess's eye. He smiles. Very briefly. But it was a smile! Jess's first thought is that she hopes no one saw him. Although he'd upset her in the past she doesn't want anything bad to happen to him. That simple gesture gives her heart a little lift and she sits for the remainder of the meeting feeling that maybe they don't all hate her. Maybe the congregation would forgive her for her appalling behaviour. It gives her a nugget of hope at a time when she really needs it.

On the bus home, after walking into town to the bus station, Marianne tells her she is proud of her for making it there and doing the right thing and that Jehovah will bless her. Jess doesn't care right now – all she wants to do is take some more aspirin and collapse into bed. Her stuffed toy cats are waiting for her on her bedspread and she just wants to snuggle up and bury her head amongst them. The flu passes eventually but the following week Marianne informs her that several in the congregation had gone down with it. *Well, it's not my fault,* she reasons. *I had to go.*

*

The weeks pass by at a painfully slow pace and Jess is really struggling. Over the few weeks since she caught the flu she hasn't felt right. A sore throat and cough seem to keep returning, a little less severe each time but still annoying. She's never felt so low. But she carries on as best she can by eating well, getting enough sleep and keeping warm.

*

Spring is moving into summer and the daffodils and tulips have gone over in the garden and need digging out and storing for next spring. Usually Jess notices and appreciates the change in the seasons. The wonders of new life springing forth with each new flower that unfolds, the fresh smell of cut grass and the volume of birdsong as they open their wings to the warmth in the air. But Jess is sinking. The thought of a long, lonely summer stretching out before her is frightening.

She feels no enjoyment in anything, sees no beauty, and wants to sleep all the time. Her workmates notice she is different to how she normally is. They comment on her miserable face and jokingly ask her, "Who's died?" She wants to joke back at them and say, "I have," but they wouldn't get it. They have no idea of the prison she is living in. The isolation and loneliness are slowing her down, making her sluggish in everything she does.

The cats understand. They listen to her gentle sobs through the night. They're always there sitting on her shelf high up or sprawled across the bed, keeping an eye on her.

Jess is slacking in her self-imposed spiritual routine and Marianne notices.

"You know, Jess, you've helped me an awful lot recently," she explains thoughtfully, feeling she should say something, even though she should technically not "encourage" her in any way. "I've never been very regular at pre-study and seeing you sitting here at the table doing yours every week has made me do more." She places a hand on Jess's shoulder as she stands there looking out into the garden. But the compliment does nothing for Jess's mood.

Jess thinks about the upcoming District Assembly in August. With no transport of her own and not being allowed to travel on the congregation coach there's no way to get there. That's the first one she will have ever missed. Thinking about it, though, the experience would not have been the least bit enjoyable, having to apologise to everyone that spoke to her and explain her position.

*

The summer passes and contrary to what Jess believes she does actually get through it. She has no choice. The swimming pool becomes her go to place and each Tuesday she asks the driver of the work bus to let her off in town so she can do some lengths. The cool of the water makes her gasp as she makes her way down the metal steps but once she's in she finds it refreshing and enlivening. Hands together as if in prayer Jess pushes her feet off the side and stretches out ahead, reaching for the other end of the pool. Her legs move rhythmically behind, kicking away the day's stresses and the tension of the two meetings since her last session. One lane is roped off for swimming lengths and right now there is no one else in it. Bliss! She can go at her own pace and not have to speed up to overtake or get stuck behind swim buddies deep in conversation.

Jess is pleased with herself that she's made the effort to do something different, a regular hobby, and she begins to view swimming as absolutely vital to her wellbeing.

Most weeks there is only usually one or two others in the lane and every now and then one of them is a familiar face from the congregation. It makes her think about getting out but instead she ducks under or turns on her back and looks at the passing clouds through the skylights, not wanting to make anyone feel awkward. There's nothing like bumping into someone to bring her back to her reality but she gets through it.

By autumn her reading of the Daily Text becomes intermittent as does her *Watchtower* preparation, and the meetings seem so boring when she can't take part. All she can do is sit there and look up the scriptures and follow along as the speaker reads them. Answering up is one of the restrictions she's under and she doesn't even feel at ease enough to laugh at any funny comments that are made.

In the Kingdom Hall the windows are high up and shallow. When it was due for refurbishment there was considerable discussion as to whether there was a need for windows at all. There had been a few break-ins previously, the sound equipment being taken. But thankfully the windows remained and during the more boring meetings Jess could look out and see the tops of the trees swaying in the wind. Over a period of three weeks a lot of the leaves had fallen and she watched each time until she saw the last one get whisked away on a gust of autumn wind. Now there was nothing but twigs and a grey sky, but at least with the windows it doesn't feel too much like a prison.

When Marianne goes to the meetings, which is irregular and unpredictable, she has to wait in her seat for her till she's ready to leave. Often she needs to speak to someone about some matter or other and it's during these times that Jess overhears people talking around her:

A sister from a neighbouring congregation is getting married soon and Arthur's wife is having her hip operation next week; Dave wants to pioneer but he's just waiting to hear about a job that he's applied for and Steve and Caren have been asked to move to 'where the need is greater,' as they speak another language. She hears it all and is the perfect eavesdropper as she can't pass it on.

She's invisible.

On occasion, Jess had been amongst the pairs of sisters selected to give the number three talk on a Thursday night. Now she sees Cassie progressing and the other young ones and knows she's being left behind. All those public speaking skills she had been learning since her childhood she fears will be forgotten and she'll have to learn them all over again once she's back. It will be hard but with Jehovah's help she'll do it: anything is possible with his help and support.

Jess has noticed that Alan has been giving number five talks and tackling some very difficult subjects. After his first one the audience had clapped, and Jess joined in feeling quite proud of him. She'd also heard he was pioneering recently too. It looks like he's really going for it, reaching out for position of Ministerial Servant perhaps. It's not unusual for a nineteen-year-old to be appointed as a Min Serv – there are Elders at twenty-five or so in some congregations. It doesn't matter that they are not married or that they don't have children, or that they have little life experience. No. To be viewed as a mature Brother with responsibilities of nurturing the congregation all they need is a love for Jehovah and a good reputation.

Jess feels so alone at the end of every single meeting.

Back home Chubbers hears her moans and worries and she takes it all in without interrupting. She's a good listener and Jess starts taking her in her bag to work, stuffing her pink fur in deep so it doesn't get caught in the zip.

*

It's been a whole year of this living hell, and having spent a long summer alone, another depressing winter lies ahead with nothing and no one to help break it up. Jess is seriously unsure how much longer she can live like this without going mad. She didn't know how such 'madness' would manifest itself, but she is convinced something will change in her irreparably if she carries on living in this spiritual prison.

She is so sick of this feeling of total rejection piled on top of the guilt she already feels from doing so much wrong. It's more than a feeling; it goes in through her eyes, triggered by the sight of someone she knows, or the magazines or the Kingdom Melody cassettes Marianne plays endlessly. It twists through her insides, down her throat, making her want to vomit it out. The path it takes through her chest, her heart, is one of ups and downs, of shakes and turns and tumbles, rattling through her body towards her stomach. She's often in pain: head, chest, stomach, back, as if her body is shouting out for help and mercy. But there's no help and there's no escape.

One Sunday afternoon as she returns from the meeting to a much-repeated boring afternoon of just her mum and the TV she reaches her breaking point. She places herself in between Marianne and the TV and with a mixture of pleading and exasperation she blurts her words out, knowing she'll feel better once they're out. With palms held wide her cry is pitiful: "I can't do this anymore, Mum! I'm too tired. I miss Peter. This is killing me."

She stomps over to the sofa plonking herself down and covers her head with a cushion, wanting to hide away for the rest of her life, or just go to sleep and not wake up.

"I know, Jess. It's hard for me as well, you know. Some sisters cross the road so they don't have to speak to me, too. They don't know what to say." It's typical of Marianne to turn the focus onto herself, her own hardships are always so much worse than anyone else's.

Jess looks out from under the cushion frowning disbelievingly at her mum.

"You are not disfellowshipped! You don't feel what I feel when they look away, when my friends won't even meet my eye. Nobody wants to sit near me at the meetings, they move away. It's like they're scared I'm going to infect them." Jess shouts in her mum's face. "Aaargh!" The cushion goes on her head again as she tries to calm herself down. A few minutes pass and all the while Marianne sits in silence with her mouth tightly shut. But Jess's decision has been made and as she removes the cushion she takes a deep breath and declares:

"I don't want to go to any more meetings, Mum. I'm sorry," she muffles.

Marianne remains silent. She knows it's Jess's choice what she does with her spirituality. She's not allowed to encourage her to continue going to meetings or to pray for her. This system of disfellowshipping is designed by Jehovah to bring her to her senses and get her to make her own mind up about what's truly important in this world. She has to make it on her own. Just Jess and Jehovah.

But maybe there's one thing she can do without going against God's rules.

"Jess, sit up. There's something you need to know."

There's nothing Marianne can tell her to make her change her mind now, she's had enough, more than enough of this treatment. It's too hard and she feels if this is what her life is to be like then she'll have to make a go of it, make new friends. It would mean having to construct a completely new life, reinvent herself, start afresh. Could she do it? Could she live a happy life without Jehovah?

I'll have to. I'm either in or out, one or the other, that's the way of the Truth. It's too hard trying to get back in when there's absolutely no help, no one to talk to. Maybe I don't belong in the Organisation anyway. Maybe I'm not good enough and this test of endurance has shown it. Mum will tell me to move out, I know she will. She won't have someone living under her roof who has rejected Jehovah. I'll go and live with Dad, catch up on all those lost years.

Suddenly, Jess's train of thought had hatched a

plan and a little skip erupts in her heart as she thinks of the possibility of reconnecting with the other half of her family. She lets her imagination wander onto a clackety Tube bound for Uxbridge and doesn't hear when Marianne announces the birth of the baby.

"Jess, you've got a niece, did you hear me?"

"What? Have Peter and Janey had a baby?" She pauses momentarily. "When?"

"She's five months old now. The night after you were disfellowshipped Peter told me Janey was expecting. I couldn't tell you, Jess, I didn't want you to feel bad about not being allowed to see her."

"Five months?!" Jess shouts. "Five months and you've known about her all this time and didn't tell me? I would rather have known! At least it would have given me something nice to think about, a reason to keep going. Thanks a lot, Mum."

Throwing the cushion down on the sofa Jess makes her feelings very clear as she storms out the front door, banging it behind her.

Her head is pounding, her brain a tumble dryer as her thoughts are thrown one way and then the other.

I have a little niece. She's my flesh and blood, my family. I love her already.

If I don't get reinstated I will never see her. Peter would never let her get to know me.

If I carry on going to meetings I could go down to Southend and spend time with her, get to know her funny little ways, take her out to the park, dance with her, play games in the garden. When she's a little older she could come up here to stay, I could show her off at the meetings and take her out on ministry with me. We could go shopping together, I could teach her about make-up and clothes and we could try on shoes and get pizza.

Her choices are clear. She knows what she must do.

Chapter Fourteen

Perhaps she should have asked to be reinstated before now, before she got to this crisis point. She hadn't been told how long she would be out for. There is no time length set down in any publication or in the Bible probably because everyone is different in how they respond to such treatment. But she's here now and proceeds to ask her mum how she makes it happen.

"First of all, what do you need to do?" says Marianne, trying to get Jess to think, satisfied that her announcement about the baby had produced the right result in her.

"Pray to Jehovah. Ask him to have me back in his favour." She knows that is the correct response. It's the first thing the Elders will ask her about.

"When you've done that, write a letter to Kevin Choi and say you'd like to be reinstated. Be humble, be accepting, say that you've learned from the experience. And tell him that you know that 'Jehovah disciplines those he loves,' as the scripture says. Provided all those things are true, of course."

It sounds so simple. Perhaps it is. A letter and then probably a meeting with the same three Elders and then it's announced. *Wouldn't it be good,* she says to her old mate Nik. Her life will change overnight. She'd have her friends Cassie and Nerys back, she'd have her freedom back, freedom to be herself again, to rekindle her other relationships and get back out on the ministry.

She could give talks again, go to the Book Study on a Tuesday night and answer up, and most importantly, get to know her niece.

It has been so long. But now maybe the end is in sight. She goes upstairs to be on her own for a while to do what she's got to do.

*

Marianne gives the letter to Kevin at the next meeting and a few days later Jess is invited to a Judicial hearing at the Hall the following Friday evening. She is nervous. Remembering the last time she sat in front of the same three Elders she wonders how intrusive their questioning will be this time.

The layout is familiar: in the same small meeting room three chairs all face her and the door is closed against the dark empty, chilly Hall on the other side. As expected the meeting begins with a prayer and Chris asks that Jehovah's guidance be upon the proceedings and that the outcome may be positive, bringing glory to his name.

"So, Jess," begins Kevin in a chirpy tone. "We've noticed how regularly you've attended the meetings since being disfellowshipped. It's a good sign as it shows where your heart is, what you see as important. And you attended the Memorial last year, that was good. So, you've been outside the congregation for about a year now, is that right?" he asks in disbelief as he turns his head to the others for confirmation. Seeing their nods, he continues, "How time flies, eh?"

It might have flown for you, Kevin, but I've been the one living in this situation all this time and I can tell you it feels more like five years, thinks Jess. *How inconsiderate of him.*

"Yes, well, so you would like to be reinstated into the congregation, is that right?"

"Yes," replies Jess.

"Do you feel you are ready to come back to Jehovah and have you expressed that to him?"

"Yes, I have, I put that in my letter." *What a stupid question, did you not read it?* she thinks.

Chris takes over the questioning and asks Jess if she has seen Ray recently and if their relationship has continued in any form.

"No! I haven't seen him since I left him in Eastbourne."

"Have you talked to him on the phone at all?" he pushes.

"No, nothing."

Chris continues: "And have you been involved with any other male in a sexual way during this time?"

Oh, for goodness' sake! Jess can't believe that they're asking such unnecessary questions. It makes her feel like a slut, as if she's jumping into bed with anyone in trousers. Perhaps their view of her has really changed now.

Bob looks directly at Chris on his right-hand side, appearing shocked by such an enquiry and then, having been silent up to now, apologetically explains, "I'm sorry, Jess, as you can understand, we have to ask these questions."

"No, I have not." She hopes by her firm tone they can tell they're being unreasonable. But it didn't seem to have the slightest effect on them, on Chris anyway, as he continues with this line of questioning.

"Obviously, your experience with Ray will have awoken feelings within you that you may not have had before and, as a young person, once they have been stimulated there can be a tendency to want more. Do you masturbate, Jess?"

She remains silent.

This is too much and this time both Bob and Kevin look at Chris in disbelief. With that one question she's got the measure of him and it just confirms to her that he's a creepy, filthy bastard. He sits there patiently awaiting Jess's answer but she won't give him the satisfaction of any morsel he can feed his fantasies with.

She leans forward, peers straight into his eyes and calmly asks, "Do you?" She doesn't flinch, doesn't break eye contact with him until he looks away.

Kevin coughs and Bob fidgets in his seat and the meeting is brought to order with a few appropriate scriptures and a closing prayer.

Now she waits.

*

The following week sees Jess pick up on her spiritual routine again with earnest effort, and the meetings take on a different tone for her with the thought that she may soon be back taking part.

Alan is still making great progress and gives the final prayer at a couple of meetings. She still has a soft spot for him but knows deep down he will never look at her in that way, not now.

A week goes by, two. There's no word.

She tells herself she has to be patient. They have to discuss it between themselves and continue to watch her to see if she keeps at it, doesn't slack off in her meeting attendance. But Jess is determined to get her life back so nothing is going to make her give them any reason not to accept her back.

*

Tuesday night comes around and Marianne is off to the Book Study. Jess thinks of Esther again and decides to give her a ring. It's been months since she called her so it's not exactly as if she's 'associating' with a worldly person. Anyway, Esther is such a lovely woman.

"Jess, how good to hear from you. I've been wondering how you are."

"Hi Esther, how are you and Will keeping? I expect it's cold down there, do you have any snow yet?"

Their conversation is light and easy, refreshing and it's just so good for Jess to talk to someone, have a physical chat about everything and nothing. Jess tells her she's still practicing her crochet skills and about how monotonous her job is.

"Are you coming down this way to visit your friends again next summer?" she asks Jess.

"Er, maybe. I'm not sure."

*

Esther is a wise woman and can hear the hesitation in Jess's voice. When she first met her on the night Jess collapsed at the restaurant she never asked her what had caused her such distress. She just dealt with her, took her home and left it at that. It's none of her business anyway. But she can sense there is something in Jess's life that isn't quite right and hearing her voice suddenly change makes her consider asking. She's not a nosey woman but likes to think she can be of help to Jess if she needs it, be that a listening ear or a shoulder to cry on

222

down the phone.

"Will's here at the moment. Want to speak to him?" she asks cheerily.

It's nice speaking to Will. His voice is smooth and unhurried and is very calming. She lets him update her on some of his more unusual photo shoots he's done recently. He talks about his camera which he has just upgraded and that he's hoping to get a good price for his old one from the advert he's placed in a photo magazine. Jess could easily let him whittle on but has to think of the cost of the phone call.

"Well, Will, it's been really nice talking to you. Hope it all goes well with your work. Where's your next job taking you?" she enquires, trying to wrap up the conversation tactfully.

"I'll be in London next week, in an office in Baker Street. It's a new business that wants some promotional pictures doing."

He pauses and Jess can hear him breathing lightly.

"I don't suppose… er, no it's OK." He falters as he changes his mind.

"What, Will, what are you saying?" Jess asks.

"Do you fancy meeting up in London? The shoot is in the morning so I'll be finished around lunchtime. We could get something to eat and have a wander round the area, go to Regent's Park if it's a nice day."

Jess allows a silence to fall while she's considering the suggestion. He's nice, kind and thoughtful – but she's met one of those before and look where it got her. She needs time to think about this. It's not as easy as saying yes, or no. There's so much at stake. So much that Will is unaware of and maybe wouldn't understand.

"Can I have some time to think about it, Will. I'll call in a few days."

"Of course, take your time. I know it's a bit out of the blue. It's next Thursday so have a think. Speak soon, Jess."

*

Chubbers!!! What do I do? Why has this happened right now? I really don't need this! Chubbers gets a great pouring out from Jess as she contemplates the possible consequences of meeting up with Will. She talks her way through it to the stuffed animal and imagines its responses as if it was a) her mum; b) an Elder c) Jehovah.

Ugh! It's Satan, it must be. He's trying to get me to give up and ruin my chances of getting back. I can't do it. It's not right. It doesn't matter how nice Will is, he's not a Witness and he doesn't love Jehovah so he's not right for me. No, I'm not going down this path again, it's caused me too much anguish. I'm going to do the right thing.

When she calls Will it's clear he's disappointed. She can hear it in his voice. Trying not to lie and to let him down gently it makes it a very tense phone call and Jess knows that he'll be thinking the worst – that she just doesn't like him enough. But that isn't strictly true.

*

Another week goes by spent in her familiar, rigid pattern of work, study, swimming, two meetings and shopping. Her head aches frequently and this waiting game is torturous. Her life is about to start again, but she doesn't know when. *Is it the same feeling people get when they know their life is about to end?* she asks herself.

Thoughts about dying had never hung around in Jess's head for too long. From childhood she had been taught to believe she will live forever – she will not die. That is, unless she gets knocked down by a bus or something similar. She and other children her age were not expected to finish junior school before Armageddon arrives. 'It's just around the corner.' Everyone knows that Jehovah has control of world affairs and he will step in at just the right time. It won't be long now.

*

Yet another week rolls by Jess and is beginning to feel this is a bit of a joke. *As if my punishment hasn't been enough,* she thinks, *they are purposely making me wait, testing me, testing my endurance.* She wonders if this part of the process is directed from the Governing Body or if they are actually making up their own rules. There is a secret Elders' rule book that she's heard about where all the standards are set out and she determines that if she can ever get her hands on a copy this is something she will have to investigate.

Thursday night meeting is fast approaching. Jess has had a busy week at work, with a huge order to complete. There was a comedy sketch being filmed in the area involving all the actors wearing a particular style of frame, so there was no slacking from anyone this week. At the meeting she takes a seat on the back row as usual and digs out her songbook and Bible from her bag. A packet of milk bottle sweets sits at the bottom, open, and some have spilled out. Eating sweets during a meeting was seen as highly disrespectful when she was a child but she's be eighteen on her next birthday and she is willing to risk being told off.

Taking a discreet look around the Hall before the meeting starts Jess spots Alan sitting in the back row on the opposite side. He seems to be back in his old suit, not his new smart one. Shame. He looks really good in it. Cassie is up ahead with her parents and is wearing a blouse she'd worn to Norwich assembly. Jess had admired it and had looked for the same in Etam but they'd sold out.

She knows what to expect. The programme doesn't alter that much from week to week: song, prayer, Bible highlights, Bible reading, number two talk, number three talk, number four talk, song and then any announcements. That was the first half over.

Everyone takes their seats following the cringe-worthy song, with some notes too high for the sisters and others too low for the Brothers. They mumble through it and settle down as Kevin Choi, still the Presiding Overseer, gets up on the platform to make any announcements. He clears his throat and stands with his hands gripping the sides of the lectern. Jess sees him take a deep breath and look up at the audience.

"Jessica Dalton has been reinstated," he declares, straight-faced.

There is silence.

Jess's heart beats faster at hearing her name and she can't stop her face from broadening into a huge smile. No one reacts – they are instructed not to show pleasure at such an announcement. To them it's no big thing – now Jessica will have to prove herself by continuing to progress spiritually. Then and only then, will people welcome her properly, once she's been judged as genuine. She looks at Marianne who has her face in her hands. She's not crying, just having a moment, and she reaches to take Jess's hand in hers, giving it a big squeeze.

But for some reason Kevin is still on the platform. He's still holding the lectern and takes another deep breath. The tension in the Hall is palpable, thicker than Marianne's custard. Another announcement?

This time Kevin doesn't look up at the audience but picks a spot in the middle distance, down the central aisle.

Exhaling heavily, his breath booms through the microphone as he informs the congregation that, "Chris Standon has been disfellowshipped," immediately followed by, "Alan Chambers has been disfellowshipped."

What?! Chris and Alan? What's going on? Jess can't get her head around it. She remembered Alan had been caught smoking at the party but that was so long ago. *And Chris? What has he been up to?*

Her innocent mind does not connect the two but she doesn't need to wait too long before more information comes forth. The giveaway talk is given in the second half, delivered to a keen audience, waiting for some juicy gossip. It was not about smoking at all. It was about sexual behaviour towards a person of one's own sex and how it is clearly condemned by Jehovah in the Bible. Jess had to stifle a snigger. This is just unbelievable. Chris and Alan have been having sex together!?

Many, many heads turn and there is a hushed, heavy atmosphere for the rest of the meeting as people absorb this shocking, disgusting news.

*

The news about Alan greatly upsets Jess and her emotions are torn between elation at finally having made it back and the sadness at not being able to speak to Alan. It was his smile at the Memorial last April that had given her a lift when she needed it and she wanted to thank him. He's got a tough time ahead, a very tough time.

But it explained a lot: he wasn't interested in her because he wasn't interested in any girl. That makes her feel slightly less rejected – if such a feeling exists. Chris had been mentoring Alan, clearly. After his slip up at the party it must have been the case that Chris took him under his wing and guided him back onto the straight and narrow path. Guided him straight into his bedroom more like. Poor Alan.

*

The final prayer over, Jess sits for a few seconds and places her books back in her bag, the sweet bag empty now. From different directions she hears several people mumble a guarded 'hello' and she replies as coolly as them, although what she really wants to do is throw her arms around each and every one of them, even those she doesn't particularly like. It feels as if people's emotions are still stunted, still stifled, all tightly controlled and so unnatural. But Cassie is different and she makes her way down the aisle with her arms open wide, heading straight for Jess. The girls hug each other for a long time, swaying and rocking, with tears streaming down their faces. A sob escapes and Jess knows her mascara is all down her face.

"Jess!"

"Cassie, I'm sorry!"

"Sshh, it doesn't matter. Come back to my house now, you and your mum. Dad will give you a lift home."

The girls catch up with each other's news and when Jess tries to explain about Ray and how she got herself into such a mess, Cassie shuts her up. She tells her it's not important, she's just glad she made her way back.

Chapter Fifteen

Marianne is thrilled and relieved that she has her daughter back in the fold, where she belongs. She'll be safe now and having learned a tough lesson, hopefully won't make the same mistake again. The stress of the last year and a half or so has built up for Marianne. She felt she needed to be the strong one, in deed if not in word, not being able to encourage Jess verbally. She had pushed herself to go to meetings for Jess's sake when she really did not feel up to it, and now, having relaxed, a black cloud descends and tells her it's time to slow down.

Jess thought that having a granddaughter would have helped her mum but it doesn't seem to have. She doesn't talk about her that much and has only been down to see her once since she'd been born.

But for Jess this is really something wonderful, her beautiful little niece named Bethany Amber. In the few photos Peter sent Jess can see a resemblance to Marianne around her sweet eyes. She has ginger hair, the Irish side of the family shining through. Jess is desperate to get down to see her and give her lots of cuddles. She's bought presents for her too, making up for lost time. She had to take advice from the shop assistant in Mothercare about what to buy a baby girl as she really had no clue about these things.

Her first chat with Peter on the phone the day after her reinstatement is awkward and full of apologies from Jess. The tears are heard by each other down the line and Peter reassures Jess that she must put it all behind her now and move forward with her life and not look back. The siblings arrange for Jess to go down soon for a visit and this time she is to catch the train into St Pancras rather than the coach, to arrive in daylight, not after dark.

Jess is so excited and realises it was worth all the effort, the tears and the loneliness to get back into the Truth, no matter how hard it was. Now she can look forward to helping her niece to get to know Jehovah and push forward to life in paradise surrounded by beauty and happiness in abundance.

*

As Jess starts to grow back into her fully active Jehovah's Witness life again, Marianne retreats into a shell of mental exhaustion. As Jess starts to attend the Book Study and give answers, make arrangements to go out on the ministry and prepare a number two talk, Marianne takes to her bed more and more with headaches as excuses, aching limbs and tiredness.

Jess doesn't know what to do to help her mum. Nothing she's done in the past has managed to bring her out of herself so Jess is inclined to just allow her time to work through it at her own pace. She cooks and cleans so Marianne can rest and encourages her to get to as many meetings as she can.

With the help of an increased dose of antidepressants Marianne slowly starts to pick herself up off the floor, so much so that she even considered pioneering. Seventy hours dedicated to preaching the good news of God's Kingdom. The thought of pioneering made her happy and this is the goal she will be working towards. She felt she was blessed for it when the Circuit Overseer and his wife chose her house to stay at during their bi-annual visit. She'd heard they liked chips so bought an electric deep fat fryer and chucked out the old saucepan and basket. While they stayed it meant that for a week she and Jess would get lifts to and from the meetings. Blessed indeed.

*

Jess thinks of Alan often. Is Jehovah still blessing him? He was there the night his disfellowshipping was announced, and she knows how hard that would have been, but she hasn't seen him since. Chris, on the other hand, hasn't missed any meetings and has strutted around like nothing has changed. No one talks to him but he looks like he doesn't give a damn. If she could just talk to Alan, maybe she could encourage him but talking face to face with him is just not worth the risk. *Not worth the risk.* The phrase sounds so mean as she explains to Chubbers what she's thinking but she has to protect herself. She decides to write him a letter. No one will know, only Jehovah. Would he mind that much? She's really doesn't think he would.

Her letter is full of empathy and understanding and reaches Alan through his letter box, hand delivered by Jess. Alan was a 'born-in' like her and had known nothing else so they have much in common. Trying not to tell him directly what to do she puts forth the pros and cons of staying out and going back in the hope that he will choose what's right. The Truth is still very much in her heart and hopes it's in Alan's and if he can just get over this silly mistake he's made and get back on track he'll be alright. It won't be easy that's for sure but it will be worth it. His life on a paradise earth is at stake, he wouldn't want to throw that away.

Winter has set in although there is no snow yet. Jess still has her job at the eyewear manufacturers and is saving up for driving lessons which she knows will give her much more freedom, freedom to visit other congregations and make a wider circle of friends, ones that don't know her past. She still hasn't seen Alan at any meetings and so concludes he won't be coming back and the day she receives a letter from him confirms it.

It was a very short letter.

Dear Jess,

I don't know how you did it.

Take care,

Alan.

Two days later her world was rocked when Marianne told her that Alan's body had been found by his dad.

Twenty-year-old Alan had hung himself from a beam in the garage leaving no note or any indication of how he had been feeling. Jess knew it wasn't just his guilt that was eating him up. To be ostracised and ousted so completely from everything he'd ever known would have tormented his mind day and night without let up. He couldn't take it anymore and had to put a stop to it somehow. The idea had crossed her own mind more than once.

No announcement was made about Alan's funeral. There were no conversations before or after meetings about Alan, no one that Jess talked to anyway. It was like he had never existed. He was dead to them, even before he'd taken his last breath. For Jess it played on her mind, this treatment of a young man who had contributed to the smooth running of the meetings, who had delivered quality talks and who had spent many hours in ministry over the years. How could he, overnight, be considered such a bad, evil person, one who hates Jehovah, one who is his enemy and be cast aside like a piece of dirt on someone's shoe? And do they not understand what pain he must have been in to take his own life?

His parents were devastated, Jess could see it in their faces and the way they held themselves. At each talk that touched on death or the resurrection in the coming paradise, his mum almost curled herself up in her seat with such emotional agony, trying desperately not to draw attention. His dad didn't move, just kept his eyes on the speaker, as if to move a muscle would open a floodgate that couldn't be closed.

Death amongst the Witnesses is a funny thing. It's as if the loss of a loved one isn't supposed to hurt as much as it does to non-Witnesses, because of their strong belief in a resurrection. They never say, 'Rest in peace,' believing that the dead are just in a deep sleep – there's no separate spirit so they would not rest any other way than peacefully, of course. Witness funerals are the only ones Jess had seen where everyone wears a smile. She always thought it was quite bizarre, inhuman.

But Alan was a different story. He had died in a disfellowshipped state, alienated from God and his congregation. He also took his own life, self-murder. The hopes his parents had always nurtured would never be as strong as they had once been and their hearts' desire to see their son again, forever dimmed. In their minds they just couldn't be sure that he would be resurrected. Jess really felt for them. She told them about her letter to him, which they had read, and they assured her that there was nothing in it that would have made him take such action. Jess was so relieved. Despite having worded her letter very carefully she thought maybe something she'd put might have pushed him over the edge.

Against her spiritual education regarding disfellowshipped ones and against Marianne's advice she attended his funeral and wept openly with Alan's parents and a few non-Witness relatives. She knew deep down the role that being ostracised had played in his decision, something no one else could possibly understand, not even the Elders who serve up such a bitter-tasting meal.

*

Slowly, painfully slowly, the Brothers and sisters in the congregation accept that Jess is back, to a degree. Individuals say hello to her and ask her how she is. But there are no accompanying hugs, not like there used to be. And there's one thing she notices which never used to exist: the married sisters are very protective of their husbands when Jess is around. She wonders if she was imagining it at first but it has continued. On two occasions Jess had noticed one of the sisters will not allow Jess to be alone in the same room as her husband when she announced she needed the toilet. She made a point of waiting till someone else was around before leaving the room. How petty! Another wife clearly couldn't bear to hear Jess having a conversation with her husband and kept interrupting, eventually dragging him away. These poor, paranoid sisters with their ugly husbands in their beige shirts. She had to laugh!

Jess was stronger now, mentally stronger, but it took considerable time to get her confidence back, especially when knocking on doors. How could she talk about the abundance of immorality in the world today when she had been guilty of it herself? The guilt she felt was still there deep down and was something that couldn't be erased, not when reminders of her former behaviour were thrown at her frequently from the platform at the Hall and at assemblies. There was no let up. She needs a break from it all.

*

She starts to make plans for her visit to Peter's. One thing she must do before she goes is call Esther and tell her about her new family member. On the Friday evening before she's due to travel she dials her number.

Esther can tell Jess is happier the moment she starts to talk. There's a freshness and a lift in her voice that she hasn't heard before. She attributes it to Christmas coming and thinks Jess has probably got some wonderful plans with her friends, meals out with her workmates, parties and shopping trips. It's good to hear her sounding so upbeat for a change.

Jess's news about Bethany Amber is wonderful! *Ah, so that's the reason she sounds so happy!* thinks Esther. When Jess tells her she's travelling down the next day and that she is crossing London around lunchtime Esther can't believe it as she and Will are in London the next day too. Esther is going shopping while Will does another photo shoot. Fortunately, he's being paid good money for all these unpopular Saturday shoots he's doing. She and Jess arrange to meet for lunch at a café just outside St Pancras station. Esther thinks Jess is such a lovely girl and is genuinely looking forward to seeing her again.

When Jess hangs up she can't quite grasp how her life has changed overnight. It feels like she's been released from prison, that she's been in a coma and the whole world has been carrying on without her. She can breathe easily and somehow the air tastes cleaner and fresher. Now she can rejoin the action and try to catch up. *It was just a little holiday,* she tells herself, *some time out, my wilderness months. Jesus did it.*

After some thought, Jess decides not to tell Marianne about meeting up with Esther. She doesn't need to know and would probably only try to talk her out of mixing with a worldly person unnecessarily. But Jess has experienced Esther's kindness and wonders why that trait is overlooked in everyone that's not a Witness. It doesn't make sense.

*

The train journey down to St Pancras only takes an hour and Jess reads a few chapters of the novel she's brought with her. *Frankenstein.* What a fascinating story! She's just got to the bit where the monster is hiding in the outbuilding next to the house of the family. He finds a discarded bag full of books in the woods and he's now teaching himself to read. No one wants to be near him because of his appearance and even he hates his own reflection. What a lonely existence.

Replacing the book in her bag Jess looks out the window and tries to focus on the world as it whizzes past. The open fields are the backdrop to untidy railway depots and metal industrial units advertising their purposes with huge nameboards. Tiny dots of white in the far distance become grass-munching sheep as the train hurtles along, clattering and heaving on parts of unlevel track.

It's so good to get away, thinks Jess as she takes a sip of her can of Lilt. The months have dragged by unbelievably slowly but now she's served her time she is determined to do good, to be a true, faithful Witness and continue doing what she knows is right. Maybe she can talk to Esther about the Truth and the benefits of serving Jehovah. *Wouldn't it be wonderful if Esther and Will had a Bible study!*

*

The heavy diesel train slows as it pulls under the cathedral-like metal roof of the station. Out of the window small mosaics of sky peek through the forest of bricks and glass and the next passengers for this train stand patiently on the platform ready to jump on and take their seats. Jess stands up, checking her seat to make sure she hasn't left anything. Her sensibly labelled case sits by her side till the other passengers shuffle down the train. Heavy with diesel fumes the air catches in her throat making her cough suddenly. On reaching the barrier she hands her ticket over and looks round as she hears her name being called: "Jess! Over here, Jess!"

It's Esther up ahead, making her way towards her.

"I'm a little early so thought I'd come and meet you off the train. How are you, my dear?"

"Esther, how lovely to see you," replies Jess. "I'm really well thanks."

They hug as if they're old friends, the age difference proving to be no barrier. Jess doesn't think of Esther as a substitute mum or as an older sister or aunt. She's just Esther.

They walk at a pace through the crowded station out to the main road and towards the café Esther has chosen, chatting all the while about the weather and how busy the town is looking in Eastbourne with Christmas shoppers out in force.

*

The café is a sizeable place, very cosy with soft pads on the wooden chairs and colourful velvet cushions on the two armchairs by the window. Pink ruched curtains hang at the large front windows adorned with long thick tassels and the light from the spring sunshine casts a warm glow onto the low table as the two take their places. *A mixture of posh and snuggly*, Jess decides, as she removes her jacket and gloves.

After placing their order with the waitress Esther moves the conversation forward.

"So, tell me all your news, Jess, tell me all about your little niece. I bet you can't wait to see her."

There isn't a lot to tell Esther about Bethany or her life back home. She has her job to explain and her swimming routine, that's about it. No exciting social life to chat about. She's waiting for the right moment to break into the Witness world and is slightly hesitant about seeing 'that look' on Esther's face. The one she sees so often from members of the public. The one that says the shutters have come down, the one that says, 'oh for God's sake, not religion. Go away, I'm not interested.' She doesn't want to see disgust in this lovely lady's eyes so skirts around the subject for as long as she can.

But Jess is delighted to show her the photos of Bethany, which are getting a bit dog-eared already, several of them showing her cute smile. She keeps them in her purse so they're with her all the time and looks at them throughout the day, every day. At bedtime she wishes her a good life and sweet dreams as she kisses her goodnight.

"I must say you look so much happier than the last time I saw you. My guess is that you were having a rough time when we saw you that first evening, perhaps you were a bit homesick?" She put her hand on Jess's. "I don't wish to pry but for someone to suffer with panic attacks there's usually a very good reason. If you ever want to talk about it, I'm here to listen."

Jess smiles. That is all she needs to start her off. Over a tasty lunch of chicken salad with crusty bread and a cup of hot coffee she bravely sets about telling Esther a short version of the story right from her childhood. How Marianne came into the Truth, about Dad leaving, how difficult it was through her school years, her baptism, how obsessed with the Truth her mum is. About Norwich assembly, running away, getting the job at the Beefeater and going to see her dad. And, wondering if she can possibly make her understand, about being disfellowshipped.

She has to pause at this point to explain what being disfellowshipped means and why it is a loving provision. Yes, it was hard, but she got through it and has now been reinstated into the congregation and is happy again.

The waitress hovers at the table with a pot of coffee and after a nod from Jess re-fills their cups.

*

Esther takes it all in, letting it swoosh through her mind as Jess explains things. It wasn't right to make any negative comments to this young girl. It's all she's ever known and is clearly unaware of the choices she is entitled to make in life. The world is far, far bigger than one set of man-made beliefs. She wonders what attracted Jess's mum to it, but then, when Jess had told her about Marianne's background she felt it was understandable to grab onto something that sounds so wonderful. She didn't blame her one bit.

Esther had met some Jehovah's Witnesses before. They had called at her door one afternoon about a year ago and offered their magazines.

"I enjoyed reading them and the two ladies came back each fortnight with the latest editions," recounts Esther. "I noticed that towards the end of every article there was a Biblical slant and I remember thinking it would be nice just to read something interesting without there being an agenda, without feeling as if I'm being preached to. But they were nice ladies, kind and gentle."

"Yes, the magazines do try to stir an interest in spiritual things. They can be quite encouraging too sometimes."

"And do you go from door to door yourself, Jess?" Esther enquires.

"Yes, I've been doing it since I was a young child."

"Really?" Esther is surprised. She'd never spotted any children down her street door-knocking. Is that kind of thing allowed for children? Is it even safe for them to knock on a stranger's door?

"There's always someone close by so there's no danger, really."

Still Esther is quite perturbed by the notion and her concern shows on her face.

"Jess, I know Witnesses are known for their door to door work but I've never agreed with it. Really I can't see how this is acceptable these days. No one knows who's behind each door. There could be a ferocious dog or a complete nutter, you just don't know. Your responsible adults are actually putting the children in a lot of danger."

When Jess makes no comment Esther sees she's thinking about it. She must have felt afraid sometimes when approaching strange houses but if everyone around her was doing it she wouldn't have seen the danger.

Esther finishes her coffee and looks at the sweet menu. Cheesecake, Victoria sponge, chocolate cake are all calling out to her and she decides to go for the one with the least amount of sugar; a fruit scone with margarine. A few pounds had found their way around her tummy over the winter and it's now time to ditch the winter comfort eating and get back on track with her weight loss routine. Walking at least three miles every day, swimming in the sea, eating healthily and getting enough sleep. Her work pattern had changed to part-time so she has no excuse.

"Are you going to have some cake, Jess? By the way, this is my treat today."

As Esther raises other questions about the beliefs of the Witnesses – the no blood issue, Christmas, Easter, birthdays – Jess is happy to answer each one with confidence and conviction. She wishes she had brought her Bible along so she could support her answers scripturally. She doesn't voice it but feels that Esther really needs to have a regular weekly Bible study and in her mind she's already picturing herself phoning the Eastbourne congregation to ask if they can send someone out to her house next week.

But Esther's querying becomes more personal and her next question makes Jess stop talking and think.

"Jess, what keeps you in it? It must have been so hard to have been put out, cut off from everyone you know and then to make your way back all on your own. I'm not sure I could do it. You must really want to be part of it. What keeps you going?"

The automatic answer that sits just behind Jess's lips involves the paradise, God's favour, it's the Truth, all the usual reasons, all the benefits. But she doesn't release the words. She opens her mouth but nothing comes out. In the silence of the following moments she realises she's said them too many times and is beginning to sound like a stuck record.

"Do you really believe in God?" asks Esther. "I mean, I believe in God but not one that treats his children like you've been treated."

Her silence lengthens and she fidgets in her chair. A woman shuffles past the steamy window jabbering away to herself.

Esther gently continues, "Is this practice of disfellowshipping truly a loving provision, as you say? What's loving about it? From what you've described you had no choice but to go back otherwise you would never have seen your family again. And as for your poor friend Alan, well, I just can't get my head around it."

Esther shakes her head, exasperated, and looks down at her hands.

Jess lowers her eyes. She's right. Esther's right in what she says.

"I'm sorry, Jess, these are just my thoughts, I'm not trying to put you off your religion. But maybe it's time to take a good look at what you're involved in. It's something you've been taught from a very young age. Is it what you want now you're getting older?"

Jess's coffee is cold but distractedly she drinks it anyway.

"You're a young woman with your whole life ahead of you. There's a whole world out there. Most people are good. Most people are honest and kind. You're missing out on so much."

Jess still doesn't speak. Another automatic response has instantly formulated but she keeps it locked away.

Esther reaches across the table and places her hand over Jess's.

"Just promise me something, yes? That you'll give yourself time to explore, investigate and really look hard at what you are involved in. Am I right in saying that your religion prides itself on not believing anything with pagan origins? Well, you need to do the same. Look at where your beliefs have come from. Look at how your religion got started. It's probably one of those American cults. Do you promise, Jess?"

Jess raises her head and looks directly at Esther. For some reason she wants to hug her, to sit on her lap and cry in her arms. No one had suggested to her that her disfellowshipping wasn't actually loving discipline from a loving god. No one had stood up for her feelings before. Any queries she'd had were answered in her own mind but to hear another person questioning the rights and wrongs of the practice created a new feeling that was warming and comforting to her heart.

"Alright, I'll give it some thought," Jess promises, not knowing where to start.

"I've got an idea," Esther announces, but is cut short when the bell on the café door jingles as someone enters.

"Will!" Jess exclaims. She stands up as Will approaches the table, backpack falling from his shoulder onto the floor. He hugs Jess and asks how she is, smiling widely and looking happy to see her.

Coffee all round – Jess doesn't usually drink so much coffee – the three chat away for another hour and Will speaks of things that are happening in Eastbourne. Sadly, the remaining few jobs at the Bird's Eye factory have now gone and the premises will be closed. That was where Ben had worked for the two years he lived in the town. But on a happier note, plans for a new harbour development in Eastbourne have been given the go-ahead. With the harbour, surrounding housing and pubs and restaurants it will create plenty of jobs. Jess is always pleased to hear news from her hometown.

"Hey, why don't you come down and stay for a few days?" he suddenly asks. "The weather's going to turn soon. You might want to go swimming in the sea."

"That's just what I was going to suggest, Will," says Esther. "We could tie it in with one of your work trips and Jess could travel back down with you. How does that sound, Jess?"

Although the invitation comes as a surprise she doesn't hesitate with her answer: "Yes. Yes, that sounds good." She feels totally at ease with these people and the chance to spend some more time with them stirs absolutely no guilt in her. Is that wrong?

The new financial year had started so Jess had plenty of holiday entitlement. Plans would be made nearer the time. *A week in Eastbourne!* She couldn't wait!

*

As she continues on her journey to Southend Jess replays their conversation several times in her head. A seed is sown. Maybe the seed has been there for a long time. Maybe it's just been watered, fed with the right nutrients, given light and fresh air and the chance to grow.

Chapter Sixteen

Bethany is a gorgeous little girl, she giggles all the time and pulls such funny faces when she doesn't get her own way. Jess went with Peter when he took her to the park and had fun pushing her on the kiddie swing and listening to her baby language.

"Not too high please, Jess."

Peter's protectiveness kicks in. *He'll be a good dad*, thinks Jess.

It's February and chilly by the sea in Southend. Adventure Island is closed and people make their way along the wide boulevard ducking into the shops for warmth. The Railway Hotel advertises live music on Thursday evenings and Sunday afternoons, and as Jess passes by she can see a roaring fire through the window. The Kingdom Hall is not far away from Peter's house and on Thursday as they walk the half mile there they pass the Railway, the pub sign squeaking as it blows to and fro in the wind. Jess smiles as she hears the warming rhythm and blues harmonica blasting out as someone enters through the door.

The meeting is a surprisingly pleasant event. It's wonderful to be sitting surrounded by her family. Bethany makes a fair amount of noise at her age especially during the prayers (the time when she's supposed to be the quietest), but she'll soon learn how to sit quietly for very long periods of time.

*

Peter is happy to be able to spend some time with his little sister, reconnecting and discussing their future plans. He's pleased to hear that Jess has good spiritual goals in mind and he hopes she can stick to them. He remembers how Marianne can be with her fluctuating moods and debilitating migraines and hopes Jess is coping with her strange ways.

"Her moods are getting worse, Peter," explains Jess. "It's like she's shutting down. The gap in between is shorter now and she spends longer in bed each time. And she doesn't really talk or do anything. Just sits in front of the TV or reads her books."

Peter's first priority where his mum is concerned is her spirituality. "Is Mum getting to many meetings? And what about the ministry? Is she managing to get out regularly?"

"It's quite hit and miss with everything really," is Jess's honest reply. "Although she always has her goal of pioneering in mind."

Peter was six years older than Jess so he'd seen a lot more of Marianne's behaviour and decline. From an early age he had been very protective of his mum, caring for her when she was down, doing a lot of the cooking and washing when he was at home.

At the age of thirteen, when Ben left, he took on the role of 'man of the house' bestowed upon him by Marianne, and took over caring for household matters; paying the bills at the post office, budgeting the weekly income, and guiding his younger sister. A heavy burden for a thirteen-year-old boy, but it was good practice for his future when he would have his own family.

Then at seventeen Peter took driving lessons,

passed his test and bought a Renault Four from Mr Laughton next door. Marianne then found she could replace an afternoon in bed with a nice drive in the country which did her just as much good, if not more. Peter was a kind and gentle young man, very popular with the girls and, when they saw how well he cared for his mum and sister, was deemed much more than dating material; he would be the perfect husband.

*

But now he's seriously worried about Marianne. From what Jess is saying it's clear she needs some kind of professional help with her depression. Perhaps some stronger medication and some counselling. He resolves to make an appointment with her doctor and travel up to go with her to discuss the options.

Medication would be easy to sort out but as for any counselling the problem is that the religion's advice is strictly against seeking any help from outside. Counsellors are 'worldly' people who will advise using strategies that would conflict with Christian principles. Or they may promote a course of action that would be deemed unchristian such as having a relationship outside of marriage. 'It's OK if it's not hurting anyone,' that's what they'd say. Peter doesn't want his mum to be led down a wrong path in such a vulnerable state and will explain her scriptural stance to her doctor. He's a very understanding doctor and besides, there have been more difficult things to explain to him in the past related to the religion.

Peter's heart went out to his mum and he felt so helpless as he saw her suffering for so many years and at the same time refusing to go against spiritual advice and find a counsellor. She's a faithful sister and would be rewarded in the long run.

From a fun perspective Jess thought what her mum needed was just a good night of passion with a handsome fella. That would sort her out. Or to get dressed up and go out for the night and get blind drunk, let her hair down for a change. Go dancing and have some fun. She wished she could do these things herself but it's all so very dangerous.

*

Jess's visit ends with hugs and kisses for Bethany, Peter and Janey and repeated promises to meet up again very soon. The time she spent there has done her so much good. Makes her feel part of the human race again, that she belongs somewhere and has a valuable role to play. She'd missed that feeling.

During the journey back through London and on the train to the Midlands Jess remembered her promise to Esther and rolled it around her mind. What if the Elders were not appointed by God after all? What if they actually made all their own decisions, and weren't guided by the holy spirit as they professed? What if their decision to disfellowship her had actually been wrong? No. It didn't bear thinking about.

*

It's March, and the forecast heavy showers hadn't arrived. A few damp dewy mornings are soon replaced by brilliant sunshine and the smell of newness as tiny buds start to appear on the branches. Jess sprinkles a mixture of seeds on the bird table, a new feature in the garden since Sophie had gone, and sits inside the house watching the birds' tiny heads bobbing as they get their fill.

Meeting night tonight. Marianne's not going. Jess is getting a lift with a family who live nearby. Her ankle has been playing up recently so she phoned and asked if they wouldn't mind giving her a lift there and back. She'd decided to ask the favour of all the people who had walked past her on the night she'd fallen in the ice. She's sure they won't mind.

It's the end of the first week in the month which means everybody needed to have put their reports in the box last week. How many hours spent in the ministry, the number of magazines and books placed, how many Bible studies conducted during the month – all necessary information to be collated and published. The Governing Body in New York needs to see the increase, needs to see the results of the Campaign in February, the invitation to the upcoming Memorial.

The Service Overseer, Lance, addresses the congregation:

"So, Brothers, reports. Sadly, the reminder given last week doesn't appear to have had any effect. There are still several who haven't put their slip in the box. Wouldn't it be a shame to think that all our hard work during this special month has been for nothing? The Brothers at the Branch need to have accurate figures to send on to Brooklyn headquarters. So I will be putting a list of names on the noticeboard of those still to hand their report in. Let's make an extra effort, Brothers, to do things Jehovah's way, and remember, 'he who is faithful in least, is faithful in much'."

What a jumped-up little man. Who does he think he is, embarrassing people in this way? Jess had never heard anything like this before and is inwardly seething. *Talk about naming and shaming!*

Out of her seat as soon as the announcement is finished Jess discreetly walks to the back of the Hall and hangs around by the literature desk for a few minutes, right next to the noticeboard. It's not uncommon for there to be at least one person lurking about, stretching their back or legs after sitting in those too-upright chairs for an hour. The rest of the congregation are fumbling about trying to find a scripture.

She watches as Lance leaves the platform and heads in her direction, papers and Bible clutched to his chest. While he's fiddling around with a pin and a piece of paper dragged from his pocket, Jess nonchalantly leans against the wall and straightens the butterfly on her earing, paying him no attention. Out of the corner of her eye she sees him stand back to admire his posting, nod his head in approval then return to his seat.

Jess's name would not be on any list, she had put her report in at the last meeting and she's not about to see her brothers and sisters being named and shamed in this way. This is not regular practice. This is not direction from God. *How dare he?* As quick as lightning Jess pulls the piece of paper off the board and stuffs it in her pocket – she's sure nobody has seen her – and she makes her way back to her seat.

Discussing it with Marianne at home later, she doesn't even look at the list as she rips it up into tiny pieces and throws them in the bin.

"It's not supposed to be about figures, is it? It's about serving Jehovah and pleasing him. What's got into Lance behaving this way?" Jess is hoping Marianne can shed some light on it.

"He's just an imperfect man, Jess, trying to do a good job."

"But that's not the way to do it, by shaming people, is it?

"We have to overlook things like this, mistakes and misunderstandings. 'Keep putting up with one another with love,' isn't that what the scripture says?"

Perhaps, thinks Jess, but it makes her look at Lance in a completely different light.

*

Lance conducts the ministry meeting at a house nearby every Saturday morning and since the 'reports' incident Jess has been finding it hard to go. It's not that the ministry is difficult. The speaking to strangers bit is easy. No, what's hard is getting out of bed on a Saturday morning when she's been working all week and just wants a lie-in. Probably everyone feels the same. She only does an hour, or an hour and fifteen minutes at the most, then back to someone's for a coffee. Maybe it's time to think about going part-time so she can spend more time in the ministry. It's what she always wanted to aim for after all, maybe pioneer. Her outgoings were minimal so financially it shouldn't be a problem. She makes up her mind to talk to Marianne about it. She wishes there was some fun to be had in this life. It just seems to be a hard slog all the time with nothing to look forward to. Everyone has their own responsibilities and no time for anyone else.

*

Out of the blue rumors of a party have reached Jess's ears. For the young ones. In someone's house. There would be an Elder or two there for safety but still, a party! As it's not the done thing to discuss social events at a meeting, when the whispers stop when she gets near she puts it down to the rule and she waits for her invitation from the host, Helen. She'll probably ring or drop an invite through the door. Any day now. She knows which evening it's on and circles it on her calendar, hoping, hoping.

She waited and waited for word about the party, what time to be there, what to bring and gave Helen the benefit of the doubt right up till the last minute. But no invitation came her way. *Maybe she thinks she has invited me already, maybe she asked someone else to tell me about it.* No word came. She sits at home that Saturday night, cut to the heart, and thinks about the music, dancing and food and fun her friends will all be having.

Jess can only surmise it's because of her history. After all this time and the effort she has put in to the Truth since being reinstated, it's a fact: people never forgive and they never forget. It's one thing being partnered up as normal on the ministry, being given talks to do, cleaning the Kingdom Hall but their true colours are shown when it comes to socialising and having fun.

That night Jess took a mental step back. She's in no man's land. In the Truth but still kept on the sidelines. Not fully a part of the congregation except where spiritual matters are concerned. Kept at arm's length. *Is this how it's always going to be?* she wonders.

*

Cassie went to the party and the following week round at her house she recounts to Jess the events of the night.

There wasn't much music played – some Cliff Richard, George Benson, some Kingdom Melodies.

"Any alcohol?" enquires Jess, curious as to what kind of 'party' this was.

"Yes, Stewart brought some cans and someone else had a bottle of wine, I didn't see much else. It was quite boring really. But I did notice Stewart and Amy were chatting quite a lot," says Cassie conspiratorially.

Stewart and Amy had met at work some time ago. They were both employed at the local Tesco and encouraged by Amy, Stewart had studied with her dad, Dave. His baptism followed about a year later and he went straight into pioneering, making such swift advancement that there were a few questions on the older ones' lips. *How come he is leading the congregation in prayer after only being baptised three months ago? And why is he accompanying Dave when he goes on Shepherding calls? He's a young unmarried man with little experience of life and, well, only Elders and Ministerial Servants have the authority to make Shepherding calls.*

"What, they were hanging out together even with her dad there?" Amy's dad was one of the Elders assigned along with another to keep an eye on proceedings. He was 'soft as shit' as Amy herself described him once. Jess saw him as wishy-washy, always flustered and would do anything for an easy life. Amy had grown up without her mum as she had left for another man in Australia when Amy was small.

"Yeh, both Elders just sat in the corner all night. When the noise got up they told us to keep it down. That was all," Cassie explains. She leans in and whispers to

Jess, "They didn't notice but I saw Stewart and Amy go out the back door together hand in hand. I knew she had her eye on him. They came back about fifteen minutes later. Wanted a bit of time alone I guess."

"Whoa! Scandal!" exclaims Jess, giggling into her drink. "They'd make a nice couple actually. Stewart needs to put some deodorant on though!"

They laugh and Cassie continues to tell Jess about the evening and to listen to her as she explained how it made her feel, being the only one out of the whole congregation of young ones not to be invited.

"I'm sorry, Jess. It's not right. You want me to have a word with Helen?"

"No, just leave it. Thanks, Cassie. It is what it is. It's my own fault after all."

*

Stewart and Amy's relationship developed quickly and they became engaged and were allowed to sit together at the meetings. They could even officially hold hands whilst in the Kingdom Hall. Jess felt quite excited about the prospect of a wedding. She hadn't been to a wedding since Peter and Janey's and looked forward to having an excuse to buy a new dress.

One Thursday night at the meeting Jess asks Amy for a copy of the wedding list.

"No idea what to get you two. Have you got your dress sorted out yet, Amy?"

"No, Jess." Amy is quite short with her and Jess wonders why. Maybe she's nervous about the whole thing.

"Can we meet up for a chat, Jess? I really, really need to talk so someone. Someone who'll understand,"

Amy whispers, and as she walks away Jess gets the feeling all is not well.

Their chat took place in a café in town and through tears Amy let it all out. She and Stewart had slipped up and two nights after the party they'd ended up doing the deed in the back of his car.

"Amy! What were you thinking?"

"I know, I know," Amy whines. "It just happened, we didn't plan it or anything like that."

"Have you told your dad?"

"No, I can't, Jess. It could be so bad for us and for my dad. He could be removed as an Elder. He'd never forgive me. No," she shakes her head determinedly, "I can't tell him."

Jess thinks for a moment before speaking, weighing up the rights and wrongs of confession. The consequences for all concerned, for Amy, for Stewart who's just about to go to Pioneer School for four weeks. Yes, it's true her dad could be removed as an Elder for not being 'master of his own house' and having a wayward daughter. There is a shortage of Elders too in the congregation, only six are considered to qualify, with mature sisters having to say the prayer at ministry meetings. It's alright as long as they respectfully cover their head with a scarf or something. This could be utterly disastrous for several people. From experience Jess knows it will come out in one way or another sooner or later, and gives Amy her best advice.

"Oh, Amy. Think how you'd feel if you keep quiet about it now and then it comes out after the wedding. How would everyone feel? You will have deceived the whole congregation. And don't forget, Jehovah knows what's happened, he will bring it out into the open if he wants to. You need to say your prayers and ask for forgiveness."

It was a situation too close to home for Jess and took her back to her own episode not so long ago – the guilt, the worry about what would happen, the judicial committee meeting, the announcement. She couldn't help wondering how this young couple would handle this situation and would the Elders deal with Amy and Stewart the same way as they had dealt with her? The resurrection of such destructive memories set her back for a while but she had to have a stern talk with herself. Tell herself that it's all in the past, and her experiences can be used for good now, to help someone else.

*

Amy spoke to Stewart and between them they decided to do the right thing and confess. Her dad was angry about it at the start needlessly pointing out what a stupid thing it was to do and why couldn't they just have waited till after the wedding? It's only a couple of months away. She felt they showed a sufficient amount of contrition, enough for Dave to soften up a bit, but when the conversation moved on to his position as an Elder possibly being affected he once again got serious. Amy winced as she heard how worried Dave was but it didn't make him delay the phone call to the Presiding Overseer. A Judicial Committee meeting was arranged.

Their joint Committee comprised Dave, Kevin, who was still appointed as the Presiding Overseer, and Arthur who was a newly appointed Elder.

Amy's phone call to Jess comes so quickly, the meeting was at seven-thirty and it comes just after eight o'clock. They hadn't messed around, then. Jess feared the worst. But Amy's relief can be heard in her voice as soon as she starts speaking.

"Public reproof, Jess. On Thursday night."

"Phew, I must admit, I thought the worst as you were in and out so fast. But why public? No one knows about it do they? Did you tell them you'd told me?"

"No, it's just that someone saw us in the car," she says through a snigger. "I won't be at the meeting for the announcement, I can tell you that. It's too embarrassing. Anyway, once that's over I can get back to normal. Dad had a good telling off from the other two about 'the conduct of his household' and that's about it."

Jess is genuinely pleased and relieved for Amy, and for Stewart. It wouldn't have been good to start their married life being disfellowshipped. She gives Amy her best sisterly advice about not being alone together and if they ever needed a chaperone she's to call her.

But her advice falls on deaf ears. The next time it happens the two of them are caught in the act in her bedroom. Dave had gone out and Stewart had turned up unexpectedly believing he would be in. Finding themselves alone in the house, one thing led to another and, hey, ho, up the stairs they stumbled and into the most disastrous situation.

Again, Amy confesses to Jess who gives her the same advice: apologise to Jehovah, confess to an Elder straight away. Get it sorted. Jess is fearful for Amy about the results of a second Judicial Committee meeting and sits nervously waiting for the phone call from her. As it's the second time they've made the same mistake there's absolutely no doubt the two of them will be disfellowshipped. Still, Jess will be there for her and has already considered if she could possibly ostracise her, knowing exactly how that feels. She knows it would affect Amy's whole life and she will lose all her friends. Amy is very popular, very outgoing and this will simply destroy her.

But she needn't have worried.

Amy delivers the news and it's the last thing Jess expects to hear.

"Another public reproof," Amy's voice is upbeat and strong. She almost laughs.

Jess is silent for a moment, trying to take it in.

"What? How come? You must have grovelled at their feet to get that result." Jess is shocked and is struggling to understand it. They had committed the same sin twice which means they're not repentant. Everyone knows how such a scenario ends up, it's used as an example in the literature all the time. Proper repentance means not doing it again, sometimes, as in Jess's case, it means not fleeing from the situation. If those are the rules then they should have been disfellowshipped. Not that Jess wanted that for them but if things were equal and the Elders were working along with the Elders' *Shepherd the Flock of God* book then this is not what's supposed to happen.

It wasn't only Jess that noticed this inconsistency. After the second public reproof announcement the murmurings in the congregation were so persistent that a Special Needs talk was given. A bi-monthly slot in the mid-week meeting programme is reserved for necessary talks and this one was delivered by Kevin Choi.

Without referring to Amy and Stewart's situation

or naming any of the Judicial Committee Elders it came in the form of a congregational rebuke, a telling off for not trusting the Elders. Elders who were appointed by Holy Spirit, who were led by the Holy Spirit and who made decisions in accord with the Holy Spirit. Who was anyone to question them? They knew all the facts of a matter. The congregation were showing a spirit of independence, dangerous and destructive. Isn't that what Eve showed back in the Garden of Eden? She stopped trusting in God and went her own way, made her own decisions, thinking she knew better. "We don't want to be like Eve, do we?"

*

"Well, that was us told," says Marianne back at home.

"I don't get it, Mum," says Jess, as she stands with a frown on her face trying to make sense of it. "I did it once, I confessed and I got disfellowshipped. Amy and Stewart did it twice, were caught in the act and they get a reproof. It doesn't add up."

"Well, you know, we can't possibly understand how the Holy Spirit works every time. There must be things we don't know and we just have to trust the Elders."

"No! It's not right." Jess raises her voice. She is getting sick of hearing the same old excuse for the Elders' actions.

"But they are God representatives on earth, Jess," Marianne replies, trying to calm her daughter down.

"Oh, you know what? So is the Pope!"

"Yes, but he doesn't…"

She didn't wait to hear Marianne's stock explanation, wasn't interested. Storming off upstairs in her anger she flung her bag at her wardrobe, the contents spilling out. Her song book lay open, her pens, notepad, her little folder full of report slips, Not at Home slips and her Bible all lay in a heap and for the first time, she really didn't care. She had always showed the Bible respect, looked after it, not allowed it to get wet when on the ministry in the pouring rain, always placed it on a bookshelf, but right now she couldn't give a damn.

Chapter Seventeen

I promised Esther I'd do some research, what did she say? Find out how my religion got started? Jess didn't know how to begin, or where. She thought about going back through the old magazines but they would be biased, of course. She needed some independent factual information, perhaps from an encyclopaedia. Maybe the local libraries would hold such a book or if not then it would be an excuse to take a trip to the National Library in London.

But how would knowing how the Organisation got started settle her mind about whether it was divinely directed or not? No, she needed to know less about the practicalities, the funding, the early days of printing books and magazines, and more about the principles of Christianity. That's what Jesus taught after all. He condemned the religious leaders of his day for burdening the people with unnecessary rules, tying them in knots, paralysing them with fear of putting a foot wrong. She could see her religion was going the same way and it wasn't right. How could it be?

Her faith in God was not in question. She had never doubted God and his effect on her life. Even when she was disfellowshipped it was the Elders she had blamed for being too harsh, not God. Looking back, she didn't believe God had approved of her treatment. She was absolutely sure in her mind that God was not at fault, that he just would not approve of the interpretation of the scriptures used to support disfellowshipping.

Jess was convinced it was God that gave her the strength to carry on and not give up. *But if that was true why didn't he help Alan to stay strong?* She could not answer that question for herself. Maybe his faith and belief weren't that firm. Maybe his own guilt was that much more painful that Jess's. Who knows? His parents would be asking themselves the same question no doubt.

*

Jess had told Marianne about Esther when she came back from her travels. She'd explained how kind Esther and Will had been on the night she had a panic attack at work. She'd hoped it would show Marianne that there were some lovely people out there in this wicked world, that they weren't all evil Satan-worshipers. She didn't feel it was necessary to tell her though that she and Esther had been keeping in touch. She had so looked forward to their Tuesday night phone calls when Marianne was out at the Book Study and although their chats were not that often they had formed a bond.

Now that Jess would be going down to Pevensey Bay to stay with Esther she felt it was time to let Marianne know how close they'd become.

"Well, that's nice, dear. She sounds like a kind person. And what about her son?"

"Will? Well, I don't know him as well as Esther but he seems just as nice. He's a photographer. Lives in Brighton and stays at his mum's now and then depending on his work."

"Right…" says Marianne, nodding her head thoughtfully.

Jess can see her mum's highly suspicious mind kick into action straight away but she didn't comment on it.

*

Jess checked her remaining Annual Leave at work and after a short telephone conversation with Esther, booked a week off beginning in two weeks' time. Late March was a nice time to hit the south coast.

She was so looking forward to going down south again, back home. The thought crosses her mind to visit Kathy and Greg and the family. How would they react to her? It had been over a year since she was reinstated. Had enough time passed for them to forgive her for dumping herself at their feet? Of course, Marianne had told them of Jess's disfellowshipping and reinstatement and word travels fast within the Organisation, so everyone that Jess had ever known would be aware. She was really not sure how they would treat her. It could go either way. She'd never put Kathy and Greg down as ones to hold grudges and, although they were quite relaxed in many areas, this was the Truth and at times it produced such unnatural behaviour.

*

Saturday. The journey down to Eastbourne by coach is so long. Eight hours from door to door and consists of the coach to Marylebone, a quick lunch at Gino's and then Tubes across to Victoria station. There is a wait of forty-five minutes before Jess can board the coach to Eastbourne and once seated she rolls up her jacket and cushions her head against the window. As the coach pulls out of the station Jess closes her eyes and doesn't want to open them till she's arrived.

She thinks about her mum and hopes she'll be all right by herself for the week. She had been sharp with

265

the Book Study conductor recently, something about not asking her to read a scripture when he'd asked everyone else that night. Petty really, but Marianne's sensitivity fed her paranoia that this was personal.

She thinks about Cassie, her dear friend. She is a smart girl, surely she can see the faults in the Organisation? Maybe she should talk to her when she gets back, help her to see that things aren't right, that Elders do get it wrong.

And she wonders how Alan's parents are coping. It's been a while now since they lost their son. They still go to all the meetings and are out on the ministry on a Sunday straight after the meeting. Maybe they put on that Kingdom smile to help them cope and then crash into emotional heaps when they get home. Do they really believe they'll see Alan again?

Should she attend the meetings during her week's holiday? Esther would be all right with that, she may even want to go along herself to see what it's all about. No ministry, though, she'll leave that for now. Perhaps just the Sunday meeting to say hello to some old friends, that is, if they are willing to acknowledge to her.

Her thoughts roll around her head merging into each other and despite the bumpy ride out of the city, Jess can feel herself falling asleep. By the time the coach is on the smooth roads south she's nodded off, bound to wake up with a stiff neck and drool on her jacket.

The driver brakes hard for some reason and wakes her up. Looking at her watch she notes she's been asleep for two hours. Another hour of the journey to go, she reckons, and considers reading her book but really she just wants to get there and get off this damn coach. On the way out of the house that morning she'd grabbed the post and, seeing a letter from Nerys, shoved it in her bag to read later. She remembers it now and digs around in her bag. Nerys's letters were always funny and cheery but this one has news for Jess that could not have been more unexpected.

It isn't Nerys White anymore, it's Mrs Nerys Barton. There had been no mention of a boyfriend in any of her letters, not even a hint. She wrote that it had all happened very quickly. She'd met Richie at an assembly a couple of months ago and they hit it off straight away. He'd been over to the house several times and they felt they were getting very close. There were so many opportunities to jump into the sack because of everyone being out and about all the time so the thought was that if they felt that strongly about each other then they should get married.

"It's the right thing to do," wrote Nerys, "at least we're safe now and everyone can relax. We had to think about the consequences if we slipped up and because you'd told me all about how you felt being disfellowshipped, well, I just didn't want to go down that route. We're getting a place together soon in London near Richie's parents so you'll be able to come and stay."

Married? At eighteen? She's only known him for a short while. And all because she didn't want to run the risk of being disfellowshipped. Oh Nerys! You bloody idiot! Jess hoped she wouldn't live to regret it.

*

Esther is waiting at the station in Susan's Road and as the coach pulls in they wave to each other excitedly. Big hugs and an offer to carry bags precede the short walk to where the car is parked. As they drive along the coast road with the evening sun behind them Jess peers past Esther's head and out to sea where the waves are making their gentle journey to the shore. A few swimmers have left their clothes in piles on the beach and the walkers skirt around them as they go. From inside the car Jess can almost hear their feet crunching through the stones. Strings of lightbulbs that hang between each Victorian lamp post sway in the southerly breeze. *I'm home,* thinks Jess. *This is where I belong.* There's something magnetic about the place, about the air, the sounds and the smells. Memories of a happier life flood back, one blending into another as they drive along at a steady pace towards Pevensey Bay.

There's the pier where she bought ice cream and played on the two pence shoving machines with Jackie and Diane; Treasure Island on the right with the huge bumpy slide that issued free leg burns on the way down. Princes Park with the swans, model boats on the lake and the blue kidney-shaped paddling pool where Karen had splashed her with the freezing water. As they drove past the Sovereign Centre Jess recalled her school swimming wins and pictured her certificates pinned to the kitchen wall next to the clock.

The pain gathers in her chest and threatens to escape from her eyes until she looks down into her lap at her bag, her pink diary just visible against the shiny lining. This week she may just do something that warrants an entry.

"I think I'll go to the meeting on Sunday if that's all right, Esther?"

"Will you need a lift there? Where abouts is the meeting place?" Esther replies, knowing she has no shifts on Sunday and therefore free to drive her.

"It's in Hampden Park, Broderick Road, I believe."

Jess had never been to the new Hall, though Nerys had told her all about it. The congregation had outgrown the old one above the fish and chip restaurant and with funds from the congregation and the Branch, had built a new one the other side of town. It backed directly on to the trainline and whenever a train hurtles past the speaker has to pause until the noise has subsided. Jess thought that was hilarious. *Why on earth did they decide to build the Kingdom Hall next to a trainline?*

Curious to understand Jess's position in the congregation after having been disfellowshipped, Esther digs a little, gently of course.

"So how have your old friends been towards you since you've been back in the congregation? Are they the sort to hold grudges or are they OK with you?"

"Some of them are just as they used to be before. Others are quite standoffish. It's quite a mixture really."

Recalling the party exclusion episode Jess explains to Esther how cruel others have been towards her.

"I find that so childish. Did the Elders have a word with Helen about how unchristian that was?"

"I doubt it. I feel like an outsider, Esther. I don't know if I belong anymore. It's like I've been away on holiday and have come back but everyone else has moved on without me. My old friend Cassie is the only one who's exactly the same with me, bless her. She is completely non-judgmental and I love her for it. But the others... there's a distance there that I know will never

269

be repaired."

Jess sighs and, closing her eyes, lets her head fall onto the headrest. Esther puts her hand on top of Jess's and gives it a squeeze.

"I'll go on Sunday and see how Kathy and Greg are towards me. That'll be interesting."

*

Esther's house sits right on the beach. Beyond the low front wall two feet in front of the house lies a pebbled public track that runs along all the properties facing the sea. On the far side of that sits each occupants' garden. Some are left open, others have a fence around and each is laid out differently, unique to the owners' own taste.

Esther's little wooden gate opens onto a decked pathway with a pebbled area either side. In amongst the stones the mauves and purples of viper's bugloss and sea holly stand out against the muted tones of the sea kale. A rusting bistro table and two chairs have their legs buried in the pebbles, and a basket of sea glass Esther has been collecting over the years sits just off centre. Next to the gate that leads onto the beach a wooden boat with flaking white paint lies at an angle displaying a pile of old rope and several terracotta pots freshly planted up. A stray oar leans against the side balanced on some large rocks and the paddle end points to the name just visible on the side: 'Pioneer.' *Can't get away from it,* thinks Jess.

Once Esther has shown her where she'll be sleeping Jess looks down at the view from the guest bedroom and smiles broadly taking in the whole scene. She can see all the way along the coast to Hastings and then to the right where the Martello towers stand, once guardians of the coastline, silently looking back at her. It's stunning. Peaceful. Inviting. Her room is spacious and pretty with delicately flowered peach wallpaper with matching bedspread and cushions. The deep orange curtains are held back with tassels and the walls hold a pair of photographs, presumable taken by Will, of some of the local birdlife.

Jess unpacks her things and hangs her meeting clothes in the wardrobe, her shoes, clean and shiny, she sets under the dressing table. Remembering to ask if she can call her mum to let her know she arrived safely she treads the open staircase in her socks down to the hallway.

She feels so comfortable here, as if she's known Esther all her life.

"Cup of tea, Jess?" Esther calls as she hears Jess put the phone down.

"Love one, thanks. Shall I make it?" Jess offers.

"Oh, yes thanks, no sugar for me. Will should be round soon. He's going to pick up fish and chips for us on his way through."

"Sounds good. I'm really hungry now, I didn't realise."

"Will always comes over on a Saturday if he's not going out with his friends. We have a takeaway and then he goes for a late swim before he goes home."

"Is the sea warm enough now then?" asks Jess, shivering as she pictures herself getting her feet in the water.

"It's refreshing shall we say," Esther giggles. "I prefer to go in the mornings. It's a great way to start the day."

And they chat about everything and nothing as they sit at the thick oak kitchen table. The side door opens onto to a small colourful garden, the dog, Shep, comes bounding in sniffing around this new strange guest. He's a collie, six years old, black and white with symmetrical markings and the brightest, most friendly eyes. Once he's decided Jess is not an enemy he clearly wants to play and drops his slobbery rubber ball at her feet, looking at her hopefully.

"You've made a friend there already," remarks Esther. "Take him out on the beach for a run if you like."

Shep runs ahead chasing the ball at top speed, darting around other walkers. She can breathe here. She can see far, far away into the distance and the events of the past seem a million miles away. For a change, it all feels so unimportant. Shep runs back with the ball in his mouth ready for the next throw. Crunching along the stones with her fingers linked behind her head, elbows out, Jess can feel the warmth of the setting sun as she lifts her head up towards it. Right now she feels completely at peace.

*

Will dumps the steaming bags of fish and chips onto the table and Esther takes the warmed plates out of the oven. Jess places cutlery for each of them and her first meal with Esther and Will feels so natural and warm. She enjoys her chat with Will about how his day has been, her journey down and how it feels to be back in Eastbourne. He is very attentive as they talk, listening to her answers, and he takes time to think before responding.

"So, what have you got planned for the week,

Jess, anything in particular you want to do?" he asks.

"I haven't thought about it really, but I'd like to head up to the Downs at some point, Beachy Head, if the weather's good. I know the bus to Brighton stops off there."

"I'm off work on Wednesday if you want some company," Will suggests.

Jess feels a tiny tingle in her chest at spending a few hours alone with Will. She knows it's the start of something that could be quite wonderful and searches her heart for the 'Go' sign. Is she brave enough to let go of her lifelong indoctrination about worldly people, and about dating without a chaperone? She looks at Esther, almost asking for her permission. Esther does not return her look, and instead stands up to put the kettle on.

Jess looks back at Will.

"Yes," comes her determined reply, "I'd like that, Will."

*

The cry of the seagulls is what wakes Jess up before her alarm goes off. Such a piercing sound which does not allow for any snoozing so she gets up with a good stretch, shaking out her muscles, stiff from sitting so long on the coach yesterday.

Esther, an early riser, has laid out breakfast so Jess can help herself to cereals, toast and jam. The pot of tea on the table is still warm so Jess pours herself a large mug and as she stirs in a spoonful of sugar, contemplates the morning ahead. She's nervous, very nervous about going to the meeting and asks herself why. *Why should I be worried about seeing Kathy and Greg? I've paid for my mistake, and heavily. I have nothing to prove to anyone except God. No, if they've got a problem with me well, then, it's their fault.*

She needs to keep this in perspective for the rest of the morning and tells herself to hold her head up, to be nice to whoever she talks to and to stay positive. She prays for strength and as she does so realises that such a prayer it quite ironic. That she should be praying for help to get through a short period of uplifting association with other so-called Christians who supposedly love her and view her as their spiritual sister. Something is not right.

*

When Esther drops Jess off on the main road just down from the Hall she thanks her, assures her she'll be fine getting the train back, and starts her nervous walk towards the building. Some unfamiliar faces going in the same direction give her friendly smiles and nods, their bags and briefcases swinging in time to their confident strides. It feels so strange to be back with her old congregation.

Once over the threshold into the foyer Jess hangs her coat up on the rail and looks around for the toilet. She doesn't need it, just wants to know where it is in case she feels the urge later. A lovely couple who had been at the Book Study meeting at Kathy's make eye contact, and for a second they hesitate. Jess is ready to say hello and ask how they are, be as friendly as she always is, but as they hurriedly walk away it's clear they've been told of her troubles. Nothing is private in this Organisation.

A smartly dressed young girl is waiting at the literature desk, being sent to pick up the family order of magazines for the month. A young brother is near the platform plugging in microphones and adjusting the lectern ready for the first speaker.

Seats have been saved by Bibles and songbooks and there's a fair number of people milling around making conversation. Jess choses a seat in the middle, not on the edge, not at the back. No, she needs to be right in the middle of the congregation. She has every right to be there. As she turns round she spots Kathy and Greg walking in together through the doors. Tentatively, Jess waves. Kathy sees her and gives a smile. Jess takes a step further: beckoning and pointing, she indicates there are spare seats next to her and they both walk towards her. *Good start,* she thinks, but at the same time bracing herself for a sharp word or two about how she had behaved.

But she needn't have worried. They meet at the end of the row and Kathy holds her arms out wide and grabs Jess folding her up in a hugely warm embrace. She holds her as tight as she had when Jess had turned up that day with Ray, and kisses her cheeks and hugs her again. No words are necessary. Tears fall discretely, dabbed away with a tissue from Kathy's sleeve. *It's all OK,* Jess sighs inwardly with relief, *she's forgiven me, truly.*

Remnants of guilt have taken a strong hold on Jess and her stern internal dialogue sometimes doesn't work. *Will it always be this way?* she wonders. Suddenly she can see clearly that these feelings don't exist when she's around Esther and Will. The supposed squeaky-clean environment when surrounded by other Witnesses creates a feeling of failure within her, that she will never be good enough, not with her history. The regular reminders of her mistake still float down from the platform through talks about adultery, fornication, dating worldly people, disfellowshipping, bad association. There's no escape from it.

Chapter Eighteen

In an effort to put all the negativity aside Jess spends the week seeking out some fun activities. This is a time for enjoyment and relaxation, a complete break from the oppression of her normal life. Swimming is at the top of the mental list she has composed and on waking to bright, sunny spring mornings she takes Esther's lead and heads down to the beach, costume on under her towel, and takes a bracing swim in the salty water.

The near freezing water strangely gives her life, energy. It lifts her up and carries her effortlessly while she lies and stares at the clear blue sky, her hair floating like seaweed around her head.

She wonders whether it's a good idea to go round to Kathy and Greg's. They appeared pleased to see her at the meeting but knowing how strict they are about doing things the right way, without a doubt the conversation would turn to the Truth. Kathy would dig around in Jess's spiritual life, asking her about her meeting attendance and ministry experiences, presenting it as 'encouragement.' It's the last thing she needs at the moment. No. Maybe next time she comes down this way she'll pay them a visit.

She needs a bike. It's flat as a pancake round there, great for cycling. *I wonder if Esther's got one she wouldn't mind me using?* she wonders. A cheeky enquiry that evening has Esther rummaging around in the shed and dusting the cobwebs off her purple Raleigh

Caprice. A spot of oil in the right places and it's good to go. The new harbour is where she heads first the next day eager to see what's going on down there. Her strong swimmer's legs make the ride easy even though she hasn't ridden a bike since before her dad left. She had loved her blue Raleigh RSW14. Daddy had bought her a Mickey Mouse bell for it and had started to teach her how to mend a puncture. Then he left and she still doesn't know.

Will said there'll be a mixture of shops and restaurants, flats and houses down at the harbour attracting buyers and renters from far and wide. There's certainly a lot of activity, the curtained windows show that many of the properties have occupants and two or three of the cafés are open already. The handwritten advert for staff on the door of one of the cafés catches Jess's eye and part of her wants to go in and ask about it. But she tucks that thought away somewhere safe.

One thing she must do is take a walk, or cycle, around the estate she used to live in, where the family were last together. The following afternoon, with the wind behind her, Jess makes her way along the coast road, turns right at the big roundabout and heads for Charnwood Close.

Seeing her old house, the path to the front door which is now green not blue, brings an eruption of tears and a single sob. Lost for a moment in her memories she can feel Diane holding her hand as she attempts to roller-skate down the slope between the backs of the houses. It looks so shallow now but seemed mountainous as a little girl and many was the time she ran in crying with a knee or elbow pouring with blood.

Holding the bike standing with her back to the house she can picture Silkie playfighting on the green with his dog-friend Robbie. Every day Robbie used to come and scratch at the door until Silkie went out to him. They tumbled around together, chased each other, jumped on and off the low wall nearby and fought over doggie treats thrown from the kitchen window. No one knew who Robbie belonged to and it didn't matter. He became part of the family.

Her memories threatening to overwhelm her and a sudden gust of warm air pushes her from behind and keeps her cycling forward, onward, away from the past and on into the future as she turns the corner and gazes at the hazy majestic Sussex Downs in the distance.

The cycle into town takes half an hour. The area is lively and colourful and already busy with tourists. Gift shops offer tins of fudge and walking canes of rock, baskets of pebble sweets and postcards with four inviting images of the town. She'd like to get something for Marianne but knows she would be far from impressed with anything edible packaged in an advertisement for the Eastbourne sun.

"Those are for the tourists," she'd say.

Jess will look later in the week for something she would appreciate. It might be quite a challenge.

*

Back at Esther's, mealtimes are a shared experience with the two women in the kitchen – Esther instructing and Jess obliging, finding her way around a multitude of utensils and gadgets. She offers to cook chilli and rice on Friday night so Esther can put her feet up and enquires if Will would like to join them.

"Yes, that's a good idea. He loves a bit of spicy food now and again but not too often. He's quite like his father, though, most of the time. Meat and two veg type of man."

"Nothing wrong with meat and two veg," remarks Jess.

"No, but I haven't had any for years, I've forgotten what it's like!"

"Esther!" Jess giggles with mock disgust.

*

Wednesday is approaching and Jess's upcoming afternoon alone with Will makes her nervous. She wonders if she's doing the right thing. She's weighed up the risks, the effects, has questioned her own motives and has come to the conclusion that there is absolutely nothing wrong with the plan. Will is a good person. He's not an evil devil worshiper, a liar, cheat, thief or murderer as she's been taught all her life. No, he's caring, hard-working, considerate and attentive. And he hasn't got a judgmental bone in his body. Unlike many of the Witnesses back in her congregation. She feels for the first time that she's made a moral decision completely on her own, and she's quite proud of herself for a change.

Jess smiles at herself in the mirror as she hears Will's key in the front door. Descending the stairs he looks up at her and she feels as if he is looking at her for the first time. Really seeing her. She's wearing some new nice fitting jeans and black trainers. The top, from Etam, was a bit of an extravagance at eight pounds but so what! She's on holiday! The new baseball cap she bought, in case it's windy up on the Downs, holds her unruly hair in place and a light touch of lipstick balances with her pink cheeks. She looks radiant.

She's ready and grabbing her jacket from the hook by the door fights the urge to giggle. This feels like a date, a real date!

Esther is at work so there's no one to wish them a nice afternoon, but Jess knows it's going to be delightful. There is a popular walk of about four miles that goes through Beachy Head past the Belle Tout lighthouse and along to Birling Gap. They park the car at the foot of the first hill and grab bottles of water from the café before ascending the steep, seemingly never-ending, grassy slope.

"This is so beautiful," Jess gasps as the hill plateaus out at long last. "Boy, I'm out of breath!"

"Been a while since I've been walking up here. I must be really unfit," Will pants as he gulps his water down. "I forget how stunning it is."

At the top they both gaze out to the wide expanse of sea before them. At around five hundred and sixty feet it's too high up to see any ripples but there are one or two boats just visible on the horizon. The early spring sunlight has a particular hew as it shines on the sprawling town to the left, South Cliff tower dominating the view.

Jess and Will carry on along the well-trodden stony path in silence occasionally stopping and turning around to take in the whole breath-taking vista from south to north.

Approaching a well-used bench, its back legs having sunk deep into the ground, Will's suggestion to sit down and have a drink was very welcome. He was very organised and had brought along some snacks and a flask of coffee. He'd forgotten to bring any sugar though but Jess excuses him. He'd brought a packet of Jacob's orange Club biscuits, her favourite.

"So, tell me about the last time you were up here, then," Jess's invitation causing a faraway look in Will's eyes.

"Came here with a few friends late one evening. Yeh, we walked right along to the pub at Birling Gap and had a few pints and didn't notice the time. Found ourselves scrambling around in the dark trying find our way on to the main road. Not a clue where the path was and kept hearing noises in the bushes as we walked by. Pretty scary I can tell you. It's pitch black up here at night, no lights. Eventually got out to the road and hitched a lift back into town. Taught us a lesson. You been up here before?"

"Yes, when I was about six I think. I was with my family and it felt like we were walking for hours and hours and my short little legs got so tired. I remember I started crying and daddy carried me on his shoulders for the rest of the time."

She's hoping for an opening in the conversation. Nice as it is talking about sweet memories there is an urge to cut to the deeper things. She wants to confide in Will, tell him of her experiences and hear his opinion.

"There's something I've never asked you, Will, I hope you don't mind but where's your dad?" Will turns his head away and immediately Jess regrets asking. Looking at the sky his soft voice replied:

"It's fine, Jess. He died when I was eight. Massive heart attack. We'd just had a great summer together, him and me. My older brother, Duncan, was always out with his friends so I had Dad all to myself. We did loads together, fishing, out in the boat, long walks. And then all of a sudden, he was gone. Mum's still not over it."

"That's awful, I'm so sorry to hear that, Will." Her Witness head jumps into action and before her mouth can follow she stops herself. *No. I'm not going to start preaching to Will about where he thinks his dad is right now, whether he thinks he'll ever see him again. About the resurrection, the paradise. If he wants to we can talk about those things another time. Not now. Leave him alone.* But she does want to comfort him. She feels the strongest urge to put her arms around him and just hold him tight.

Now she realises they have something in common, sort of. They'd both lost the love of their fathers at an early age. As the sun moves across the spring sky they talk openly about their feelings, unwittingly forming a bond, the type that comes with shared tragedies.

"So how did you get into photography? Was it something you always wanted to do?" she enquires.

"I used to play around with Dad's camera. He'd let me hold it round my neck when we went out for walks then he started teaching me how to 'see' an object properly, see what surrounds it, how to frame it. Then he showed me how to use different lenses and filters. It went on from there really. After sixth form I searched high and low to find a photography course and eventually found one in Brighton. Contacted newspapers and magazines and basically put myself out there. The work is steady, sometimes the days are long depending on where I go but, I love it."

How satisfying to have set a goal in life and to be living it out, thinks Jess, *something interesting and exciting. And to be getting paid for doing something you already love. What could be better?*

They keep walking, stopping occasionally to absorb the stunning views. The Belle Tout lighthouse is up ahead but still a long way off. The ground is littered with sharp bits of flint and lumps of chalk in amongst the trodden grass, evidence of what lies beneath their feet. Watched over by the sparkling white of Beachy Head cliffs, the lighthouse stands sturdy and proud and walkers pose for photos dangerously close to the cliff edge.

A lush, rich shade of green spreads out as far as the eye can see, sinking and rising with the contours of the hills. Hedgerows create shadows and distant sheep graze all day oblivious to the intruders around them. A roughly chopped wooden fence encircles an out of bounds area marked by a sign and the path skirts around the edge, guiding them towards another steep slope. Looking down upon the wide grassy area ahead it invites them to challenge each other to a race. Like two children they look at each other and assume a starting position and off they go, all the way down and back up the other side. They arrive breathless at the strategically placed bench and plonk themselves down, gasping and laughing.

The couple sit side by side and enjoy the quiet as a warm breeze tumbles around their legs. The blustery wind has picked up and Jess is glad she'd worn her hat. A few high-pitched barks from behind makes them turn their heads. A little west highland terrier jumps around in a frenzy chasing leaves and growling as they float about. Its owner walking on ahead, calls its name: "Sophie, come along, Sophie!"

"Ah! My cat was called Sophie!" Jess tells Will.

"Sweet name for a cat, not sure about a dog though. What happened to her?" he asks.

This is the opening Jess had been waiting for. It gives her a pathway to take Will down and on their journey she tells him of her beloved cat and her adorable kittens, her upbringing in the Truth, about her adventure away from home and about Ray. He frowns as he listens to her description of the way she was dealt with on her return but he doesn't interrupt. Not knowing if he can understand she explains how things have changed since she's been reinstated, how her old so-called friends have distanced themselves from her. And she speaks of the suffocating trap she now finds herself in, that if she were to leave the religion she would be giving up everything and everyone she's ever known.

He listens without commenting and doesn't ask questions until she's finished.

"Jess, let me ask you something. Do you believe in God?"

"Absolutely," comes her immediate reply.

"Why? You sound very sure. Is it purely because you were brought up with that belief?"

It's a question she's never considered before. But of course she believes in God. She begins to formulate an answer but Will doesn't allow her to voice it before he poses a second question.

"And what else about your religion do you feel so sure about? Is there anything?"

"The words of Jesus Christ, definitely." She nods as she speaks, "No one can argue with the things he said – you know, love your neighbour, treat others how you would like to be treated, those kind of things. What he said makes so much sense."

"I'm sorry, Jess, I'm not trying to get you to answer me in particular but maybe these are things you need to answer for yourself."

He pauses, waiting for that suggestion to sink in. They both raise their faces to the warm sun.

He continues: "In my opinion if anyone is going to believe in something they need to know where that belief came from. How does it get into a person's head in the first place? For instance, can you think of something, some teaching or rule that seems, I don't know, hard to understand or just totally ridiculous?"

"Ha! There are loads!" she laughs. "sisters are not allowed to work behind the literature desk, hand the microphone round, give a talk directly to the congregation. I could go on, Will," and she does, getting into a rhythm of no-nos, counting them off on her fingers. "The Brothers have to wear a suit, which means matching trousers and jacket, not contrasting like brown trousers and a cream jacket. We are not allowed to eat hot cross buns or black sausage. No discos, no parties with more than ten people, no mixing with anyone not a Witness. Don't listen to Michael Jackson's 'Beat It' cos it's all about masturbation. And don't get me started on the whole disfellowshipping thing. That *has* to be wrong." She suddenly blushed as she realised she'd said the 'm' word.

"OK, OK, Jess," Will smiles and signals with his

hand for her to slow down. "So, if you think about each one of those rules, where did it come from? Where did you first hear it? Was it in your magazines? From your mum? Did you hear other people in your congregation talking about it?"

She ponders, looking down in her lap, turning a lump of chalk she'd picked up from the path.

"I can see what you're saying. It's the same as what we tell people on the ministry – check what you believe against the Bible. If it's not in the Bible then it can't be right."

"Well, there you are then. Maybe you need to start from scratch and use their own advice, check everything you hold in your heart against the scriptures. Sounds to me like you know your Bible well enough."

Will makes it sound so simple.

"But that would take forever! Deep down I know they're right, Jehovah's Witnesses are the only true religion and the only ones that will be saved at Armageddon. But what if they're not, Will? What if I've believed this stuff and trusted this Organisation my whole life only to find out it's not true, that it's a big money-making hoax? What would I do then? Where would I belong?" She shakes her head as if to banish such an frightening idea.

An expression appears on her face that makes Will take her hand. He turns to face her, concerned that he might have upset her with all these questions.

"What is it, Jess?"

"Will," she whispers. "Who am I? All my opinions have been formed for me, I've been told how to feel, told what's right and wrong, told who to mix with, who to avoid. I've never been able to develop a hobby or an interest that isn't something spiritual. I've just realised that I don't know who I am! I'm scared, Will." Her eyes are pleading with him for his understanding.

"Look, don't think too deeply about it, Jess." His hand tightens around her fingers.

"You wouldn't be completely alone. You've got your mum and Peter and Janey. And your little niece. You're in touch with your dad again and your sisters." His voice softened as he adds, "and you've got me and Mum, if you want us."

She looked into his eyes and shuffled along the seat closer to him. With his reassuring arm around her shoulder she let her body sink into his embrace.

"And just think, finding your true self could actually be a lot of fun."

*

This girl needs to get out more, Will thinks, considering which club to take her to first. How sad to get to the age of eighteen and to never have been to a school disco, an activity club, parties, never celebrated Christmas or been spoiled on her birthday. Birthday! He must find out when her birthday is.

She's got a lot of catching up to do, and he wants to be the one to show her what real life can be like. What it's like to have fun.

"Shall we head back? We could stop for a drink at The Castle on the way home," Will suggests.

"Yeh, let's go." She chucks the chalk away into the gorse bushes and they walk in silence back the way they came, hand in hand. This feels so nice, different to holding Ray's hand. The town now stretches out before them and a small pang of loss floods her heart. She definitely left a big part of herself here when the family moved away. The slope back down to where the car is parked is so steep they have to step sideways, avoiding chunks of flint and chalk which would take their feet from under them.

Back at the car she raises her head to look at Will as he holds the door open for her. Good, kind, thoughtful Will. Maybe there is hope. Maybe she's not as stuck in her suffocating life as she thinks she is. They smile at each other through the window as he closes the passenger door.

*

The remainder of her week moves slowly, peacefully punctuated with swimming, dog walks, cooking and lots of talking with Esther. She thinks about her empty life back home, about her stifling spiritual routine and false friends. She wonders how her mum has been coping on her own this past week. Marianne's life has been empty for years, no wonder she's depressed.

Jess prays. She prays for the strength to return home and for ideas about how to make life better for herself, more enjoyable, more real. *Surely this can't be what you intended, Jehovah? This isn't really living, it's just an existence, waiting for Armageddon to come, and meanwhile, I'm missing out on so much of the beauty of life.*

*

On the final evening after the chilli Jess has cooked, out of the blue Esther hands her a glass of wine. Will disappears into the TV room, Shep following him as he clicks his fingers.

"Come and sit in the lounge for a moment, Jess, there's something I want to talk to you about."

This sounds serious, Jess thinks.

"You've only been here a few days and already I can see you look a lot more relaxed. Forgive me for saying but it doesn't sound like you're happy where you are and with the people you mix with. It's like you're carrying a heavy burden around with you and that's not good for a young woman just starting out in life."

So far Jess couldn't disagree with Esther on any point. But she wondered what she was getting to.

"Why not come and live here? You can have that room up there, make it how you want it. There are plenty of jobs going in the restaurants down at the new harbour, it won't take you long to find something. You belong down here, Jess."

Esther paused, allowing Jess to take in her offer for a moment.

"Will you think about it? Talk to your mum, have a heart to heart with her and tell her how it all makes you feel. In your own time let me know what you decide."

Jess doesn't know what to say. She can't quite believe it and sees it as an answer to her prayer. It is the perfect solution. She can't thank Esther enough and through tears and giggles, she talks about all the things she could do down here. There's a local magazine on the table, *The Pevensey Post*, and taking a quick flick through she can see there are loads of activities to be involved in: charity work, amateur dramatics, a cycling club, swimming clubs (she thinks about lifeguard training), she could help out with an afterschool club at her old junior school. There are so many options!

Will pops his head round the door and asks what all the giggling is about. Esther tells him what they've been discussing and he adds his opinion stating that it's a 'no-brainer'.

"By the way, Jess, when's your birthday?"

"April the fifth," she replies nonchalantly, sticking her nose back into the magazine. In her peripheral vision she sees him wink at Esther. "That's tomorrow! Why didn't you tell us? Oops, sorry, you don't need to answer that, I know why."

*

Her last day is the day after tomorrow, the train to Victoria leaves at midday. Jess is dreading going back, saying goodbye to Esther and Will. Whatever happens she knows they will remain firm friends and will never lose touch. Braving the cold water she takes a short final swim before packing up her things and tidying her room. Taking a look around she wonders what it would be like to live right on the beach, to go swimming every morning, to watch the little boats out on the water. To hear the gulls calling and smell the salty air. *Wonderful, just wonderful,* that's what it would be like.

But the thought of her mum crosses her mind. How can she possibly leave her all alone up there? What kind of daughter would that make her? She'd already let her down once by being selfish and running away. Is she being selfish now too? She would need to think seriously about such a big decision and how it would affect Marianne.

*

Back at home Jess unpacks and sorts her washing out and, while she does so, tells Marianne what she's been getting up to in Eastbourne all week. Knowing what Marianne's reaction would probably be she leaves out the afternoon she spent with Will. She would just worry unnecessarily, believing in her own mind that her fornicator daughter had been at it again and was in line to be disfellowshipped. Poor Marianne. Her imagination was just too strong sometimes.

The next day is Sunday.

As Jess gets herself ready that morning, she is unaware that this will be her last meeting – ever.

Chapter Nineteen

There will be no more preparation, no more answering up during the *Watchtower*. No more Book Study meeting on a Tuesday evening. No more door-to-door ministry. No more cold shoulders to put up with. No longer will she give any Witnesses the chance to treat her as the odd one out, to point the finger, or for sisters to shuffle their husbands far away from such a fornicator.

She would listen to no more made-up rules from the platform, never have to put in another ministry report, feel no more eyes boring into the back of her head during talks about the consequences of fornication. So complete will be her detachment from the congregation, from the Truth, from the Organisation, it will feel like her life is starting from scratch. That she's been born again.

*

The congregation settles down before rising to sing the opening song. A prayer follows and the speaker arrives on the platform to deliver his talk entitled: 'Jehovah Will Carry it Out.'**

It's about how Jehovah's enemies with be dealt with in the future at Armageddon and the first scripture referred to is Psalm 37:20:

But the wicked will perish: Though the Lord's enemies are like the flowers of the field, they will be consumed, they will go up in smoke.

Charming, thinks Jess, remembering she'd heard this scripture being discussed before. It was explained as symbolic, representing an everlasting, permanent destruction of God's enemies. And this was written in the time of King David when regular bloody battles were fought. *So, is there now some new understanding? New light?* she wonders. For forty minutes the speaker explains who God's enemies are: those that have rejected the True God, have turned their back on him and have joined forces with Satan and become apostate. He explained:

"Fire would be such a suitable means of elimination of such refuse. What a fitting picture of the final end of all God's enemies. It's sobering, but something we all look forward to. And how reassuring for God's people, not that we rejoice in someone's death, but, when it comes to God's enemies – fine, they're out of the way."

He pulls a box of matches from his jacket pocket.

"I thought it would be a fitting memory aid to help this verse stay in our minds. Here's what Jehovah has promised…"

He takes out a match and strikes it dramatically. Holding it high so the audience can see. The small flame licks its way up the stick and as he blows out the flame he focusses on the rising smoke. There is an expectant silence as everyone watches.

"Puff! Gone."

The audience gives a hearty laugh, and then applauds.

They actually applaud!

Jess is incensed. *Why are they clapping?* Blinking

hard and shaking her head, she's trying to make sense of what this Elder has just said and done.

So, clearly they are teaching that this scripture has a literal meaning now. Anyone who chooses to leave Jehovah's Witnesses is an enemy of God. And they are going to take such delight in their destruction!

What about my dad? My sisters? They went to meetings, had Bible studies but they chose not to continue. It sounds like according to this man they are God's enemies and will all go up in flames and we are expected to cheer about it!

This is the final straw for Jess. She's had enough of this twisted, sadistic bullshit and she's having no part in it anymore. This is encouraging hatred, hatred of people like Esther and Will, anyone who has shooed away the Witnesses at their door, calling them 'refuse' and looking forward to their deaths. It's disgusting.

The talk is nearing its end but Jess urgently wants to get out of this place. She gathers her books, shoves them into her bag and hurriedly stumbles out of the row and towards the exit. She can't believe what she's just heard. *Does God really approve of this view of his children? Would a loving God do this, really? What about forgiveness, understanding, the right to question things?*

Kevin Choi has seen her thunderous face and follows her out through the heavy glass doors to the foyer.

"Is everything all right, Jess?" he enquires softly.

"No, everything is not all right," she whispers angrily, hands on her hips.

"Has someone upset you?" he asks, unaware of the

blood bubbling up in Jess's veins.

She says it.

"Has someone upset me? Ha! Have a guess. You lot have no idea how much you've upset me!"

Shocked at her own words she breathes deeply, contemplating how to proceed with this chance she's been given. A chance to tell him exactly what she thinks of him and his cronies, the so-called Truth and the Organisation. A chance to voice her innermost thoughts that have been buried for so long. Putting the talk she's just heard to one side, there's something far more important that needs sorting out.

"Tell me, Kevin, why did you disfellowship me?"

"Jess, why go over the past, eh? You're back in the congregation now, just put it behind you."

"No, I'd like an answer," she persists, and asks again, pointedly: "Why did you disfellowship me?"

"You know why. You simply weren't repentant for what you'd done. There are guidelines we as Elders have to follow. It wasn't personal."

"So why didn't you follow those guidelines when you dealt with Amy and Stewart? Were they repentant? Were they truly sorry when they went off and did the same thing again? Why were they only reproved and not disfellowshipped? I'd like to know, Kevin."

People's heads are turning to watch them through the glass doors and Jess moves making Kevin move too, blocking their view. He shakes his head and pauses before she hears his lame answer.

"Their circumstances were not the same as yours, and, well, they're married now. Move on, Jess."

"I'll tell you why, shall I? Because Amy's dad is

an Elder. It looks like there's one rule for Elders' families and another rule for everyone else. That's the only reason they didn't get kicked out and you know it. It's called 'Elder Privilege' isn't it?"

She then proceeds to state some facts he needs to know: "You stole my life, Kevin. You used me as an example for the other young ones that were getting a bit feisty. Well, thanks a lot for that. I had nobody, *nobody* to talk to. No family except Mum, no friends, no company for months and months. How would you like that? I felt so alone I wanted to die. I didn't want to carry on." Her breath is coming in short bursts as she tries to keep control.

Kevin stands there looking at the floor but she continues. How can she possibly make him understand?

"You did the same to Alan and look what happened there. You killed him! You're despicable. How can you Elders truly be led by Holy Spirit when you play games with people's lives? Do you really think Jehovah approves of this kind of treatment of young people, of anyone?"

"You don't understand, Jess. We have to keep the congregation clean from people like you."

"What did you say? People like me?!" she almost shouts. "And what kind of person do you think I am?"

He looks at her from top to toe and taking a step back he meets her eyes.

"A little whore."

Jess was at boiling point but desperately trying to keep control of her emotions and her mouth. Perhaps she should just let it all out. Why be worried about offending him now? He'll never admit they were wrong. Never.

And she'll never receive an apology, not for herself or for Alan.

Her rising anger and a torrent of thoughts bunch together and began to burn inside her head.

Be Christian. Be Christian, she desperately repeats to herself.

No! He needs to understand what he's done!

She feels her arms lifting up and places her hands on his shoulders. She looks into his eyes and as sharp and as hard as she possibly can knees Kevin in the groin. While he stands there holding himself and wincing in pain she brings her right fist back and punches him full force on the nose. She hears a loud crack of bone on bone. He tumbles backwards and crashes through the glass doors falling to the floor writhing in agony. Blood pours from his nose and he lies there as Jess looks down on him in disgust. This sniveling, bloody pathetic excuse for a man.

The speaker on the platform has stopped and the audience has swiveled round in their seats to see what all the commotion is. All eyes are on Kevin as he lay on the floor and a couple of brothers rush to his side. Their attention moves to Jess but she ignores their gasps and looks of disbelief. She gives them what for in her most authoritative voice:

"You're no loving shepherds. You Elders are murderers, and so is this whole Organisation. Open your eyes, people!" Jess blurts out. "This is not the true religion, this is not the Truth, it never has been!"

Fuming with anger Jess turns, picks up her bag from the foyer and walks out of that Hall with her head held high. Shaking from head to foot, it takes her the four-mile walk home to calm herself down. She needs that time, needs that space to get her mind off the past now that she's dealt it a severe blow. No amount of time will erase her mistake from the memory of these people. They will never let her forget. She has to leave this toxic environment. And soon.

*

Back at home, after making a strong coffee for herself and a tea for Marianne, she asks her: "Come and sit down for a minute, Mum, I need to talk to you." She hopes nothing of what she's just been through remains visible on her face.

Coffee cup in hand Jess sits at the table opposite Marianne. She speaks softly, slowly, and doesn't want to alarm her mum, wants her to work it out for herself as she regales the wonderful week she'd spent with Esther and Will and how much at home she had felt. Jess sees the penny drop in Marianne's eyes and she doesn't look surprised at all.

The phone call to Peter later that afternoon is awkward and with Marianne being within earshot Jess is trying to choose her words carefully. She wants to hear his thoughts on Marianne moving in with him for a while. Her plan is to eventually rent a house where her mum can come and live if she wants to. Peter, shocked to hear of Jess's move, eventually agrees it's a good idea. It would give her a new start but she must stick to the Truth, go back to their old congregation and stay close to the brothers and sisters. Jess doesn't comment. She knows she will never set foot inside a Kingdom Hall again as long as she lives. He says he'll need to talk things through with Janey of course, but doesn't see a problem with Marianne coming to stay.

Marianne is sharp when she wants to be and she can decipher what they are saying from Jess's half of the conversation. In a raised voice so Peter can hear she tells the two of them to hold on just a minute and stop making plans for her. She wants to stay right where she is. Well, it's her choice. She has the option if she ever changes her mind and Jess feels comfortable with that for the moment. However, why Marianne wishes to stay up here with no family is difficult to understand.

*

Her clothes, shoes and Chubbers is all Jess packs. No books, except her Bible, no magazines. No smart meeting clothes, her calf-length skirts and flesh-coloured tights can all go in the bin. No ministry bag – she wants to buy a nice bright slouchy bag when she gets down there, one with buckles and a long handle.

Cassie has a bag like that. Poor Cassie. Jess will miss her terribly. She's the only friend who was genuine and when she's settled into her new home Jess will contact her and explain. There was no time to say goodbye, she had to get out of there as soon as she could. Her boss was satisfied that Jess had to leave suddenly due to family issues and assured her she would be provided with a good reference.

*

Esther meets Jess at the train station and is ready to shower her with hugs and kisses, knowing she's done the right thing. She is thrilled. She has grown to love Jess and looks on her as the daughter she never had. She's known for a long time how Will feels about her and tries not to get excited about the thought of them getting together. Her pity for this young woman turns to pride as she listens to her making plans for her future on the drive to Pevensey Bay.

*

Will is at the house when they arrive and he opens the door before Jess puts her new key in, a beaming smile spreading across his tanned face.

"Jess, hi, good journey? Let me get those," he says after a big hug, grabbing the handle on Jess's suitcase and large bag.

Following a welcome cuppa and a sandwich Will suggests a swim.

"Great, see you down there in ten minutes," Jess agrees, and runs her bags upstairs to her room.

She can't wait to get into the water, to feel the cleansing liquid encircle her body, feel it cool the top of her head. Hopefully it will be slightly warmer than last week – but probably not.

The tide is out. The ridged honey-coloured sand stretches out to beyond human vision and is scattered with grey and white pebbles, strings of black seaweed and feels chilly underfoot. Jess can see Will up ahead by the top of the groin, one huge towel laid out with his trainers holding down two corners, large stones secure the others.

Eager to get in the water they pad across the dry sand, their toes sinking in at the end of each step.

All of a sudden Jess stops.

She turns.

Behind her, beyond the mound of stones pushed up by the strength of the tide is a row of eight beach huts. Elders in their suits, all dressed the same, peering out to

301

sea to check what's going on.

They stand there, rigid and strong, like sentries, all looking in the same direction – straight at her. Their window-eyes reflect the warming sun but she knows their insides are dark and dusty. They are deceptively welcoming with their flowery curtains and brightly painted wooden slats, their pointed roofs like hands held in deep thought. A feeling of being watched falls across Jess and roots her feet into the sand.

But she resolutely turns back and looks up into Will's eyes. She shakes her head, shakes away the judgement and the last remnants of guilt that she knows will stop her living her life.

He holds out his hand for her to take. They connect whole-heartedly, and squeezing each other's hands take off towards the water at a pace. They run straight ahead, out further and further, till the water takes their weight.

And Jess doesn't look back again, only forward, only at Will and the sky and the sea and the sun. Only at the real life.

The Beginning

Further reading:

Author: Robert Crompton
Pathways to Freedom
Leaving Gilead

Author: Jonny Halfhead
The 1975 Apocalypse
Nine Pills
The Offence of Grace

Author: Bonnie Zieman

Exiting the JW Cult: A Healing Handbook for current and former Jehovah's Witnesses

References:

1. *Examining the Scriptures Daily 2017*. Published by Watchtower Bible and Tract Society.
   Thurs 2nd February.

** Online Video Library | JW.ORG Videos English. Morning Worship, Anthony Morris III "Jehovah Will Carry it Out."

Printed in Great Britain
by Amazon